Praise for *From Beer to Eternity*

Nominated for an Agatha Award for Best
Contemporary Novel

Featured on Buzzfeed Books!

Listed as a Mystery Maven's Favorite Whodunits,
Thrillers, and Capers of 2020 on Goodreads

"*From Beer to Eternity* is a terrific start to Sherry
Harris's Chloe Jackson, Sea Glass Saloon Mystery
series. I absolutely loved it. Can't wait for Book 2!"
—Susan Santangelo, *Suspense Magazine*

"Boasting an eclectic cast of characters, a small-
town atmosphere and engaging dialogue, this was
an entertaining book to read, and I can't wait to
see what new adventures await Chloe and her
friends in this pleasantly appealing debut series."
—*Dru's Book Musings*

"I already love these characters and this setting,
so I will definitely be back for the next round.
From Beer to Eternity is the first in what promises
to be a great new series."
—*Carstairs Considers*

"*From Beer to Eternity* is Sherry Harris at her best. It
has a great love interest, a layered backstory, fun
and some hysterical laugh-out-loud lines. I can't
wait until my next visit to Emerald Cove."
—Kellye Garrett, author of the
Detective By Day mysteries

Praise for *Three Shots to the Wind*

"It's a fascinating look into how personality skews perspective, handled deftly by Sherry Harris as she spins this entertaining yarn."
—*Criminal Element*

"An enjoyable cozy read with plenty of suspects, romance, and a beachy vibe."
—*Kirkus Reviews*

Praise for *Absence of Alice*

"*Absence of Alice* is a roller-coaster of a mystery that I couldn't put down. Wow! What a read!"
—*Suspense Magazine*

"Sarah Winston has yet to disappoint me with one of her adventures, and *Absence of Alice* is no exception. Sherry Harris has once again penned a winner. Fans will delight in the latest addition to the series. If you haven't met Sarah yet, fix that today."
—*Carstairs Considers*

"Fans of Harris are used to her deft management of tension and humor and will find the author's considerable skills on full display here."
—*Washington Independent Review of Books*

Best Book of the Week pick
—*Woman's World*

Praise for *All Murders Final!*

"There's a lot going on in this charming mystery, and it all works. The dialogue flows effortlessly, and the plot is filled with numerous twists and turns. Sarah is a resourceful and appealing protagonist, supported by a cast of quirky friends. Well written and executed, this is a definite winner. Bargain-hunting has never been so much fun!"
—*RT Book Reviews,* 4 Stars

"A must-read cozy mystery! Don't wear your socks when you read this story cause it's gonna knock 'em off!"
—*Chatting About Cozies*

"Just because Sherry Harris's protagonist Sarah Winston lives in a small town, it doesn't mean that her problems are small . . . Harris fits the puzzle pieces together with a sure hand."
—Sheila Connolly, Agatha- and Anthony-nominated author of the Orchard Mysteries

"A thrilling mystery . . . Brilliantly written, each chapter drew me in deeper and deeper, my anticipation mounting with every turn of the page. By the time I reached the last page, all I could say was . . . wow!"
—*Lisa Ks Book Reviews*

Praise for *The Longest Yard Sale*

"I love a complex plot and *The Longest Yard Sale* fills the bill with mysterious fires, a missing painting, thefts from a thrift shop and, of course, murder. Add an intriguing cast of victims, potential villains and sidekicks, an interesting setting, and two eligible men for the sleuth to choose between and you have a sure winner even before you get to the last page and find yourself laughing out loud."
—Kaitlyn Dunnett, author of *The Scottie Barked at Midnight*

"Readers will have a blast following Sarah Winston on her next adventure as she hunts for bargains and bad guys. Sherry Harris's latest is as delightful as the best garage sale find!"
—Liz Mugavero, Agatha-nominated author of the Pawsitively Organic Mysteries

"Sherry Harris is a gifted storyteller, with plenty of twists and adventures for her smart and stubborn protagonist."
—Beth Kanell, Kingdom Books

"Once again Sherry Harris entwines small-town life with that of the nearby Air Force base, yard sales with romance, art theft with murder. The story is a bargain, and a priceless one!"
—Edith Maxwell, Agatha-nominated author of the Local Foods mystery series

Praise for *Tagged for Death*

Nominated for an Agatha Award for Best First Novel

"*Tagged for Death* is skillfully rendered, with expert characterization and depiction of military life. Best of all, Sarah is the type of intelligent, resourceful, and appealing person we would all like to get to know better!"
—*Mystery Scene Magazine*

"Full of garage-sale tips, this amusing cozy debut introduces an unusual protagonist who has overcome some recent tribulations and become stronger."
—*Library Journal*

"A terrific find! Engaging and entertaining, this clever cozy is a treasure—charmingly crafted and full of surprises."
—Hank Phillippi Ryan, Agatha-, Anthony- and Mary Higgins Clark-award-winning author

"Like the treasures Sarah Winston finds at the garage sales she loves, this book is a gem."
—Barbara Ross, Agatha-nominated author of the Maine Clambake Mysteries

"It was masterfully done. *Tagged for Death* is a winning debut that will have you turning pages until you reach the final one. I'm already looking forward to Sarah's next bargain with death."
—Mark Baker, *Carstairs Considers*

Mysteries by Sherry Harris

The Chloe Jackson Sea Glass Saloon Mysteries
THREE SHOTS TO THE WIND
A TIME TO SWILL
and
Agatha Award nominated Best Contemporary Novel
FROM BEER TO ETERNITY

The Sarah Winston Garage Sale Mysteries
ABSENCE OF ALICE
SELL LOW, SWEET HARRIET
LET'S FAKE A DEAL
THE GUN ALSO RISES
I KNOW WHAT YOU BID LAST SUMMER
A GOOD DAY TO BUY
ALL MURDERS FINAL!
THE LONGEST YARD SALE
and
Agatha Award Nominated Best First Novel
TAGGED FOR DEATH

Rum and Choke

Sherry Harris

Kensington Publishing Corp.
www.kensingtonbooks.com

KENSINGTON BOOKS are published by

Kensington Publishing Corp.
119 West 40th Street
New York, NY 10018

All Kensington titles, imprints, and distributed lines are available at special quantity discounts for bulk purchases for sales promotion, premiums, fund-raising, educational, or institutional use.

Special book excerpts or customized printings can also be created to fit specific needs. For details, write or phone the office of the Kensington Sales Manager: Attn.: Sales Department. Kensington Publishing Corp., 119 West 40th Street, New York, NY 10018. Phone: 1-800-221-2647.

The K and Teapot logo is a trademark of Kensington Publishing Corp.

First Printing: January 2023
ISBN: 978-1-4967-3438-9

ISBN: 978-1-4967-3439-6 (ebook)

10 9 8 7 6 5 4 3 2 1

Printed in the United States of America

To Bob
Always and forever
and to Clare
The Angel on my Shoulder, I miss you

Heritage Businesses

Sea Glass—owner, Vivi Jo Slidell

Briny Pirate—owner, Wade Thomas

Redneck Rollercoaster—owner, Ralph Harrison

Russo's Grocery Store—owner, Fred Russo

Hickle Glass Bottom Boat—owners, Edith Hickle,
Leah Hickle, Oscar Hickle

Emerald Cove Fishing Charters—owner, Jed
Farwell

CHAPTER 1

Have you ever walked into work to find your boss and coworker staring at you with over-eager expressions? Me either—until today and I immediately realized something was up. It wasn't just their expressions, but the fact that they were both here before me. That was highly unusual. I'd found, since I'd moved to Emerald Cove, Florida, that unusual was rarely good.

Joaquín Diaz, head bartender, and Vivi Slidell, my business partner and boss, both stood behind the bar in the Sea Glass Saloon. The looks on their faces reminded me of my nieces and nephews when they knew they were in trouble but hoped they weren't. I was tempted to walk right back out into the April sunshine and return tomorrow. However, knowing Joaquín and Vivi the way I did, I figured they'd just follow me out. So whatever was up with them, I might as well just stay and find out.

"What?" I asked as I stowed my purse under the bar. Although the Sea Glass was called a saloon, it was more tiki hut. Its wooden walls were dotted with vintage photographs and signs. The concrete floors made it easy to sweep the sand out at the end of the day. The south side of the bar faced the Gulf of Mexico, and the entire wall was sliding glass doors that could be pushed back to open to the deck. Almost every day, I looked out at the water and told myself, *Chloe Jackson, you live in paradise.* Although right now, I was afraid my day was going to be more like the Hardy Boys book *Trouble in Paradise.*

"What do you mean by 'what'?" Joaquín asked. His eyes sparkled, making them match the emerald color of the water along this stretch of the Florida Panhandle. His Hawaiian shirt was the same emerald green and had a giant flamingo on it.

Mr. Innocent. "I can tell something is up with you two. Just tell me so we can get this place open for the day."

"We haven't won for *four years,*" Vivi said, emphasizing the "four years" with head nods that made her sleek silver bob brush her slim shoulders. You'd never know the woman was in her seventies. She could be a model if she wanted to.

"And you're perfect for it." Joaquín raised his beautifully groomed eyebrows at me. His dark hair was wind-tousled. Probably because he'd just gotten back from his morning of fishing.

"So we signed you up," Vivi said.

"Because we knew you'd say yes," Joaquín added.

"The deadline was nine this morning. And like Joaquín said, we were sure you'd agree."

"You wouldn't let us down." Joaquín's face had moved to a "pleading for a treat" expression of a three-year-old.

My eyes were starting to ache from darting back and forth as first one spoke and then the other. "What did you sign me up for, that I'm perfect for, and you knew I'd say yes to?" My voice was a tad bit impatient. Maybe they'd signed me up for bartending school, although that would be a bit of a surprise, because my drink-making skills had grown by leaps and bounds since I'd started working here ten months ago.

"The annual Florida Panhandle Barback Games," Vivi said.

I swear, they both took a step back like they expected an explosion, which was weird, because I didn't normally have a temper. Although all of this might bring one on or, at the very least, bring on a headache. Instead, I raised an eyebrow—well, both eyebrows. I'd never managed to raise just one, even though I'd practiced in front of a mirror when I was a teenager. "Annual. Barback. Games."

They both nodded. Being the barback was part of my job. A barback did a lot of the prep work for the bartender, like cutting fruit; making sure liquor, or *spirits* as Joaquín called them, were stocked; making sure glassware was clean and readily available; anything that would assist the bartender and make their job easier.

"Why haven't I heard anything about this before?"

"You moved down after the games last year. We do it at the end of spring break season and before the busy summer season," Vivi said.

"Before it gets too hot and humid," Joaquín added.

"Why don't you do it, Joaquín?" I asked.

"He won four years ago, and you can only enter every five years," Vivi said.

"What does the competition entail?" I asked. My eyes were narrowing. My voice sounded wary. Bolting became a very real possibility.

"It's an obstacle course," Vivi said.

"Easy stuff," Joaquín said.

Obstacle course. Are you kidding me? "Like what?" I asked. I knew I'd cave and say yes, but I might as well make them suffer a bit for not consulting me first.

"Carrying three full beer mugs in each hand while running through tires," Joaquín said. "Fastest time with the least spillage wins the round."

Oh, yeah, like that sounded easy. I was going to need a round of drinks just listening to all of this.

"Fruit chopping," Vivi offered.

That sounded too easy. "What's the catch?" I asked.

"You have to stand on one leg," Vivi said.

My mouth dropped open. People with sharp knives standing on one leg? I started picturing all kinds of disasters, most of which ended up with me bleeding.

"Sorting vodka brands from least to most expensive. No catch on that one," Joaquín said.

"Running a tray of drinks from one station to another without spilling." Vivi watched me carefully, as if trying to gauge what my answer would be.

"Creating a drink from mystery ingredients," Joaquín said. "Don't worry, I'll train you."

As if that was all I had to worry about.

"And then rolling an empty keg up a hill to the finish line." Vivi put her hands up in a *see how easy that will be?* gesture.

"What's the catch? I have to roll it with my nose? Do it blindfolded? Feet tied together?"

"No."

"Of course not."

They both actually sounded indignant. I almost laughed. "What's in it for me?"

"The glory," Vivi said.

"A cool trophy that you get to keep forever," Joaquín said.

"It brings in more business, which means more money for all of us," Vivi said. "In fact, that starts as soon as the competitors are announced, because everyone wants to size up the competition."

"I'll train you," Joaquín offered. "You've got this."

I needed training? What was that about? "When is the competition?" How much time did I have to prepare? Or quit and hightail it back to my hometown of Chicago to avoid catastrophic embarrassment? There were plenty of bars there. It should be easy to find a new job, or maybe by now, the Chicago Public Library system was hiring again, and I could return to my old job of children's librarian.

"It's ten days from now," Joaquín said. "Plenty of time."

Only ten days? I did a mental grimace. How could I say no? "Fine. I'll do it."

"Great."

"Excellent," Vivi said.

"So who is the competition?" I asked. I was thinking of the bar Two Bobs just down the walkway that ran the length of the small harbor. "All of the staff at Two Bobs look pretty young and fit."

"Did you bring the dossier?" Joaquín asked Vivi.

"*Dossier*? What have you gotten me into?" I asked.

"It's in the office," Vivi said, not answering my question.

"Why is there a dossier?" I asked seconds later, when we were all seated in Vivi's office. Joaquín and I sat across from Vivi. We faced a beautiful painting of the Gulf of Mexico.

"Some of the bars bring in ringers," Joaquín said casually, like it was no big deal.

"Ringers?"

"Professional athletes." Vivi reached into her gold designer handbag and pulled out a manila folder. She put on a pair of reading glasses and, with pursed lips, opened the folder.

"Professional? *Athletes?*" Good grief. I kept repeating what they'd just said. "I thought this was just local people who worked in the bar already."

"Any competitors have to work in the bar they are representing for at least thirty days."

Vivi withdrew three eight-by-ten photos from the manila folder and placed them in front of me. All of the photos looked like they'd been taken with a telephoto lens without the subject's knowledge. I'll bet Ann Williams had something to do with these photos. Ann was known locally as a fixer, and I knew Vivi relied on her when she needed help with something.

Vivi tapped the photo on the left. It was a muscular Black man. Shaved head, hands so large the rocks glass in his hand looked like a shot glass, and a smile that would melt ice cubes. I felt a little warm just looking at him.

Vivi pulled out a piece of paper. "This is Jean Claude LaPierre. He's representing Sandy's in Dune Allen. Olympic gold medalist in the shot put. Six-two, from Des Moines, Iowa. Darling of the reality TV show circuit. He's danced with stars, cooked on the Food Network, and had his heart broken as runner-up on *The Bachelorette.*"

"I can't compete with that." I gestured toward the photo, a bit of panic in my voice.

"Achilles' heel is that he can't run fast. That's no worry for you, Chloe," Vivi said, looking over her glasses at me.

Oh, gee, that made me feel *sooo* much better. While I did run every day, one of his strides was probably three of mine.

Joaquín tapped on the middle picture as Vivi handed him a piece of paper from her folder. This picture showed a woman with inch-long hair and brightly painted nails. Tough-looking, but not in a mean way. And stunningly beautiful. "Lisa Kelley.

Retired Hollywood stuntwoman. Semi-finalist in *American Ninja Warrior.* Gray's Tavern in Grayton Beach signed her up."

"Does she look kind of familiar?" I asked.

Joaquín looked uncomfortable. That couldn't be good.

"Spit it out," I said.

"She was Gal Gadot's stuntwoman."

CHAPTER 2

"*Wonder Woman?* I can't compete with Wonder Woman." It was more of a wail than a statement.

"Of course you can," Vivi said. She flicked her hand like she was flicking away my worries.

"What's her Achilles' heel?" I asked.

"None that we know of," Joaquín answered.

I don't know what kind of expression I made, but Joaquín and Vivi both looked alarmed.

"Yet," Vivi added hastily, "I'm sure she has one."

"If she's retired, maybe she has some kind of injury that will slow her up," Joaquín said.

"And she hasn't worked in a bar as long as you have," Vivi added.

Yeah, right. I was doomed to disappoint.

Vivi tapped a pink fingernail on the last photo. This guy was running out of the water with a surfboard under his arm. Long, flowing sun-streaked hair suitable for the cover of a romance novel.

High cheekbones. Full lips. Long, lean body. Abs that were so defined his picture probably appeared next to "washboard" in the dictionary.

"So a surfer dude." Maybe I could take a surfer dude and not come in last.

Vivi took another piece of paper out of the manila folder. She pursed her lips again while she perused the document. Surely she'd already read this, so why was she procrastinating?

"Champion surfer Enrique Laurier. Now working at Two Bobs. Also a world-renowned triathlete."

"Come on. I don't have a chance. Where did they find these people? Why don't we find someone? Surely one of us must know someone."

"It's too late. Like we said, registration closed this morning. The contest is in ten days," Vivi said. "Besides, we don't have to cheat to win."

"So you couldn't hire someone?" I asked.

"They fell through," Vivi admitted.

"Ha. So does Enrique have any known problems that might help me win?"

"He's a bit of a lothario," Vivi said.

Joaquín choked back a laugh.

Lothario? Who used that term anymore? "So he likes his women? How does that stop him?"

"Well, if he was worn out the night before the event, it might help." Vivi grinned.

I smacked my forehead. This was too much information. "Are you suggesting that I—"

Vivi's face turned bright red. "No. Absolutely not." She shook her head. "That's not what I meant. At all. Never. Not you, anyway. Maybe someone willing who likes him, though." Vivi paused. "Everything I'm saying is making this worse. Right?"

"Most of it," I replied.

"So your mission today—" Vivi said.

"If I choose to accept it," I quipped.

"Is to go to those three bars and chat up Jean Claude, Lisa, and Enrique," Vivi said.

This situation just kept getting better and better. "I have to work."

"That's why I'm here. To fill in for you," Vivi said. "The more information you can gather, the better we will know how you need to train. Just flirt a little."

Really? "Rip won't like that," I said. Rip Barnett was my boyfriend. Vivi wasn't a fan, although she was coming around.

"Be your vivacious self then. You always charm our customers," Vivi said.

I pinked a little at that. Vivi wasn't one to give a lot of compliments.

"Just call Rip and explain the situation. He'll understand," Vivi said.

I looked at Joaquín, hoping for back up. He shrugged. *Traitor.* I guess they both really wanted that trophy. "Are there only four of us?"

"No," Vivi said. "There are others, locals, but you could take them blindfolded."

"Won't they know what I'm up to if I try to go check them out?" I asked.

"The list hasn't been announced yet," Vivi said.

"Then how did you . . . oh, never mind." Vivi had gotten the information, and she wasn't about to tell me how. Ann Williams. Had to be. I was going to try to track her down before I started on this crazy journey.

We all stood and walked back into the bar.

"Why don't I just chop the fruit at least?" I asked.

"No, no." Vivi shook her head. "You just go home, get ready, and chat up your opponents."

I looked down at my polo shirt and khaki capri leggings. I guess she didn't think I was dressed for success. "Okay, whatever. I'll report back later."

It was 11:30 by the time I'd gotten home, fixed my short brown hair by slicking it back with some gel and tucking it behind my ears, and then put on a ton of makeup. My eyes were smoky, my lips full with a dark red lipstick I rarely used, and I'd added fake eyelashes. My widow's peak was more pronounced with my hair like this, and I was afraid my look was tilting toward vampire instead of sexy. I put on a flirty little sundress. Good thing it was warm out today.

Once I was ready, I tried calling Ann Williams to talk to her about the competition. She didn't answer. I took a deep breath and called Rip. We'd been seeing each other steadily since January, but were taking things slow. Some days I couldn't decide if I was relieved or upset that he didn't seem to want to rush into anything, either. Things were good between us, and I hoped this call didn't upset the basket or anything else.

After we said our hellos, I plunged into my conversation with Vivi and Joaquín, repeating as much as I could verbatim. There was a long silence, and my stomach started to swish around with dread.

"Do you want to do all this?" Rip finally asked. "You'd be great at it."

I thought for a moment. I weighed making a fool of myself against making Vivi and Joaquín happy. While I didn't like how they'd roped me into this, it did sound kind of fun, and I had a competitive streak. "I guess so. Yes. It will be interesting."

"Then go get them, and let me know if you need back up or a ride."

My heart melted a little. I couldn't believe I was seeing this amazing man after a really horrible engagement that had ended badly. "Thank you."

"And Chloe," Rip said.

"Yes."

"You're my Wonder Woman." The line disconnected.

I fanned myself a little while I stared at the phone, smiling like a goofball. I ate an early lunch. Day drinking and I didn't always get along, so a full stomach seemed like a good idea.

When I couldn't procrastinate any longer, I walked outside. A shiny black truck that I didn't recognize was parked in my driveway, blocking my car. I took a step back. There'd been three murders since I'd moved here, and I'd become more cautious. More scared. I plunged my hand into my purse and started digging for my phone. A man climbed out. Ah, he worked for Ann Williams. He picked Ann and me up last October, but what was he doing here?

He was a big, burly guy. Clean-shaven and wearing a khaki-colored button-down shirt, but the sleeves had been cut out. He wore loose-fitting jeans that he hitched up as he walked toward me. He had pretty brown eyes.

"Ann thought you might like a ride so you didn't have to worry about drinking and driving."

Well, that confirmed that Ann was involved in all of this. I wasn't too surprised, but what was her interest in the whole thing? It seemed outside the realm of my idea of what a fixer would do. But then again, what did I really know about what the job title of "fixer" entailed?

"Thanks," I said. Beats using a rideshare app.

"Where to?" he asked when we were buckled into the truck. The seats were luxurious—rich leather that almost molded to my body.

"Let's go to Gray's Tavern first. It's the farthest east, and we can work our way back." Grayton Beach was a small town east on 30A. Gray's Tavern wasn't as popular as the Red Bar and wasn't as nice, from what I'd heard.

He started the truck, and it purred like a contented cat. I only wished I felt the same. I was more like the cat on the proverbial hot tin roof.

We'd driven a couple of minutes in what felt like an awkward silence. As far as I could tell, he had the advantage of knowing who I was, while all I knew was that he was somehow associated with Ann.

"What's your name?" That seemed like a fair question. If he was going to drive me all around, I couldn't say "hey you" all afternoon.

"They call me Dex."

"Is that your real name?" There were some unusual names down here, but something about his use of *they call me* led me to believe his name was something else.

He cut his eyes towards me for a moment before refocusing on the road. "Poindexter." Dex shook his head. "I have no idea why I told you that. Ann's one of the few people who knows."

Ann knew everything, and there's no way she'd hire someone whose background she hadn't thoroughly checked out. At least that was my impression of her. Ann took risks but in a cautious, careful way. "My lips are sealed."

Dex gave a quick nod.

"Did you grow up around here?" I asked.

"Nope."

Chatty. Dex turned up a jazz station loud enough that it ended my attempts at conversation. I guess he was a "one confession per trip" kind of guy. I was fine with that. No, I really wasn't, because now I had to focus on how to approach Wonder Woman.

CHAPTER 3

Fifteen minutes later, I stood just inside the entrance to Gray's Tavern, scanning the room to get a feel for the place. Dex had declined to join me but had given me his cell phone number in case I needed anything. I couldn't decide if that was reassuring or if he felt like I was going to get into some kind of trouble. Great. Just when I needed a boost of confidence.

The bar wasn't all that different than the Sea Glass, with its weathered walls and an easy-to-clean concrete floor. The walls were decorated with the occasional swordfish, but no one had gone to any great effort to make the place charming. However, it lacked the Sea Glass's beautiful view and wasn't as bright or cheery inside. It didn't smell as good, either. The air wasn't tanged with as much salt, the cleaner they must have used was bleach-forward, and the hints of beer smelled old.

The patrons looked like a mix of hardworking locals—although how hardworking were you if you were day drinking?—and tourists who probably didn't want to pay what drinks cost in a place with a good view. The rule of thumb here was the closer you were to the beach, the more expensive the drink, and often, the more watered-down. Of course, that wasn't the case at the Sea Glass. There were more men than women in here. Possibly because Wonder Woman supposedly worked here.

It didn't take me long to spot Wonder Woman, even without her Bracelets of Submission and costume. I really needed to try and think of her as Lisa, because Lisa was such a friendly name, not nearly as intimidating as thinking of her as the Princess of the Amazons. She sat alone at the end of the bar, reading a book. She had two drinks in front of her. One was clear liquid with a lime floating in it. The clear liquid could be water, gin, rum, vodka—the list could go on and on, so who knows what it was. The other was a dark shade of green and looked more like one of those healthy smoothies some people love.

The men in the room ogled her. One swaggered up and said something. She slowly lifted her head from the book she was reading, put a bookmark in, and set it on the bar. Lisa turned in her seat, grabbed the man by the collar, almost lifting him off his feet.

She said something I couldn't hear, but he paled and put his hands up in surrender. She gave him a little shake and let him loose, which caused him to stumble back. He slunk back to his table, where his buddies were all laughing. I'd observed all this from near the front door as I tried to figure out how to approach Lisa.

The man who'd slunk back to his chair noticed me, said something to his friends, and they all turned to stare. I was now wishing I'd worn an oversized turtleneck and loose pants instead of the flirty sundress. I'd never been so ogled in my life.

"Hey, mama. Want to come over and make daddy happy?"

Ick. I didn't get that men-calling-themselves-daddy thing. "Not in a million years."

Lisa looked my way. Maybe this was my in. I walked across the room and took a seat next to her at the bar.

"Why do men always think a woman alone in a bar wants company?" I asked as she picked up her book.

Lisa shook her head. "No idea."

"I hope you don't mind if I sit here. I'm alone, too, and really don't want to be bothered." I paused. "And don't worry, I'll leave you to your book." Up close, she looked even stronger and more intimidating than she had in her pictures or even from the entrance of the bar.

"No worries."

She picked her book back up and started reading again. I glanced at the cover. Lisa was reading a mystery by V.M. Burns. It didn't look like she actually worked here if she got to sit around reading all day.

The bartender came over then. "What would you like?"

What *would* I like? Nothing too strong; I had a

long day ahead of me. The man kept glancing over at Lisa. I couldn't decide if he was irritated because she was getting paid to sit there and read or fascinated because she was so beautiful. At any rate, something was making him uneasy. The bartender turned his attention back to me.

"How about a Bushwacker?" I asked. Bushwackers were like milkshakes for adults. They'd been invented in 1975 on St. Thomas in the Virgin Islands. So while some drinks' histories stretched back hundreds of years, this one was a relative newcomer. The bartender who had come up with the drink named it after his dog, Bushwack. They could be strong drinks, but places like this tended to skimp on the alcohol while also adding a lot of crushed ice and half-and-half. I should be okay. Plus, the dairy should coat my stomach. I knew that was wishful thinking but tried to convince myself that it would help. Although in this kind of bar, maybe this was too complicated a drink.

The bartender reached into a mini fridge and pulled out a plastic jug of premade drink labeled Bushwacker. Joaquín and Vivi would shudder at its use. They both believed in making all of our drinks from scratch. On the one hand, we had the best drinks on the beach, but on the other, it took a lot of extra time. I'd once suggested we could make up our strawberry daiquiri recipe in the morning and got a lecture on freshness.

The bartender poured the mix over ice and added some half-and-half. He gave the blender a whir, poured the drink into a disposable plastic cup, and handed it to me. Lots of bars around here used these kind of cups so people could take them down to the beach. Or maybe they were just lazy and didn't want to wash glasses.

I took a sip, and just as I suspected, it was light on the alcohol, which was fine with me. Now I just had to find a way to have a conversation with Lisa since I'd said I'd leave her alone. Why did I say that? What was I thinking? Why had I agreed to Vivi's absurd plan in the first place? It was one thing to enter the competition and another to sneak around checking out the competition.

"Are you okay?" Lisa asked. "You keep sighing." She put her bookmark back in her book, set it aside, and took a drink of the green smoothie-looking thing.

Her drink was probably healthy unlike mine. "Do you ever agree to do something for someone and then regret it?" I said.

"Rarely."

Figures.

"Unless it comes to men. I have a terrible track record then. Is that your problem?" Lisa asked.

"Not this time. For once, I'm actually in a stable relationship with a good man."

"How'd you manage that?"

I smiled as I remembered the first time Rip and I had met. I'd been snoring away on a boat. Rip had walked by and thought there was a wounded animal under the tarp. It wasn't the best first impression, but who didn't like a man who didn't mind a bit—a lot—of snoring. And who was also handsome and kind.

"Oh, you've got it bad," Lisa said. "I'm Lisa, by the way."

"Chloe. I guess you're right, I do have it bad."

From there, the conversation took off, with Lisa regaling me with stories about men she knew out in Hollywood, including some from the Wonder Woman movies.

"You're a stuntwoman? No wonder you almost lifted that guy off his feet." We both turned to look. I almost shuddered. "Wow, if looks could really kill."

"He thinks I'd be lying on the floor, but he doesn't intimidate me."

We laughed, which didn't make him any happier. We both ordered Bushwackers and toasted each other and continued talking. Lisa's life was fascinating and tough at the same time. During a pause in our conversation, and after another Bushwacker, I remembered Dex was sitting out in the truck waiting for me, and this was business, not pleasure.

I left a big tip for the bartender, who'd hovered around us most of the time we were talking. I slipped off the stool. "It was nice meeting you."

"You too," Lisa said. "I hope we run into each other again."

I felt a little stab of guilt. I'd been vague during our conversation about what I did. "I'm sure we will." I just hope my deception wouldn't make her hate my guts. She seemed like a nice woman, but also like someone I wouldn't want mad at me.

Dex grilled me about what I'd found out from Lisa. I figured the least I could do was answer, since he was driving me around. I also knew that indirectly, I was letting Ann know what was up, because I was certain that Dex would report back to her. Seven minutes later, we pulled up in front of Sandy's. The building was a drab cement block. The gutters were dented and bent. It had a screened door, which hung at an odd angle.

Several Harleys were parked on the crushed-shell-covered parking lot. They gleamed in the April sun, and heat wafted off some of the chrome gas tanks.

Dex looked over the situation. "I'm going in first to make sure you'll be safe. If I don't come back out in a couple of minutes, come on in. Act like you don't know me."

That shouldn't be hard to do, because I really didn't know him. "Okay." I watched him walk in. He had a confident stride, and something about the set of his shoulders said *Don't mess with me*. It seemed kind of silly. This was Dune Allen, for goodness' sakes—a place that was more affordable than a lot of the surrounding towns and certainly not some seedy area, even if the bar itself looked run-down. But I appreciated the gesture.

I waited the required "couple" of minutes before walking in. Sandy's was dark inside, so I stood by the entrance to let my eyes adjust. The bar was directly across from me at the back of the building. The room wasn't much bigger than an elementary school classroom. Jean Claude was behind the bar. He had a white hand towel slung over one shoulder and was chopping fruit. The lime in his hand looked like a walnut. I was kind of hoping the angle of the photo had exaggerated the difference between his hand size and the glass he'd been holding.

Dex sat in a corner with his back to the wall. He could see the entire bar from where he sat. I looked over at him, but he didn't make eye contact. Dex had what looked like an iced tea in front of him. I was guessing it was alcohol and sugar-free. How was I going to ever get a chance to talk to Jean Claude? There were only three barstools at the bar, and three women were sitting in them. They laughed and flirted with Jean Claude. He was smiling and chatting with them.

I sat at the last empty table, alone and feeling awkward. It was about half a foot away from the table of men, whom I assumed belonged to the Harleys. I took the Harley-logoed T-shirts, bandanas, and boots as a sign. My back was up against the wall, too—in more ways than one.

"Jean Claude, some help out here. We have customers who want to order," a harried-looking waitress yelled from across the room.

Once Jean Claude looked at her, she jerked her head toward me in a "go wait on her" kind of way. *Yes*, this was my chance. Jean Claude didn't hurry over, and it was more of a strut than a walk. As far as I could tell, pretty much everyone in the room was watching him, because he was a sight to behold. Jean Claude wore a yellow T-shirt with the Sandy's logo on it and black shorts. He had a bruise under one eye and some marks on his arm that made it look like he'd been in a tussle.

A few seconds later, he stood by my table, and I tipped my head back to look up at him. Up close, I could see the dark lashes that curled probably without the use of an eyelash curler. He'd probably never yanked all his eyelashes out by accident in sixth grade. Jean Claude smelled like a fresh-cut Christmas tree, and he had an easy confidence that made me—a happy, in-a-solid-relationship girl—want to cast that aside and leap on him. I really hoped I didn't fan myself.

"What can I get for you?" he asked.

His voice was a low rumble. Jean Claude grinned at me as I gaped at him. I could never compete against him. I'd be too distracted. Maybe that was Sandy's plan. I finally remembered I was supposed to be ordering.

"A Bushwacker," I said. "Please."

"Coming right up. I'll just write down *Bushwacker* for the woman with the pretty brown eyes." He started writing on a pad that looked like a Post-it Note in his hand. "That helps me keep everyone straight, because I'm new at this."

I almost burst out telling him that's what I did, too, but I didn't want him to know I worked at the Sea Glass, so I just nodded and smiled. Like an idiot. Until he swaggered back up to the bar. I would have smacked my forehead for not chatting him up, but I didn't want to look more ridiculous than I already must. I'd do better when he brought my drink to me. A few minutes later, the harried-looking waitress brought back my drink, slopping a little of it on the table as she whooshed by. Rats. Foiled again.

CHAPTER 4

I took a sip, trying to subtly study Jean Claude over my plastic Solo cup. Oh! This drink was stronger. Almost unpleasantly strong. My eyes watered a little. Interesting. The margins on alcoholic beverages were slim, so I was surprised at the heavy pour. I sipped and watched, trying to come up with a plan to talk to Jean Claude without being too obvious.

"You okay?"

It was the Harley rider next to me. My eyebrows drew together for a moment before I relaxed them. "Yes." But it came out more as a question than a statement.

"You've been sighing a lot and staring at Jean Claude."

What was with me and the sighing today? I wasn't normally a sigher, but then again, I wasn't normally out on a secret mission to size up the competition with a chauffeur named Poindexter.

"What'd he do? Break your heart?" The man had a scraggly reddish beard, and pretty, pale blue eyes, with a sympathetic look in them. The sleeves were cut off of his Harley T-shirt, and his biceps bulged.

"Not yet," I said. But if I didn't figure out a way to talk to him, it might break my heart. When I was given a task, I liked to fulfill it. No matter what.

"You could join us," he said.

While joining a motorcycle gang and running away held some appeal in the moment, it wouldn't work out for me long run. My thighs always got chafed on motorcycles, and once I'd burned the heck out of my calf on an exhaust pipe. "I'm not sure I'm ready to become a motorcycle mama." I hope that didn't offend him.

He threw back his head and laughed. "I meant for a drink. Maybe we can help you with Jean Claude." He held up his hand. A wedding ring shone on it. "We're all doctors in Alabama, but like to get out on our bikes when we can. All happily married. Well, between us, I'm a little worried about Greg's situation. He's been quiet lately."

He tipped his beer toward the end of the table. A man with a neatly trimmed black beard stared glumly down at his beer. A gang of Harley-riding, happily married—except for Greg—doctors. That made me smile.

"Now why don't you finish that drink and let me order you another one."

"I'd better sit out this round and have water."

"Sounds good." When the waitress came over, he ordered a round for his boys, a water for me, and he also ordered several platters of nachos, which he said he'd share with me and his friends. The food and drinks showed up fast.

"What's a nice girl like you doing in a place like this?" The doctor asked me as he pulled another chip loaded with chicken, beans, cheese, and jalapeños off the plate of nachos. He laughed to show he was joking around.

I took another nacho, too. They were surprisingly delicious. "I work for a beach bar in Emerald Cove called the Sea Glass Saloon."

"Checking out the competition?" he asked.

I almost choked on my nacho. Worse yet, I almost answered. That's the problem when I drink in the day, but loose lips might sink me. "Something like that. What kind of doctors are you?" I hoped my question would turn attention away from me.

I nursed my Bushwacker and was laughing with the doctors as they told motorcycle riding stories while I kept an eye on Jean Claude. He stayed behind the bar most of the time, and other than chopping a bit of fruit now and then, he mostly just chatted with whomever was across from him. None of that helped me find anything out about him. Every once in a while, I'd glance over at Dex. He didn't seem to take any notice of me.

The doctor next to me nudged me. "Look, two women are leaving the bar seats. Run up there while you can and good luck."

I stood. "Thanks for the drink and the nachos. Stop by the Sea Glass in Emerald Cove sometime. The view is better and the waitress is friendly." I winked and hustled over to the bar, slipping onto a stool. Winking and sighing. What was with me today? What was next, whistling? Humming? I promised myself, no more sighing today.

Jean Claude loomed across from me. "What can I get you? Another Bushwacker?"

"I'm surprised you remembered, and yes, please."

"Big brown eyes. Hard to forget."

Joaquín was a flirt at work; maybe Jean Claude was, too. "I'll bet you say that to all the women."

"Not the blue-eyed ones." He winked. Jean Claude relayed the message to the bartender and turned back to me. "I was getting a little jealous watching you with the motorcycle dudes."

"Oh, you were, were you?" I tilted my head in what I hoped was a coquettish angle. "It looked like you had your hands full with the ladies at the bar."

"Is your neck okay?" he asked. "I could massage it for you if you turn around."

So much for coquettish. I pictured those big hands and my little neck. Picturing that was a little bit scary, even though Jean Claude had said it in a flirty way. "It's fine." I smiled. "Thank you."

Fortunately, the bartender handed my drink to Jean Claude just then. He did a slow twirl and put my Bushwacker in front of me. I took a big gulp and felt a burn right down to my toes. Yikes, that was strong. It felt like my brain did a little spin before I focused back on Jean Claude.

"Wow. That's a drink." My eyes watered a little.

"I hate it when they water drinks down."

"Me too."

"I'm new here. What's fun to do?" Jean Claude asked.

Glass broke somewhere behind me, and someone yelped. Jean Claude jerked his head up and sprinted out from behind the bar. I turned to see the doctors making a rapid exit as a full-blown fight between several tables broke out. Now I knew why Jean Claude looked like he'd been in a tussle. Before I could even stand up, Dex was at my side, grabbing my arm, hustling me around the bar. I glimpsed the bartender crouching behind the bar and punching numbers on his cell phone. Hopefully, he was calling the sheriff's department. We hurried past the bathrooms and toward a back door. The sounds of tables being overturned and people shouting followed us.

Dex dropped my arm when he realized the back door was locked. He put his shoulder into it, but the door didn't budge. He threw open the door to the women's bathroom, strode to the window, and fumbled with the lock on the frosted-glass window. Two seconds later, he had it open. I stood there stunned for a moment, trying to process the last few seconds, still listening to the crashing and shouts from the front of the bar.

"Come on," Dex said, gesturing me to the window.

I ran over, threw a leg over the sill, dropped to the ground, and sprinted toward the truck. I could hear Dex thundering along behind me. He beeped the truck open, and I dove into the front seat as he yanked on the driver's-side door. We almost bashed heads in our haste. Dex started the truck, cranked the wheel, and we were out of the parking lot before the first of the sheriff's cars we passed pulled in.

I looked back over my shoulder and saw other

people pouring out the bathroom window and front door. My breath was ragged.

"What happened?" I asked. Dex had been seated closer to the start of the fight.

"You okay?" Dex asked. He glanced over as if assessing if all my body parts remained intact.

I'm not sure he really cared if something had happened to me, but I'm sure Ann would. "I'm fine. Thanks for getting me out of there. What started that fight?"

He shook his head, and I didn't think he was going to answer.

"They were placing bets on premier-league soccer games. It got heated."

"British soccer? At Sandy's?"

Dex nodded. "There seemed to be more to it than that, but I'm not sure what. You learn anything about Jean Claude?" Dex asked.

"While he might not be fast at long-distance running, he's quick off the start. That's not something you can teach. It's inherent." He would be more competition than I hoped.

Dex parked near the Sea Glass. Time to head to Two Bobs. Another drink sounded about as appealing as being in the middle of a bar fight. We walked down the walkway that ran along the harbor. We passed the boat I'd inherited from my best friend Boone, Vivi's grandson, along with twenty-five percent ownership of the Sea Glass, and his beach cottage where I lived.

The water sparkled, and a dolphin splashed out of the water as a pelican landed on a post, swallowing a fish it had caught. The sun felt good. After the scene at Sandy's, it was idyllic. Two Bobs was a two-story, newish building with decks on the back and front. They also had a rooftop seating area with fantastic views of the harbor, the outlet from the harbor to the Gulf, and of the Gulf itself.

As we neared the entrance, Dex said, "I'll be around if you need me."

I hoped to the heavens I wouldn't.

CHAPTER 5

I nodded and headed in by myself. The décor, unlike the other bars, was industrial chic. Lots of stainless steel, reds, and blacks. The bar to the left ran the length of the room, but I didn't catch sight of Enrique. He hadn't been on the back deck when I'd crossed it, either. Being here was the riskiest, because I might run into someone I knew. They could blow my stealth cover. I ordered two Bushwackers, because I felt committed to them by this time, and maybe I could use the extra as a means of introducing myself to Enrique.

I hoped these weren't too strong, because I'd consumed a lot of alcohol in the past couple of hours. Good thing I ate before I set out on this sojourn. However, even with lunch and the nacho snack, I was starting to feel a little giggly, which meant I'd probably just about reached my limit of alcohol. When I started at Gray's, I didn't think about the calories I'd be consuming. I'd have to do an extra long run tomorrow morning.

Once I got my drinks and left a good tip, I carried them to the front deck. No sign of Enrique there, either. I scanned the inside tables. The place wasn't packed today for some reason. I guess everyone would rather be outside than in, so I headed up to the rooftop. Several tables had people at them up here. I spotted Enrique at a corner table by himself. He stared moodily out at the Gulf, his long, tan legs stretched out and resting on the chair across from him.

I weighed my options and decided to go with the direct approach. I plopped down beside him and handed him my extra Bushwacker. These were topped with whipped cream and a maraschino cherry. "You look like you could use this," I said.

He straightened a little and ran his eyes over me. It was kind of creepy. I hoped that didn't show on my face. I swept my eyes over him before looking into his pale brown eyes. I smiled. Enrique smiled back. He had a lovely smile.

"To what do I owe this pleasure?" He pointed at the drink. "Whatever that is."

"It's a Bushwacker. I was supposed to meet someone, but they canceled. So I thought I'd share."

"And what bush did someone whack to come up with this?" he asked.

It sounded pretty naughty put like that. Heat rose in my face, and Enrique grinned at me. He flicked back his flowing hair.

"I'm not sure I should accept a drink from a stranger. My mama told me not to."

I held out my hand. "I'm Chloe." He took my hand in his and held it for a few moments too long. I tried not to squirm.

"Enrique," he said.

"See now, we aren't strangers. Plus, you can trust me. I'm a former children's librarian, and we're harmless." Until you crossed us. I smiled at him again, hoping it looked sincere and not strained.

"Can I trust you, Chloe? Isn't that what all the bad people say?" He smiled back at me.

"Of course," I managed to say. I took a drink of my Bushwacker. Not as strong as the last one. Not as weak as the first. Definitely not as good as the ones Joaquín made. I was starting to sound like Goldilocks. Only in this case, Joaquín's drinks were just right. "It's what all the good people say, too."

He reached over and swiped a finger down my nose. "Whipped cream," he said. Then he sucked it off his finger.

Yuck. That seemed creepy to me instead of romantic. It was like the sun had gone under the cloud, and dark shadows were gathering around us. Where was Dex when I needed him? I glanced around. There were plenty of people within shouting distance, but no Dex.

"I feel like I've seen you before," I said. At least his picture, but it seemed like Enrique was the type of man to respond to flattery.

"I've done a bit of modeling." He smiled modestly. Or attempted to seem modest, at least. "And if you follow surfing, I have a little bit of a reputation in that world."

I snapped my fingers. "Oh, wow. You're *that* Enrique. I love to watch surfing."

"Do you surf?"

"I've attempted to, but I'm terrible at it." That wasn't necessarily true; I actually wasn't bad. I may be short, but I'm athletic.

"Maybe you need the right instructor."

The Bushwackers in my stomach roiled around. He might've thought he was playfully flirting, but I wanted to deck him. Enrique leaned back, picked up his phone, and used the keyboard for a few minutes.

"What are you doing here?" I asked. "This isn't exactly the surf capital of the world."

We both gazed out at the Gulf, where the waves were barely a ripple. Even on the windiest days, the waves were rarely bigger than three feet, and they broke too close to shore to be good for surfing.

"Can you keep a secret?" Enrique asked.

"It's my middle name."

He leaned in. Scotch wafted over to me. "I'm here to win an annual competition for barbacks. Bringing the glory to Two Bobs."

I raised my eyebrows and tried to look impressed. "Oh, I've heard about it. How hard it is to win?" I batted my eyelashes, hating myself just a little. Vivi better appreciate this. "Does that mean you work here?"

"They hired me," he said. "But this is about as much as I do." He winked. "I'm good for business. People flock in when they find out I'm here."

I'd hardly call the number of people here right

now a flock, but whatever. I gave a breathy sigh—
on purpose this time. "They are so lucky to have
you."

"They are." He laughed to soften the words and
winked at me again.

Maybe he wasn't creepy. Maybe it was just the
Bushwackers talking. A waitress appeared with a
Bushwacker and what looked like scotch, carrying
them on a tray with one hand. I'd drop them if I
tried that. Even after ten months, I usually had a
death grip on any trays I carried. She placed the
scotch in front of Enrique and the Bushwacker in
front of me. She had short, bleached hair gelled
up in little spikes with red tips that made it look
like her hair was on fire.

Enrique looked at me. "I hope you don't mind I
ordered another for us?"

Yes, I did. "Not at all." He must have texted the
order.

"Is there anything else I can get you?" The waitress was staring at Enrique.

I was pretty sure she wasn't talking just about
drinks. She bent over, and her cleavage was on full
display. And when I say full, I mean enviable. I wasn't
flat and could fill out a bikini, but she was Hooters
material. From the way Enrique was staring, I think
he liked what he saw.

"Not now, cara," Enrique said in a silky voice
that caused the waitress's arms to break out in goose
bumps.

"I'll be around when you need me," she said.

He grabbed her hand and brushed a kiss
against her knuckles. "Thank you."

She seemed reluctant to leave, but someone from one of the other tables called to her.

I grinned at Enrique. I couldn't help it. He looked so satisfied with himself. "What a burden for you."

"You can't begin to imagine." But he laughed. He lifted his scotch. "To us."

I touched my glass to his. "There is no us."

We both took drinks. Mine was a little stronger than it should have been. I needed to slow down.

"There will be," he said.

This guy had more confidence than a newly elected politician. "Not going to happen."

"What are you doing for dinner tonight?"

"I'm having it with my boyfriend."

"I think it's a little early in our relationship to call me your boyfriend."

This time I laughed. "And I think it's a little early to assume I'd have dinner with you, even though you are the famous Enrique." I rolled my *r* when I said his name. All those years of Spanish classes, finally paying off.

He narrowed his eyes for a moment, but then laughed, throwing his head back and letting his hair dangle behind him. The wind shifted, and instead of the smell of salt, the air was tinged with barbeque wafting over from the Briny Pirate, which was next to the Sea Glass. My stomach rumbled loudly in response. Enrique barked out a laugh. I'd have been embarrassed, but I'd always been this way, and I wasn't going to start apologizing for it now.

The Bushwackers took another lap around my stomach. A wave of dizziness swept over me. Lunch had been a long time ago, and I needed to eat. I was sure I wasn't going to learn anything else about Enrique other than what I'd already seen. He was handsome, he'd hit on anyone, and he gave off a slightly creepy vibe that made me uncomfortable.

I stood and swayed a little. I'd like to say it was the wind, but all we had was a gentle breeze. "Nice meeting you," I said. "See you around." He had no idea how soon or under what circumstances.

Enrique stood, too. "Don't go."

"I have to meet someone," I said. "I'm sure we'll see each other again." At least we would at the barback competition.

"Do you need me to walk you out?"

"Nope. I'm fine." I paused. I was feeling a little worse. "But thank you." I turned and hustled down the stairs.

As I headed back toward the Sea Glass, Dex fell in step with me. He walked on the waterside of the walkway and kept herding me in a straight line toward the Sea Glass. How nice, because my feet seemed to be leading me in a serpentine pattern.

"You're nice," I said, feeling a little happier than normal from all the drinks.

I felt, more than saw, him roll his eyes. I wondered how often he had to babysit drunk women. And how had I gone from feeling a little tipsy to the sidewalk seeming to roll in waves in front of me? "I need to order some foods." Foods? "Food. Lots of foods." I stopped and dug around in my purse for my phone, found it, dropped it, and bent to pick it up, almost toppling over until Dex grabbed the back of my dress, holding me up. He scooped up my phone and handed it back to me. I put it to my ear.

"Briny Pirate. Barbequed pork, potato salad, cole slaw, an order of mac and cheese, and hush puppies. Lots of hush puppies." Food would make this awful feeling go away.

"You might want to punch in the number first," Dex said. "Do you want me to order?"

"Yes, puhaleeeease." Wow, I sounded like a native, dragging *please* out to a four-syllable word. But I didn't like how that came out, and I was a little concerned that something more than just day drinking was happening to me.

I turned to Dex. "Do you think I'm having a stroke?" The words came out sounding the way Charlie Brown's parents sounded on the cartoons. *Wah, wah, wah wah.* My knees felt mushy, and everything went black.

CHAPTER 6

I heard Ann Williams yelling at someone, and my eyes flew open. I was on a cot in Vivi's office. Where the heck had it come from, and how had I ended up here? My mouth felt like someone had stuck hot stones in it. There was a wet, cool rag on my head.

"You were supposed to make sure she was okay," Ann yelled. She stood in the doorway next to Dex. All up in Dex's face. His normally passive face was red as he looked down at her.

She was dressed in her usual black—leggings and a T-shirt. Occasionally she'd break up the black with a bit of red trim. Her dark hair flowed around her in perfect waves.

"She was fine when she walked into Two Bobs," Dex answered.

I sat up, and my head felt like someone was playing Olympic-worthy ping-pong in it. They both whipped their heads toward me.

"Dex is right. I was fine when I walked in Two Bobs." Well, maybe *fine* was a bit of an exaggeration, but I'd gone from happy to passed out awfully fast. "It wasn't his fault," I said. "I'm a lousy drinker. Especially during the day."

Joaquín and Vivi hurried over.

"Are you okay?" Joaquín asked.

"You gave us a scare, seeing Dex carry you in over his shoulder," Vivi said.

I looked at Dex. He'd carried me back here? "Thank you, Dex. I'm so embarrassed."

I smelled barbeque, and my stomach growled again. "I need to order some food."

"I ordered for you," Dex said.

"When?" I asked. I didn't remember that.

"After I got you back here. It's in the kitchen. I'll grab it for you." Dex ducked out of sight.

Perhaps he wanted to get away from Ann's wrath, because she almost looked like one of those cartoon characters with steam coming out of her ears. He reappeared and put the food on Vivi's desk. Everyone either piled into her office or stood in the doorway. I sat in one of the chairs at Vivi's desk and lifted the lid off the tray.

"Yum," I said, looking over the array of food.

Everyone laughed. Dex had brought a huge glass of ice water, too. I chugged about half of that.

"You must be feeling better," Joaquín said. "You were snoring like a beast. Our customers thought there was an incoming tsunami." He kissed the top of my head. "I'll head back out to the bar."

"Anybody want some?" I asked as I forked in a bit of the pork. Heaven on earth. Wade, who owned the Briny Pirate, was a genius with a smoker.

Next, I had a bite of potato salad, mac and cheese, cole slaw, and then I ate a hush puppy.

Vivi sat in her big office chair across from me. She put her elbows on her desk and leaned forward. "My doctor's on the way."

I stopped my fork midway to my mouth. "Why?"

She tilted her head to Dex. "He said you went from seemingly fine to passed out fairly quickly."

That's the same thing I'd thought.

"We're worried that someone slipped something in your drink," Ann said. There was still a lot of anger in her voice.

Slipped something in my drink? I shoveled in more food while I let that thought roll around in my head. My hand shook as I put my fork down.

"My doctor is going to do some tests and check you out," Vivi said. "I thought you'd prefer that to going to the hospital."

Who would have put something in my drink? I knew about how quickly drugs could kick in. It would had to have been Jean Claude or Enrique. The bartender I ordered from at Two Bobs or that waitress who brought up the Bushwacker and scotch. But why would she do that to me? Why would any of them? Did she want Enrique? All indications were a yes, but that seemed an extreme way to get rid of the competition—not that I was. The whole episode was terrifying. I nodded. Hospital food wouldn't be nearly as good as this. Plus, I didn't think there was any reason for me to go. "How long was I out?"

"Thirty minutes," Ann said. Ann had a small pirate flag tattooed on her ankle. She was a descendent of Jean Lafitte, pirate and war hero.

From what I'd read about roofies, they affected different people in different ways depending on the dose and the person. Symptoms ranged from nausea to passing out for hours and not remembering anything that happened. I shuddered. Vivi, Ann, and Dex watched me.

"I probably just drank too much," I said. "I should have been more careful." I ate some more, because I was ravenous.

Ann glared at Dex again.

"I'm sorry," Dex said to me.

"None of this is your fault. You protected me, swept me out of the bar at Sandy's at the first sign of trouble." I turned to Ann. "He was wonderful."

Dex pinked up.

Ann relaxed a little and nodded. "Thanks."

Dex drifted out of the office and turned toward the bar. I'll bet he needed a drink. I ate another hush puppy and pushed back the tray of food. By the time the doctor came and went, it was almost seven.

"Go home and get some rest," Vivi said. "The doctor said rest would be good for you."

The bar was still full of people here on spring break. "I'd rather work." Working would be so much better than wondering if I'd been drugged. The doctor had said it would be a few days before we would know the answer to that.

Vivi frowned but nodded.

"I saw some coasters online the other day that we could order that can be used to see if there's anything in your drink or not. You put a little bit of your drink on the coaster, and if it turns blue, you know there's something in your drink."

"We've never had a problem here," Vivi said.

"I know that, but after the scare today, it seems like it might be smart to order them. At the very least, they'd be a deterrent."

"That's a great idea. Let's buy some."

"I'll do that, and then I have to make a phone call." I needed to call Rip and let him know what had happened. The last thing I wanted was for him to hear about what may or may not have happened to me from someone else. He was a volunteer firefighter and on duty tonight. I took a deep breath and dialed. Rip answered on the second ring. A lump formed in my throat at the sound of his voice. It took me a moment to be able to say anything.

"Hey," he said, "are you okay?"

"Yes." But it came out a little shakier than I wanted it to. I explained to him what had happened and emphasized that I was fine. "I've been well taken care of," I said as I wrapped up my telling of the events of the day.

"I'm sorry I have to work and can't be there. Do you need anything? What can I do?" His voice sounded more tense than usual.

"Just listening to me and not judging me helped a lot. Thank you." I heard the alert sound that there was a fire through the phone.

"I have to go. I'm sorry."

"Don't be. I'm good. Just hearing your voice made me feel way better." We hung up. Most of me believed what I'd said about the possible drugging. But a little part of me worried about what could have happened and how much worse things might have been.

* * *

I grabbed an apron, pad, pen, and started around the room, checking on customers and taking orders. Dex and Ann sat at a high-top table together, both reading. Dex had a dog-eared copy of *The Art of War,* and Ann was reading a novel by Catriona McPherson. Both of them ordered iced tea. I ran back and forth from 7 to 8:30, getting last rounds of drinks and reminding people we closed at nine. While that was much earlier than most bars, it worked for us. By 8:50, the bar was almost empty. Dex and Ann were still sitting reading with untouched iced teas by their elbows.

Joaquín was polishing glasses as I wiped down tables using our lemon-scented cleanser. I looked up to see what sounded like the start of a bad joke. What happens when a stuntwoman, a surfer, and an Olympic shot-putter enter a bar? I now know the answer to that joke: everyone stopped midmotion.

Ann Williams looked pale and grabbed Dex's arm. He jerked his head up, eyes narrowing at the sight of the three. They both stared at Enrique. Lisa walked over to me with Jean Claude and Enrique trailing her. They stopped in front of me like they were the Justice League and I was the bad guy. My only weapon was my spray bottle of cleaner, but I wasn't afraid to use it if need be. I felt Joaquín move to my side. Ann and Dex slipped out of their seats and stood by their table.

"We're closed," I said.

"Checking out the competition today?" Lisa asked. "The list of competitors for the barback competition was posted tonight. It wasn't hard to figure out once we were having drinks and talking about our day. All of us met a cute little brunette, and then someone named Chloe was on the list."

Busted. That was the only thought in my head for about two seconds until I realized that either Jean Claude or Enrique might have spiked my drink. I wouldn't let either of them have the satisfaction of knowing I was a little freaked out. And by a little, I meant major-league freaked out. I didn't realize that seeing them again would impact me the way it was. My knees wavered a little, and so did the rest of me. I managed a shrug.

"You could have just been upfront with us," Lisa said.

"Every athlete needs a competitive advantage," I replied.

Jean Claude snorted at that. "Honey, you're hardly an athlete."

A stream of curse words circled through my head. My years of training as a children's librarian meant I held them in. "We'll see about that. I may just be a barback, but you're all ringers. Don't worry. I'll beat you anyway."

Now Enrique laughed in a dismissive way. "Doubtful."

I suddenly wanted to win the stupid competition way more than I had earlier today. Wiping all those superior looks off their faces would be a pleasure.

"Rick Laurier?" Ann had moved up behind the trio.

What the heck was she talking about? Enrique whirled around with a startled look on his face. I was mystified.

"Ann?" He took a step toward Ann.

She took a step back. I'd never seen her do anything but stand her ground. Dex stepped up until he was right behind her.

"I can't believe you managed to transform yourself from Rick to Enrique without anyone figuring it out. Are you still running from the law? Or has enough time passed that you're safe now?"

Enrique/Rick got paler with every question. Vivi came out of her office. Joaquín put a hand on my shoulder and was squeezing it. Hard. I'm not even sure he realized he was doing it.

"How did you know?" Enrique asked.

"There was something in the angle of your head when I took your photo that got me thinking, remembering. I'm not the scared little teenage girl I once was. The one that could be threatened into silence."

She took a step forward, and Enrique took a big step back, bumping up against Lisa and Jean Claude. Neither of them budged for him.

"How many others were there?" Ann asked.

"N-n-none," he said.

Enrique sounded like he was lying.

"I've found some of your victims," Ann said. "And you're going to pay." She whirled around and left, with Dex not far behind her.

Enrique shook himself, like he was trying to shake off the encounter with Ann. He turned toward Lisa and Jean Claude.

"Is she telling the truth?" Lisa asked. There was a frightening note of fury in her voice.

Jean Claude's massive hands were fisted on his hips.

"It's nonsense," Enrique said to them. He gestured to Ann. "We went to high school together, and she followed me around like a puppy. When I rejected her, she made all kinds of accusations."

Ann wasn't one to fling around unfounded accusations, and even though high school was a long time ago, I couldn't imagine her doing it then, either. I didn't buy Enrique's story.

He looked over at me and smiled. "We'll be seeing you around."

"Not if I can help it."

CHAPTER 7

Ann was sitting on my front porch when I arrived home. Maybe she was worried about me. I was fine. Fully recovered. Physically, anyway. I hoped she wasn't too mad at Dex.

Ann stood once Dex dropped me off and I walked up to her. "How are you feeling?"

"Back to normal. No more day drinking for me. What about you? Are you okay?"

"Yes." We stood there for a moment. "When we were seniors, Rick ran a poker game. It was a big thing to get invited, and I did one night. I figured out quickly that it was a scam to take money from people who didn't know the game." Ann smiled briefly. "What Rick didn't know was that I'd been playing poker since I was three. I won about five hundred dollars that night.

"I drove home, and as I got out of the car, I was shoved to the ground and my purse was ripped out of my hands. Even though the man wore a mask, I knew it was Rick. I managed to grab his hand and scrape my nails down it. He kicked me in the ribs, took the money out of my purse, and said 'tell anyone and you're dead.' Then he left."

I could only imagine how scary that would have been. Especially in high school. "What happened?"

"Nothing. That cheesy line scared me. When I went to school the next day, Rick had scratches on his hand. But I never told anyone about it, although I made sure none of my friends ever went to one of his poker games."

"That's terrible."

"I found out several years later that I wasn't the only one."

"I'm sorry you had to go through that."

"After college, I started looking for him, but it was like he'd disappeared."

"Until now."

"Yes. He must not have changed his name legally, or I would have found him." She gave a brief nod. "It's not why I came here tonight. I have a favor to ask."

Wow, that was a first. I was usually the one asking Ann for help. "Go ahead."

"I'm a bit hesitant because of what you've been through today."

I gritted my teeth. I was so over people asking me if I was okay. "I'm fine." Ann couldn't have missed the tension in my voice.

"I want to go diving in the morning. Early. I need someone on the boat for safety and hoped you'd come with me. We'll be back before you need to get to work."

That was puzzling. Why wasn't she asking Dex or any of the hundreds of other people she must know in this area better than me? Was this an audition of some sort? Did she want me to join her band of merry men and women? If she had one. I hope that didn't mean she'd fired Dex.

"Why me?"

She looked at me for a couple of moments. "Because I trust you. You won't slip up and say anything. The locals tend to talk too much."

Wow. "Okay." I was usually up early, anyway.

"I'll pick you up at six."

"Wouldn't it be easier to meet at the harbor, so I can just go into work when we're done?"

"We won't be leaving from the harbor. I don't want anyone to know we're going out."

Well, that was mysterious, but then again, Ann often was. Hopefully, some time out in the Gulf would wash away the rest of the cobwebs from today. "Okay, then. I'll see you in the morning."

The Gulf the next morning was calm, but a storm was coming in this evening, and clouds gathered on the horizon. The weather service had already issued all kinds of warnings—riptides, severe thunderstorm watch, high winds, and the possibility of tornados. I didn't like storms so was happy for the distraction this morning. I poured more coffee into a mug from the thermos Ann had brought along.

I held up the thermos. "Would you like some more?"

Ann shook her head. She'd picked me up at six on the dot in an old Jeep. We'd driven down 30A, past Dune Allen toward Blue Mountain Beach. She'd turned right onto a long private drive lined on either side with well-spaced live oak trees. When I'd first moved down here, I'd been curious about why they called them live oaks instead of just oaks. I looked them up and found out they are considered almost evergreens.

At the end of the drive, a large house sat to the right and a small cove to the left. We'd launched the boat from a private dock with several boats. The house seemed unoccupied. No cars parked outside. No lights on. I was curious if it was Ann's house, but she was preoccupied, so I hadn't asked. The house was three stories, with stunning views of the Gulf on a huge private acreage that had to be worth millions.

The boat was bigger than the one I'd inherited from Boone and much more powerful. The nose lifted when we first took off, and for a minute, I'd been afraid we were going to flip. Of course, we didn't, but we'd flown across the water. The sun had just burst over the horizon and warmed me. It was going to be a hot day, which the beachgoers would love, and it would be good for business.

Ann slowed twenty minutes later. She studied her phone. It looked like there was a photo of a map on it. A very old map. Ann noticed me watching.

"While I was home in New Orleans in January, I was cleaning out a relative's house."

I'd helped my parents clean out my grandmother's house. It was never easy.

"I found this map from the late seventeen-hundreds." She handed her phone to me.

The part that looked somewhat like this area was marked Ba de S. ta Rosa.

She took a deep breath. "I also found old papers about a shipwreck. It looks like Jean Lafitte ditched a ship in this area when he was being pursued by the British Navy during the War of 1812."

"That's amazing." There were plenty of shipwrecks in the Gulf. There was even what was called a Shipwreck Trail for divers, but none of those wrecks were as old as this map. "Is there treasure?" I teased.

"Gold," Ann answered, her voice serious. "And who knows what else."

Holy Harvey Wallbanger. "No one knows about it? There's some reason there's no record of it?" That seemed almost impossible, especially this close to shore.

"As far as I can tell, there's no other record. I've been studying this for the past three months."

"Can anything possibly remain at this point?" I remembered reading that one of the ships that had been deliberately sunk for a reef had had a dump truck on top of it. The dump truck disappeared, never to be seen again, during a hurricane.

"Of course. I've been waiting for the right moment to search. I set up a computer program to run how storms would have impacted the Gulf's floor. And that storm we had two nights ago? It might have uncovered something. That's why we're out here this morning before the next storm comes in tonight."

We both glanced at the horizon. The clouds looked lovely and pink from the sunrise and still very far away. The storm we'd had two nights ago had been terrifying. It awoke all the fears I'd experienced during a storm when I was a ten-year-old and had been out on Lake Michigan. My best friend had died during the storm. I'd been so glad that Rip had stayed over that night. I clung to him like I was Saran Wrap and he was a bowl. He'd distracted me in the best way possible.

"So what's your plan?" I asked.

"I'll dive and see if I can spot anything. You'll stay up here to keep an eye out."

"For what?"

"Anything that could spell trouble, including me not resurfacing in the amount of time I'll specify."

Minutes later, she was in her full diving gear and leaped off the boat into the water. I looked at my phone, not that it had a signal out here, and set a timer for forty minutes. The boat rocked gently, the sun was rising, and I scanned the area around us. For what I wasn't sure. The shoreline was barely visible. Some pelicans skimmed the water, managing to stay just above the waves. Far out on the horizon, I could see small white specks of boats, probably fisherman. Joaquín would be out among them. The water whispered against the side of the boat. Other than that, it was deadly silent.

Thirty-five minutes later, I stared at my phone, willing Ann to come up. Wondering what I'd do if she didn't. I'd taken a scuba diving class at a swimming pool in Chicago, trying to overcome my fear of being below water. But I'd never managed a dive in open water. I couldn't bring myself to do it. So here I was, counting seconds until at last Ann popped her head back above the water and climbed aboard, water shedding from her like mini rivers.

"Any luck?" I asked. I tossed her a towel as she removed her mask and breathing apparatus.

She shook her head.

"What now? Are we headed home?"

"I have a couple of more spots to check out. There are so many variables that play out when searching for something from so long ago."

Ann took the steering wheel, and we headed farther south for fifteen minutes. After another dive that yielded nothing, we headed northwest back toward Emerald Cove. We passed a few fishing boats. Ann gave them as wide a berth as she could while studying them.

"Is something else going on?" I asked.

"Someone broke into my house last night."

"Are you okay?" That would be terrifying.

"I was staying out at my camp. I have company and didn't want them to stay out there alone."

Ann had what she called a camp on a bayou north of Choctawhatchee Bay. I'd been out there once last fall, but hadn't seen a house. "Did they take anything?"

"Nothing."

"That's odd." I was surprised that Ann didn't have a security system at her house. She's the one who helped set up mine when I moved into Boone's house last June.

"I think they found the map, because it had been moved. I'd made a lot of notes that were next to the map, and they had been moved, too."

"It's odd they didn't take them. Old maps can be worth a lot of money." The Chicago Public Library had lots of valuable maps, including the David Perlman Collection, which had maps dated as early as 1670.

"It is odd. I don't think they wanted me to know they were in the house. They left something, though."

My thoughts went to very dark places, like horse heads in beds like in *The Godfather*—movie and book.

"A red rose on the doorstep."

"Does it mean anything to you?"

"No."

"What did the sheriff say?"

"I didn't call. The less people who know what I'm up to, the better."

"You must have a security system, right? How did they get around it?" I'd think she'd have an amazing security system, but maybe she was cocky enough to think no one would mess with her. Ann did have quite the reputation around here.

"State of the art." Ann frowned. "But someone managed to get around it somehow."

Ann cut the engine then, put her diving gear on, and went back in the water without saying anything further.

It didn't surprise me she hadn't called the sheriff. She'd prefer handling things on her own. We were about three football fields from the nearest boat. I scrounged around and found some binoculars. One of the boats was trolling along, fishing lines dangling, with no one paying any attention to us. I went to the next and the next and the next, relieved they all were fishing. Going farther east away from us. A flash caught my eye, and I turned toward it with my binoculars. Someone was staring at me through their own set. A chill went through me.

A splash made me put down the binoculars as Ann's head emerged.

"Did you find anything?"

"Yes," she said. "Give me a hand."

I was expecting a treasure chest, but she had her arm around the neck of a body.

CHAPTER 8

We stared down at Enrique once we got him on the boat. Me in horror, while Ann's face stayed neutral. My stomach roiled more than it had yesterday. We'd both held our fingers to his neck, hoping for a pulse, even though it was obvious that there wouldn't be by his color. So pale.

"I need to call the Coast Guard. I don't want to use the radio and broadcast this to the world." Ann grabbed her satellite phone and punched in a number.

Interesting that she had the Coast Guard number memorized. I picked the binoculars back up and scanned to see if anyone was still watching. All the boats had moved on, and we were out here by ourselves. I wasn't sure whether to be relieved or frightened. The waves slapped gently at the side of the boat, but other than that and the sound of Ann's voice, it was silent.

Ann set the phone down. She looked almost as

pale as Enrique. "They're coming, but it will take a while."

"Was he the one who broke in your house and looked at the map?" Puddles formed around him. I looked away. "It's too big of a coincidence for him to be in this exact spot otherwise. He must have come looking for the treasure and had some kind of catastrophe with his diving equipment." My worst diving fear. Except where was his diving equipment?

Ann shook her head. "He didn't have an accident."

"How do you know that?"

"I guess he could have, but he wasn't out here alone." She glanced down at Enrique. "His body was weighed down with diver's weights. I had to remove them to bring him up."

I gasped at that. "Then his death was deliberate. It was murder." Diver's weights. I remembered that some people in my scuba diving class had to use them because they were so buoyant. They needed them to be able to stay under water. Lots of boats would have them on board.

Ann nodded. "I have to make some calls. Because of my altercation last night with Rick or Enrique, as he calls himself now, I'll be a suspect. I need to call my lawyer."

Last night seemed long ago, but Ann had said she'd make him pay, and now he was dead.

I shook my head. "That doesn't make sense. Why would you bring me out here to find the body with you, if you were guilty?"

"You'll need representation, too. They'll think you are in on it, especially since you were seen with him yesterday. People know that he possibly drugged you."

"No one will think that," I said, with more confidence than I was feeling. "If we were going to kill him, why would we discover his body." I used air quotes around *discover*. "We'd leave him until there was no evidence." I shuddered at that thought, but it was true.

"Or we'd find him to try to make ourselves look innocent," Ann said, using her own air quotes when she said *find*. "I'm so sorry I dragged you into this mess. And I broke my promise."

"What promise?"

"That I'd have you back to work on time."

I almost managed a smile at that. It broke the tension for a moment.

Ann handed me her phone. "Call Vivi. You need to let her know you'll be in late. Ask her to recommend a lawyer for you. She knows everyone."

I took the phone. I couldn't believe I needed a lawyer. It was one thing to hire a lawyer to contest a will, which I'd done in the past, but this was different. I needed a criminal defense lawyer. "Thanks." If I didn't call Vivi, and she heard the news, which she would, she'd probably call the governor like she had in the past. I dialed. "Vivi, I'm going to be late." I might as well fill her in, so I did. "No! You don't need to call the governor. Yes, I need a lawyer." I listened for a few minutes. I looked over at Ann. "Vivi's going to call someone for me."

"Put her on speaker."

I complied.

"Who are you calling, Vivi?" Ann asked.

"Johnny McCellan," Vivi said.

"He's a shark," Ann replied.

"That he is," Vivi said. "I guess I don't need to call the governor. At least for now. Keep me posted," Vivi said.

"Tell him to meet us at the Walton County Sheriff's Department," Ann said.

"I will. I can't believe you got Chloe caught up in this mess."

"I didn't mean to."

Ann and I looked at each other and said our goodbyes to Vivi. While Ann called her lawyer, I pondered why she had a criminal defense attorney on speed dial. She didn't talk for long.

"Why did you tell Vivi to have the lawyer meet us at the sheriff's office? Won't the Coast Guard handle this case?"

Ann looked around. "We aren't far enough out to be in international waters, so the locals will take care of it. The Coast Guard has probably already contacted them, and they'll be on their way out here, too, with their dive team."

"But that's good, right? Deputy Biffle will know that you, that I—we wouldn't murder someone." Ann had some kind of relationship with Biffle. I'd seen them together in a couple of soft moments in the past. There had definitely been some kind of crackling sexual tension between them at the very least.

"Dan knows I cross lines when I need to."

"But there's crossing lines, and there's murder." Ann wouldn't kill someone. Would she? "When you were diving, I was scanning around with your binoculars. Someone was watching us through their own set of binoculars."

Ann's eyes widened. "Who?"

"I don't know. I just spotted the person when you came up with Enrique."

Ann stood still for a moment and then shook herself. "That could complicate things."

"Or provide a much-needed witness."

"Or someone who will lie about what they saw."

"I hadn't thought of that." Things seemed to be getting worse instead of better.

"I'm sorry. My brain always goes to the darkest scenario. I need to call Dex and let him know I won't be available for a while."

You bet I listened in on Ann's call to Dex. I was feeling uneasy, and it wasn't just because the waves had gotten bigger, and the boat was rocking more.

"I'm going to be tied up for the rest of the day. I'll need you to check on the projects I have going," Ann said after briefly filling Dex in on what happened this morning.

Darn, she didn't go into more detail about her "projects." My curiosity level was high—anything to keep from thinking about Enrique lying dead only feet away from us.

By the time Ann ended the call, we could hear the whine of boats racing toward us, and two specks appeared, one coming from the north and the other the northeast. The second must be the Coast Guard, because they had a station in Destin.

"Would you be comfortable not mentioning the map and why we were out here?" Ann asked.

"Why?"

"I'd rather not talk about the shipwreck yet.

Once word gets out, everyone will be out here searching for it. I'd like a chance to find it first."

I studied her for a couple of seconds. "What about the break-in at your house? That could be tied to this."

Ann nodded. "You're right. I'll mention that and that nothing was taken. I'd rather not mention the map. If your moral code doesn't allow that, I'll understand."

I did some calculating in my head, weighing the pros and cons. The boats were closing in, and I had to decide.

"What do you think, Chloe?"

I looked Ann in the eye. "What map? I came out here so you could dive." If it became apparent that the map and Enrique's death were connected, I'd say something. However, Ann being out here to dive was true enough. For now.

"We'll need to figure out who had a better reason than us for killing Enrique," I said. "And after what I heard about him last night, that doesn't seem like it will be all that hard to do."

Ann stared out at the horizon for a couple of moments. "There's something else you need to know."

I braced myself. This didn't sound good.

"I killed a man."

Oh. The boat we were on seemed smaller all of a sudden. Claustrophobic.

"It will come out as people dig into my past." We could see the boats now. One was a Coast Guard boat. Lights flashing. "I went through a trial, but it was self-defense. Fortunately for me, the jury realized that."

"I'm sorry you had to go through that."

"It was after the incident with Enrique."

We both glanced over at him.

"I took every kind of self-defense class I could afford. I swore there'd never be another Enrique in my life again. Then one night, a man attacked me as I left a bar around midnight. Dragged me down an alley. I managed to slip out of his grasp and tried to make a run for it. What is it they tell schoolkids these days? Hide, run, fight. He tackled me. We fought, and I won. If one can call killing someone winning."

My heart hurt for Ann. I now knew why she liked to fix things for other people. "You're very brave."

"Not really. Inside I'm just a scared girl who fights."

The Coast Guard and sheriff's team had arrived.

"Don't say a word about anything until Johnny is with you. Name and address only. Nothing else," Ann said. "Lawyer up. First thing."

That sounded like she'd been through this before. "Okay."

"I'm going to tell them where I found the body so they can find any evidence that's down there that may help us. But that's all."

CHAPTER 9

We were separated immediately before either of us could speak. Ann to the Coast Guard boat and me to the sheriff's. Deputy Biffle was staring down at me. His ever-present mirrored aviator sunglasses in place, so I could only see my eyes and not his. Mine looked scared and worried. No way to tell what he was thinking. Although the few times I had seen him without the sunglasses, it was almost impossible to tell then, either. Except when he was with Ann.

He'd made one quick glance at her, when she'd stepped from our boat to the Coast Guard boat, but then focused on me. "Tell me what happened here this morning."

"I want my lawyer."

Deputy Biffle's mouth tightened. "That's how you want to play this? A man is dead." He gestured toward Enrique. "Don't you want us to get to the bottom of this as soon as possible?"

Oh, yes. Good job trying to play on my emotions. I almost cracked. "Lawyer."

"This makes you and Ann look like suspects."

I almost nodded in agreement, but managed to hold myself still. "Lawyer." I hated myself a little bit. It wasn't how I usually operated, but I was trusting Ann on this one.

"Do you have a lawyer?"

I nodded.

"Is it Rip?"

I shook my head. Rip used to be a criminal defense lawyer but had walked away from it over a year ago. I wondered if Rip already knew what was going on out here. Probably, since he was a volunteer firefighter. Unless he was out on a call.

"Who?"

I was frightened and tired. I didn't want to add *murder suspect* to my resume. My mind froze, and I couldn't think of the man's name. Shark. That's all I had. Wait. "Johnny someone." I didn't have to tell Deputy Biffle that, but giving him something felt right.

"Johnny McCellan? Please say no."

What the heck? I nodded. "That's his name. Why shouldn't I work with him?"

"He's underhanded. You're not."

Deputy Biffle took another look over at Ann. She was pointing to the water on the other side of her boat.

"She's talking."

"I thought once I asked for a lawyer, you couldn't ask me any other questions."

Deputy Biffle lifted a shoulder and then dropped it. He took off his sunglasses and looked down at me. His brown eyes were friendly. "This had to be a terrifying experience for you. Come on. We're friends. Help me out here."

Maybe we had been friendly on occasion, but we were hardly friends. Deputy Biffle was very good at witness manipulation. Cops lie. They use whatever they can to get answers.

I looked up at him. Softened my features. "Lawyer."

That Deputy Biffle hadn't tossed me overboard, I thought two hours later as I sat in an interview room at the Walton County Sheriff's Department, showed his great restraint. He'd been tempted. I'm sure. I would have been if our roles were reversed. We'd left the site about fifteen minutes after the last time I'd said, "lawyer." More boats had arrived, and divers from both the Coast Guard and sheriff's department had gone in the water just before we'd left. I'd been sitting here since.

Amazingly, Deputy Biffle hadn't taken my phone. I'd called Vivi again and told her what I could. I'd checked the news on my phone. There were stories labeled BREAKING NEWS that said a body had been found off the coast of Emerald Cove, but little else. I daydreamed about what a shark named Johnny would look like—dark hair, slicked back with gel, some gray at the temples, sharp features, intense eyes, and sharp teeth. Lean, predatory. I hoped he'd show up soon, because every moment of waiting made me more anxious.

The room I sat in wasn't that far off from something you'd see on a TV show like *Bosch* or *NCIS*.

Table, two chairs, the obligatory two-way mirror. I kept my back to it, wondering who was on the other side, if anyone. I shivered in the cold, or maybe from the adrenaline receding from my body. I'd alternately sat on my hands, blown on them, and tucked them under my armpits in an attempt to warm them up. Nothing helped.

Once, I'd heard Anne's voice out in the hall. It hadn't sounded happy. I'd sent a text to Rip. Not saying much, since who knew if my phone records would be subpoenaed or not. I told him I'd found a body with Ann and where I was. So far, he hadn't responded, but maybe he knew better.

I hadn't gone to check if I was locked in here or not. The answer might be too depressing. It didn't seem possible that someone would actually think I could kill someone or help kill someone. Or that I'd be involved in some elaborate cover-up where we'd killed someone and then "discovered" the body to try and throw people off the scent.

More voices outside. The handle on the door moved a bit, paused, moved again, and the door swung open.

"Chloe, is it?" a man asked. His voice had an Irish lilt. He had light red hair and the palest green eyes I'd ever seen. A bit of a paunch showed behind his black T-shirt and khaki cargo shorts. "I'm Johnny McCellan."

He reached out his hand, and we shook. Johnny's was warm against my cold one. So this was the shark?

"Chloe Jackson," I managed when I found my voice, feeling a tad disappointed that Johnny didn't match up to my imagined image of him.

"I'm sorry you caught me out. I was mowing my lawn this morning. Mowing on a Sunday morning instead of attending church. My sainted mother will be rolling in her grave." He crossed himself and smiled a cheeky smile at me.

"Am I going to be charged with murder?" I asked. A tear rolled down my cheek, and I swiped angrily at it.

Johnny pulled out the chair across from me and sat. "Now let's not be going there with your thoughts. I'm just wrapping my arms around this situation. Tell me what happened."

"Don't I have to pay you to retain you as my lawyer so anything I say will be confidential?"

"We'll sign an agreement later. For now, we have a verbal one. Vivi's taken care of the financial part. She feels responsible for pulling you into this situation."

That was a surprise. Vivi had accused Ann of being the one to pull me in, but I guess she realized she had a role in it, too, by sending me to check out the competition in the first place. I glanced around the room. "Are they recording us?" I gestured to the two-way mirror. "Or watching?"

"No. I took care of that. Now start your story where you think it's important."

"Are you going to take notes?" I asked.

He tapped his head. "I'll keep it up here for now. Don't worry. I'm sharper than I look." He flashed his charming grin.

I couldn't help but smile back. If Ann and Vivi thought this man was a shark, I guess I'd just have to trust them. And since Vivi hadn't sent anyone else along, I guess that meant something, too. I started with yesterday morning, when I'd agreed to go check out the barback competitors, and went from there just in case any of it was important.

Johnny leaned forward and listened with an intensity that bordered on frightening. I guess that's what sharks did. He shook his head when I told him that I potentially had been drugged and that I was awaiting the results. After rattling off most of the story, I paused, thinking about the map. I'd promised Ann I wouldn't tell the deputies about it, but made no such promise about telling my lawyer.

"Out with it, now," Johnny said. "Don't hold anything back that could affect your case."

The man was intuitive. "There is something more. Something that explains why we were out there."

"Are you going to share? Because it would certainly help me mount my defense." His accent lilted, and he sounded more Irish than ever.

"Ann's house was broken into last night before the dive. Nothing was stolen, but she believes that someone took photos of an old map and papers she has."

Johnny gave me an intense look. "What kind of map?"

I sighed. "An old family map that might lead to a potential treasure. I went out there to help her search."

"And did you find anything other than Enrique?"

The treasure wasn't really his business, but whatever. "No."

"Why in the world didn't you tell Deputy Biffle?"

"Because Ann wants a shot at finding the treasure, before the word gets out about it."

"You could both be charged with murder," Johnny said. His voice calm. "What treasure is worth that?"

CHAPTER 10

I soaked in Johnny's question. Part of me knew he was right. "We both could be anyway. I felt terrible, not saying anything to Deputy Biffle. I want to help them find who murdered Enrique, but I promised Ann I wouldn't mention the map for now. Some part of me understands her wanting to keep that secret."

"Okay then. We'll stick with that story for now." Johnny stood. "We'll call him in. Don't answer any questions until I give you the go ahead."

I nodded. Johnny went to the door, looked out into the hall, and gestured to someone I couldn't see.

Deputy Biffle walked in a few minutes later, looking grim and different without his hat and sunglasses. He leaned against the wall and started asking questions.

Twenty minutes later, I'd gone through the basics of the morning and Ann confronting Enrique last night at the Sea Glass. I hated talking about that part, because it made Ann look bad. But it would come out at some point, and maybe it already had if Deputy Biffle had already questioned Ann.

"Ann mentioned that her house had been broken into. What do you know about that?" Deputy Biffle asked.

I glanced at Johnny, and he nodded to go ahead. "She told me her house had been broken into and that nothing was taken."

"That's it? It seems like that must have been a very upsetting experience for her."

For most people, it would be, but Ann definitely wasn't most people. "You'd have to ask Ann about that." I almost forgot to tell him that I'd possibly been drugged, so I explained what had happened.

"I'm sorry that happened to you." He studied me for a few moments. "It must have made you angry," Deputy Biffle said.

I knew telling him about this would make things look worse for me, but not telling him and having him find out later wouldn't have gone well, either. I opened my mouth to answer, to defend myself, but Johnny shook his head.

"I think we're done here," Johnny said.

"Not quite," Deputy Biffle said to Johnny.

I looked between them, trying to pick up on cues and thinking of one of my dad's rock songs that had a lyric about staying or going. I wasn't sure at this point which I should do. Johnny finally gave a little *go ahead* nod, although I think Deputy Biffle would have gone ahead, nod or not.

"Who else was in the bar last night?" Deputy Biffle asked.

Johnny gave me a nod. I closed my eyes for a moment, picturing the scene. "Joaquín, Vivi, Ann, Dex, and a couple of tourists who were lingering."

"Do you know their names?" Biffle asked.

I shook my head. "I don't. If they'd been in before, they weren't memorable. It's been so busy with spring break that I might not have noticed them." Not being memorable was good. That meant they hadn't been drunk or obnoxious or loud. My favorite kind of customers, just like when I'd been a librarian. "And like I said, Jean Claude LaPierre and Lisa Kelley were there. They're both in town for the barback competition and came in with Enrique."

"Is there anything else?" Biffle stared at me with those brown eyes.

It felt like he was looking into my soul and could tell I was holding back. I wanted to look down, to get away from his intensity. I'm guessing smarter people than me had cracked under that look. *Don't think about the map*, I told myself. *He doesn't know.* I lifted and dropped my shoulder. "That's it." *For now,* I added silently.

Johnny stood, so I did too. I guess I wasn't going to be arrested. At least not right now. We walked out into the hall. Ann stood there, looking as calm as if she'd just walked out of a lovely tea instead of an interrogation.

"No words until we're out of here, ladies," Johnny said, ushering us down the hall.

I was almost surprised when we stepped outside to find it was still daylight. It was like that weird sensation when you go to a movie during the day and expect it to be dark out when you leave. The sun felt good after sitting in the cold. Dex leaned against Ann's truck, here to pick us up was my guess.

"I'll fix this," Ann said to me. "Don't you worry."

"I don't expect people to fix things for me. I can fix my own problems." I paused. "And help you with yours."

"Ladies," Johnny said, looking back and forth between us as if he expected us to brawl.

What kind of clients usually hired him?

"Meet me in my office tomorrow morning at nine sharp, and we will go over some strategies," he said. He handed me a business card.

I nodded as Johnny walked off. I guess he was used to people doing what he told them to.

"I'm sorry," Ann said. "I can't believe I got you into this mess."

"It's okay. You had no idea." At least I hoped she didn't. I'd had a lot of time to think while I waited for Johnny to show up. Could Ann have killed Enrique and taken me out with her this morning as cover? I didn't want to believe that of her. I chose not to. "We'll figure this out. Why don't you stop by tonight? I'll be home by ten-thirty. I think we should talk before I see Johnny in the morning." And I had questions. Not ones I wanted to ask out in the parking lot of the sheriff's department.

Ann agreed with me, and we headed over to Dex. As we did, a car wheeled into the parking lot. Rip's car. He threw it into park and leaped out. He wore shorts and a T-shirt. There were smudges of smoke on his face. When he got to me, he pulled me into his arms. He reeked of smoke and sweat, but I'd never smelled anything so wonderful in my life.

"I got here as soon as I could." He held me away from him and looked me over, as if I might have some outward injury. Then he pulled me back to him, and I snuggled against him, wrapping my arms around his waist and enjoying the heat of his body.

"I'm okay. We haven't been charged." I left the *yet* unspoken, but Rip hugged me even tighter. "Excuse me. I need to breathe."

Rip laughed. "I'm sorry. You have a lawyer?"

"Yes. A man Vivi knows. Johnny McCellan."

"Okay. He's good at what he does."

"So I've heard." I worried that I needed better than good right now.

"I can drive you home."

"Thanks."

When we got in the car, we laced hands as Rip drove. My stomach rumbled. Loudly. But Rip was used to it and somehow didn't seem to mind.

"Can I take you out to lunch?" he asked.

"I need to clean up and go to work."

"After the morning you've had?"

It didn't come out judgmentally, just curious. "I need a distraction."

He glanced at me. The corners of his mouth quirked up. "I'd be happy to distract you."

Oh, so tempting. "Thanks, but I don't want to leave Joaquín and Vivi in a lurch. Spring break has been so busy, we've barely had any time off."

"Trust me, I've noticed."

"It's not like you sit around without anything to do." I paused. "Are we going to fight?" We rarely did and usually only about something unimportant like where we were going to eat or who made better Brussels sprouts.

"No. We aren't going to fight. I just worry sometimes, because you never seem to let up."

I nodded. It had been wildly busy last summer and over spring break. The between times were more leisurely, and he'd liked it. Me, too. "We've been talking about hiring some part-time help."

"Should I apply?" Rip grinned at me.

"Oh, yes. I'd love to boss you around."

We pulled up to my house.

"You can boss me around anytime." Rip leaned over and kissed me. Suddenly, going to work didn't sound like such a great idea.

CHAPTER 11

An hour later, I stood behind the bar in the Sea Glass. Tempting as an afternoon with Rip was, I felt obligated to be here. I'd already had the "why are you here" and "go home" conversation with Vivi and Joaquín. Although at best, their attempts were half-hearted. They knew me well enough by now to know I wouldn't listen. Besides, I was more likely to pick up information in here than by sitting home stewing. This place could be a hotbed of gossip at times. Mostly on days that have a *d* in them.

The heritage business owners were gathered at a table often reserved for them. They were Vivi's oldest friends, and their family businesses dated back to at least the fifties, if not earlier. Vivi went and sat next to Wade. I'd noticed a change in Vivi lately; she seemed more affectionate around Wade, and I hoped they were finally going to be together. Wade was obviously in love with Vivi. I'd noticed that right away when I'd moved here ten months ago. Vivi had always seemed fond of him, and he was her confidant, but this was new. Wade put his arm around Vivi, and she didn't pull away. That made me smile.

I went over to take orders. When I had first arrived last June, this group had been highly suspicious of me. I couldn't blame them. I'd lied to all of them, but once I helped find the real killer when Vivi had been accused of murdering a customer, things had thawed between all of us.

"What can I get you, Ralph?"

"Sweet tea." Ralph Harrison had a deep voice and a short Afro, and owned the Redneck Rollercoaster, which was really a trolley that took tourists around the area from beaches to bars and back. He also worked as a volunteer firefighter with Rip and was married to his high-school sweetheart, Delores. She owned the local diner and was a 911 dispatcher.

I gave him a look, because Delores had him on a strict diet limiting his sugar.

"Don't start with me," he said. "It's bad enough that Delores is always hounding me about what I'm eating; I don't need you to pile on."

I laughed. "Feeling guilty, are we?"

He narrowed his eyes at me and then smiled. "How are you? That seems more important."

"I'm fine." But Ralph's question made all the others at the table turn to me, eyebrows up, interested looks on their faces. Last June, it would have been sheer curiosity, but now it was concern for me.

"We heard you were drugged," Edith Hickle

said. She owned the Glass Bottom Boat with her father and daughter.

"*Possibly* drugged. Honestly, it was probably the alcohol." That was way more comforting to think of.

"We heard you found a dead body this morning," Fred Russo said. "Who was it?"

Fred owned Russo's Market, a fabulous small grocery store that always struggled to make ends meet against the big chains. I shopped there whenever I could.

"I can't say. Deputy Biffle's orders." They all knew and mostly respected Biffle. I hoped that would make them quit asking questions.

"I heard it was one of the ringers they brought in for the barback competition," Fred said.

Everyone looked at me expectantly.

I used my neutral librarian face on them. Of course, they'd somehow heard. Telegraph, telephone, tele-a-heritage-business-owner. "I still can't say anything. And why did none of you warn me that Vivi and Joaquín were cooking up a plan to get me to represent the Sea Glass in the barback competition?"

They all started babbling reasons, including they had no idea, Vivi swore them to secrecy, and they'd been too busy to pay attention. At least I got them off the topic of the body.

I laughed. "No more excuses, but you are all on my naughty list. What can I get you to drink?" I took their orders, made the rounds of the bar, and took the orders up to Joaquín. I didn't manage to pick up any gossip. I might as well have stayed at home with Rip and let him distract me.

"Did you just fan yourself?" Joaquín asked.

Oh, brother. That was embarrassing. I was supposed to be pouring beers and filling the orders for wine. Joaquín did the more complex drinks, even though I was getting better at making them after months of practice.

"Maybe?" I said.

"Thinking about Rip?" Joaquín asked, giving me a little nudge with his hip. Joaquín had been a professional dancer in Los Angeles before he moved back here and started his fishing business and working at the bar for Vivi. He still danced his way through the day, and our female customers loved it. In fact, a line of them were sitting at the bar admiring him as we spoke. Not that it would do any good. Joaquín was happily married to Michael.

"You know me too well."

"Have you heard anything about the body?" I lowered my voice so no one could hear the question as I put beers, wine, Ralph's sweet tea, and a couple of cocktails on the tray.

"I heard it was Enrique."

If Joaquín knew, everyone else must, too. Why had the heritage business owners given me such a hard time?

"Was it?" he asked.

"I can't say."

"Blink twice if yes?"

I smiled at that. Deputy Biffle hadn't covered blinking, and I knew I could trust Joaquín. I blinked twice. Then I took the drinks and distributed them. When I returned to the bar, Joaquín was polishing glasses. I joined him.

"Do you know anything else about you-know-who?" I asked.

"Funny you should ask that question. Last night, Michael and I decided to go have a drink at Two Bobs."

CHAPTER 12

"No way." Two Bobs was known for their watered-down, overpriced drinks. Joaquín could make a better drink with his hands tied behind his back and blindfolded.

"I was uneasy after what happened with Ann last night. She seemed so upset. And since she spends a lot of time there, I wanted to check on her."

I knew she hadn't been there, because she'd been at my house. "And?"

"She wasn't there. But Enrique was with an entourage of women."

"Anyone stand out?"

"He managed them very well. Took turns dancing with them and somehow managed to keep most of them happy. I think they all understood the drill, but hoped to be the one to capture his heart. Or maybe just his body for a night."

"Yuck. Although he had a fabulous body. You said *most of them*, though."

"A couple of women sat off to one side, alternating flirting and pouting. But one woman actually dumped a drink on her competitor's head and stormed off."

"What did Enrique do?"

"He excused himself and took off after her. When he reappeared about fifteen minutes later, he had a smudge of lipstick on his cheek, and his hair was mussed."

"What did she look like?"

Joaquín described her. She sounded a lot like the woman who'd brought the drinks to Enrique and me yesterday. A woman desperate for attention from Enrique—but the question was, desperate enough to kill him? What had he called her? Cara? Was that her actual name or just a general term of endearment he used for women so he didn't call them by the wrong name? Maybe I needed to go down to Two Bobs after work and find out for myself.

"What?" Joaquín asked.

"What do you mean?"

"You narrowed your eyes and then nodded."

Geez, I wasn't usually this obvious about things. I was good at poker and keeping people from knowing what I was thinking. I must be more shaken than I realized. "I was just wondering if that woman could have anything to do with Enrique's death."

Joaquín started shaking his head. "Maybe you should sit this one out. You're already involved, and this could make things worse for you."

"I'd like to say you're right, but I think I have a bigger stake in this. I'm not content to sit back while Deputy Biffle pins this on Ann and maybe me."

"It doesn't really seem like he's that kind of deputy—one that takes the easy way out."

I sighed. "I agree. But you need to tell him what you know." And I had to do what I had to do.

"You're right. I'll call him when things slow down." Joaquín put away the glass he was polishing. "When are we going to start your training for the barback competition?"

"We're really going through with this? After what happened this morning?"

"I can't imagine why we wouldn't. It's not like they're going to cancel the competition."

"It's not going to be easy with our schedules. You fish at the crack of dawn, and then I'm in here. And then you are. The only time we're both off is after we close, and that's kind of late for practice."

"Hmmm, that's going to be a problem. Maybe Michael can help out."

"In the bar?" He had in the past. "Or as my trainer."

"Oh, he'd never agree to train you. He knows how freaking sassy you are. Former Navy man versus Chloe." Joaquín shook his head. "I don't see that ending well."

"Please, you make me sound like a monster."

"Honey, you're too short to be a monster. Maybe a Tasmanian devil. They're short and full of energy."

I shook my head at him. "I don't know why Michael puts up with you."

Joaquín grabbed me and spun me around in a couple of quick dance moves that I could never manage on my own but had me feeling like signing up for *Dancing with the Stars*. The women at the bar clapped and *ooh*ed.

"That's why, Chloe." Joaquín winked at me and then went over to the ladies at the bar to check for refills.

Two hours later, I was worn out and hadn't found out anything since Joaquín had mentioned the woman at Two Bobs. The heritage business owners were really letting me down with their lack of information. They'd all left about an hour ago to get back to their businesses. I approached a man I called the Whiskey Sourpuss. He was a regular, a curmudgeon on the outside, but I kept hoping he had a softer interior.

He and another regular had an ongoing sparring match. They both usually came in right after we opened and sat on opposite sides of the bar. They called each other "old man" and "old woman." Today, they walked in together and were sharing a table. Will wonders never cease?

One time I'd made the mistake of getting the Whiskey Sourpuss his usual old-fashioned. I'd placed it front of him with a flourish. He denied having a usual against all evidence, because he always ordered one. The first old-fashioned I'd ever made had been for him. There I'd been, all proud of myself for recognizing a regular and managing to make him a not-disgusting drink, only to have him yell about it. He ordered a whiskey sour that day—thus, the nickname I used for him. Only in my head, of course. I hoped it never popped out by accident.

"Hi," I said when I got to their table. "Nice to see you two sitting together."

"It's only 'cause it's crowded," the Sourpuss said. "When are these spring breakers going home? They trash the beach, party all night, and generally make a nuisance of themselves. Why can't they just stay home?"

I didn't think he expected me to answer, because if I explained everyone loved the beautiful white sandy beaches and aquamarine-colored waters, he wouldn't appreciate the observation. Or that their tourist dollars helped keep this town afloat, which is why there was a good school system, great library, and new fire trucks.

"And it seems like spring break starts in February and doesn't end until it's almost May." He shook his head with regret.

I couldn't argue with that. It started when New England had their February break and rolled on as various schools and colleges let their students out, with March being the peak month.

"What can I get for you today?" I was so tempted to say *the usual* just to see his reaction but managed not to.

"I'll have an old-fashioned."

"In other words, his usual," the woman said.

I tried to hide my smile, but it just didn't work. He blustered for a moment, but then laughed.

"I hate to think of myself as predictable," he said.

"Predictable isn't always a bad thing," the woman said. She nudged him with her arm.

Hmmm, they've moved from opposite sides of the room, to walking in together, to nudges. It seemed like there was definitely a lot of romance in the air this time of year.

"I'll have a mimosa," the woman said.

"Mimosas are for sissies," the Sourpuss said.

"You might do with a little sparkle in your life."

For once, the old man smiled. "Maybe I could. I'll try a mimosa too, Chloe."

Wow, something was definitely going on there. First Vivi and Wade, and now them. Had Cupid been flying over Emerald Cove?

They leaned toward me.

"We heard you and Ann Williams found a body this morning," the woman said.

"And that you got roofied last night," the man added. "Hope you're okay."

Wow, it only took ten months for this man to say something kind to me. But I'd found some people down here were reserved. I think it came from that old fisherman's way of life. They could be a tough, silent lot. "I'm fine, thanks. I can neither confirm nor deny the part about the body." I placed their drinks in front of them.

"Which means she did," said the Whiskey Sourpuss.

"Have you two heard anything about it?" I asked. Trying to sneak around listening to conversations hadn't gotten me anywhere.

They exchanged a look, which must mean they'd heard something. Now, was what they knew accurate?

"I guess one of the other ringers for the barback competition had a bit of a past with Enrique," the woman said.

"How so?" I asked.

"That I don't know. If I hear anything, I'll tell you," she said.

"Where'd you hear that?" I asked.

"We stopped by Two Bobs before we came here. Not really our kind of place, but morbid curiosity and all that." The old man waved his hand around.

I was seeing a different side of him today.

"There were a lot of women in there crying," the woman added.

"It seemed like there was a competition going on there to see who could wail the loudest," Sourpuss said. "Had to get out of there. Plus, Joaquín actually knows how to mix a drink. Speaking of drinks . . ." He gave me a sharp look.

"Coming right up," I said. If they knew that Enrique had a past with one of the other ringers, Deputy Biffle probably did, too, but why leave anything to chance? I put in their order and sent Deputy Biffle a text, telling him what I'd heard this afternoon. That bit of news along with Joaquín's information about the flock of women would at least make him look at people other than Ann and me. And if it didn't make him look, it certainly would make me dig in.

CHAPTER 13

At 9:10 that night, I stood in front of a shrine of sorts at Two Bobs. It was by the back deck that faced the harbor. There were pictures of Enrique, flowers, stuffed animals, and candles flickering a bit precariously. My instinct was to blow them out, but there were enough people milling about that it was safe enough. I walked up on the deck, where I could study the faces of the people looking at the shrine. Although this wasn't exactly the scene of the crime that a criminal would supposedly return to, it was the closest thing right now.

A few people had tear-streaked faces. A man blew his nose. Some of the crowd just seemed to be curious and stood with drinks in their hands. No one had a sign on them that said I DID IT. Nothing to see here, so I went inside. The place was packed, techno music was pounding, and lights flashed like streaks of lightning. When I lived in Chicago, I hated being in bars like this, and the few times I'd been in here, I'd never seen anything like this.

I worked my way through the crowd to the bar and ordered a drink. I didn't believe in going into a place and not ordering anything. It was almost as bad as leaving a library without a book. As I waited for a soda, which is what they called pop down here, I looked for the waitress who'd waited on Enrique and me, the one Joaquín said was crying. With the crowd and the flashing lights, it wasn't going to be easy to find anyone. The bartender put my soda on the bar.

"On the house," he shouted.

Bartenders often did that with soft drinks. Perhaps he thought I was a designated driver. I left five dollars for a tip. Something else I often did. Over-tipping had become a habit since working at the Sea Glass.

I moved around the edges of the crowd, trying to spot the waitress. It wasn't easy in a crowd with me being vertically challenged. I went out on the deck on the beach side. The noise level dropped, the breeze had picked up, and I saw lightning flash out on the horizon. Ann often sat at a table in the corner, but she wasn't there now, and neither was Dex, who sometimes held the table for her. The waitress wasn't out there, either.

I went back in—the music was still cranked—and headed up the staircase to my left. It was quieter up here, although the floor vibrated from the music below. High-top tables were scattered along the walls. Lights were strung and blew in the breeze. There was a space in the middle for dancing, and couples swayed to soft rock that was piped in. The band Looking Glass sang about Brandy and her being a good wife. As I recalled, Brandy served whiskey to sailors, so we had something in common. Although her love wasn't that into her. I really hoped that wasn't the case with Rip and me.

Someone waved from one of the tables. I realized it was Leah Hickle, one of the co-owners of the Glass Bottom Boat. She was married to one of the volunteer firefighters and sat with a group of them at a table that overlooked the harbor. Rip was on duty tonight, so not among them. But my friend Smoke was. I went over and stood between Leah and Smoke.

"Want to dance?" Smoke asked after I'd greeted everyone and declined a beer. He had blue eyes that were almost violet and thick eyelashes with blond tips. Smoke's shoulders were broad and strong.

"Oh, Rip's not going to like that," one of the men said.

I had to meet Ann at 10:30, but I had time for a dance before then. "Sure," I said.

I loved to dance, and Smoke was an excellent dancer. Rip wouldn't care. He knew that Smoke and I were strictly in the friend zone. I just hoped Smoke did. He stood, grabbed my hand, and swirled me out on the dance floor. He danced us away from the table full of firefighters, even as catcalls and comments followed us. Soon we were on the beach side of the deck, and more lightning streaked across the horizon. It was mesmerizing to watch when it was that far away.

"Are you out here nosing around?" Smoke asked.

I looked up at him. "You know me a little too well."

"I heard about Enrique. You're something, Chloe. Most people would be huddled in their beds crying after seeing a dead body like that."

"Trust me, that was tempting." Especially if Rip would have been huddled there with me. "But what good would that do?"

"I get it. Although, I'd be on the couch with a pint of ice cream and a romantic comedy on."

I laughed. "Right. I think it would be more likely you'd be busting down doors and taking names."

"Have you found anything out?"

"Nothing." Maybe a couple of whispers of gossip, but that's all they were at this point.

Smoke pulled me a pinch closer and I just enjoyed the dance.

"Would you make a good wife?" Smoke asked as Brandy played on. He pulled back a little so he could see my face.

I stuttered and stepped on his foot. Smoke saved me and whirled me around. Brandy in the song was supposed to be a good wife. Had he and Rip been talking about me? Or was he asking for himself? I hoped it was neither. "I don't plan to find out for a very long time." I was happy with my life. Why rush things?

The song ended, and we went back to the table. I said my goodbyes, because although I knew I'd have fun if I stayed, it wouldn't help me figure out who killed Enrique, and Ann was going to be waiting for me. As I headed down the stairs, one of the male waiters was carrying drinks up.

"Excuse me. Does someone named Cara work here?" I asked.

"Everyone who works here is named Cara since Enrique's been here. What's your Cara look like?"

"Spiked, gelled hair with red tips, and uh, she's um, busty."

"Sounds like Cindy Reynolds."

"Is she here?"

He shook his head. "No. She called out tonight."

"Thanks." *Cindy*. At least I had a name.

By the time I parked my little red Volkswagen Beetle in front of my house, the wind had picked up, the lightning was closer, and the air smelled like salt and ozone. Ann was sitting on my porch, blinking in the security lights set off by my driving up to the house. Frankly, I didn't need this, even though I'd agreed to meet her here. I was exhausted. I should have stayed home from work today, but I was just too damn stubborn to admit it.

Ann looked weary, too.

"Come on in," I said. Once inside, I disabled the security system. The two-bedroom, two-bath cement-block house sat on top of a dune. It was open concept, with the beds and baths on either side of the house. "Coffee? Pop? Water? Or something stronger?"

"Water sounds good," she said.

I poured two glasses of water from a pitcher I kept in the refrigerator. "Let's sit out on the porch." A long screened-in porch ran the length of the house. Floor-to-ceiling windows provided dazzling views during the day. I liked sitting out here right before a storm hit. Once it hit, I cowered inside, either in my bed or on the couch. Ann led the way and unlocked the door to the porch. A rush of cool air hit us. The storm was closer than I realized, but I hated for people to know how much storms unnerved me, so I sat on the love seat. *Perched* might be a better word. I forced myself to relax into the cushions. Ann settled on the chaise lounge, looking way more relaxed than I was.

She sat, taking in the scene. I hadn't turned on any of the lights. We didn't really need them. The storm seemed to be halfway between the horizon and here. When the lightning flashed, you could see the massive clouds surrounding it. It lighted a container ship that seemed closer than most. It was stacked high with containers and pitched in the water. Although I'm sure it had seen rougher seas than this.

"I want to go back out and try to look for the shipwreck again," Ann said.

"There has to be some connection to the map and Enrique being there." I just couldn't call him *Rick*. "But this storm isn't supposed to be done in the morning. Plus, I have an appointment with Johnny and then work."

"I was thinking Tuesday morning. Would that work for you?"

"Yes. I'm off."

Ann stood. "Thank you. I wouldn't blame you if you didn't want to take another shot at this."

"That's what friends are for."

Ann gave me a half-smile. I'm not sure we really were friends, but I was up to my neck in this already. I stood, too. Ann headed to the front door, and I followed. As Ann left, the rain started pounding down. I got in my jammies, found a good book, and huddled in bed. Storms came in many forms—ones like this and the emotional ones that made someone kill Enrique. There wasn't much I could do about the one swirling outside, but I had an idea of what I could do about Enrique.

CHAPTER 14

Monday morning rain still pounded outside when I woke up at seven, but at least the thunder and lightning were taking a break. And I'd been so exhausted last night that I'd slept through most of the storm. The occasional extra loud clap woke me, but each time, I'd gone right back to sleep. I looked out. The Gulf was riled up and gray. That's how I felt.

I poured a bowl of cereal, topped it with milk, and sat at my small dining room table. Usually, I ate out on the porch, but it was too wet to be out there today. I grabbed my phone and did a search for Enrique. Word of his death had already hit, and there were hastily written obituaries. He wasn't trending on social media, but there was a lot of activity. People posting were girlfriends, surfer friends, self-proclaimed geek friends, high-school friends, Hollywood types, and random posters. Lots of the comments were lovely—over the top, even. You'd think that Enrique was a saint. But there were some haters, some women with broken hearts, and some people who seemed to hate him for no reason. I took screenshots of the negative posts and texted them to Deputy Biffle.

Where was Enrique from? While Ann had said they went to high school together, it didn't mean he'd always lived in New Orleans. There wasn't much about his past, but then again, his real name was Rick Laurier. I needed to check under that name. Thank heavens it was an unusual last name. He was born in Kentucky but moved to Louisiana when he was ten. There wasn't much else.

When I'd exhausted that search, I decided to look up Lisa Kelley. If Enrique had a past with one of the ringers, it must be Lisa. Lots of articles started springing up. Most talked about her life as a stuntwoman. She'd worked with a lot of big celebrities and was a bit of a celebrity in her own right.

There was more than one picture of her on red carpets, in stunning gowns that showed off her amazing figure and muscles. Muscles that would serve her well in the barback competition. She was born in Delaware and had lived there until she graduated high school. Lisa and Enrique hadn't known each other growing up then. Lisa had been very athletic in high school, running track, playing basketball and volleyball. There was also an article that said she'd tried out for the boys' wrestling team and made a huge protest when she wasn't allowed to be part of the team. Lisa went out to UCLA for film school, but at some point, dropped out and became a stuntwoman.

According to one article, she'd finished her degree with a double major in film and business by the time she was thirty. Good for her. While all of this was interesting, it didn't tell me much about her personal life. I typed in her name plus *boyfriend*. Another list of articles came up. She'd dated a lot of men in LA; some were film stars, and some were stuntmen. None of them were Enrique.

I switched to images and scrolled through photos of her and Gal Gadot, her in a few of the Fast and Furious movies. She'd even worked on a romantic comedy or two. What a fascinating life. Just as I was about to give up because pictures of other people named Lisa Kelley started to pop up, I noticed one at the beach.

I made the image larger. It was Lisa with Enrique. They had just come out of the water. Both were laughing and carrying surf boards. The photo looked like it should be an ad for living in Los Angeles. The sky was cloud-free and blue with no traces of smog. Big waves crashed behind them.

I typed in *Lisa and Enrique,* which I should have done in the first place. There were several pictures of them—kissing on the beach in a shot that looked like it was taken right after the one with the surfboards, them out at dinner, out dancing at a packed club, and finally, a picture of Lisa throwing a glass of wine into Enrique's face. There was even video of the incident.

Lisa called him a lying son of a female dog, and Enrique gave her the "baby don't get worked up" treatment, guaranteeing that she'd get worked up. After the wine coated his face, Lisa stormed out, holding her hand up to a photographer who tried to block her. The camera refocused on Enrique. His jaw was set, a vein stuck out at his temple, and his face was red. His look of fury was frightening.

The video ended when he shoved the camera person and the picture jarred around and then went dark. This all happened about five years ago. I set my phone down and ate some more cereal. Five years was a long time for anger to fester. Most people would be over whatever it was by now. When they'd come into the bar with Jean Claude, they didn't look angry. The three of them had seemed like a unit. Had something happened later that night that led to another, more violent encounter between them?

I sent the link to the video and some of the other pictures to Deputy Biffle. I went back to my search, this time focusing on Enrique. He'd been charged with assault for attacking the person who was recording the incident between Lisa and him. It wasn't the only time he'd been caught in a kerfuffle. I couldn't tell if he'd ever served time or if he'd wormed his way out of it. There were even incidents in other states at surfing events when he'd gotten into it with other surfers. Maybe some of that old trouble had followed him here. I forwarded more information to Deputy Biffle. I didn't care if my texts annoyed him or not. But it was unusual that he hadn't responded to any of them. In the past, I'd either gotten a *thanks* or *stay out of it.* But Deputy Biffle had gone text-silent. That was worrisome.

Once I washed my bowl and spoon, I got ready for the day. I'd been growing my short hair out, and it was chin-length now. Growing the bangs out was a pain, but I needed a new look. It seemed like every time I'd had a major life event, I decided to change my hair to go with it. I'd been engaged once. Back then, my hair was long, hanging below my shoulders. After I'd broken the engagement off, I'd cut it short—really short.

Last winter, my ex-fiancé had been murdered down here, and now I needed a new look. I'm not sure why, but it seemed to renew me. After a shower, blow dry, and slapping on some makeup to try to cover the circles under my big brown eyes, I ran through the rain to the car. I felt a bit off and realized I hadn't run yesterday or today. My daily runs kept me sane, so I hoped I could hold it all together for the next few hours. Just before I headed out to see the lawyer, my phone binged. It was Deputy Biffle, telling me to stay out of this. As if.

Johnny's office was vast and had, what on a clear day would be, a beautiful view of Choctawhatchee Bay in Destin. He had a vanity wall with photos of him and a bunch of people I didn't recognize. Perhaps local dignitaries. His desk was glass, his chairs were comfortable, and the coffee his assistant served us was excellent.

Johnny's back was to the view, and I sat across from him. The space was definitely designed to impress. The rain continued coming down in sheets and blurred the outside world. My hands kept fluttering around until I finally clasped them together.

"So run through what happened yesterday again," Johnny said. He had a yellow legal pad on his desk and fancy-looking fountain pen poised in his hand.

I took him step-by-step through Saturday and Sunday morning. He knew most of it from our time at the police station. I'd forgotten to tell him about the other boats that were around while Ann was diving, right before she found Enrique.

"Did any of them have any identifiers that would make them stand out?" Johnny asked. He sounded hopeful.

I shook my head. "Typical white fishing boats."

"Did you see their names?" Johnny asked.

I pictured the scene in my mind. "I don't re-member noticing." I added the bit about someone looking our way, or at least he seemed to be.

"Did you recognize the person?" Johnny asked. His voice had lost the hopeful note.

"I didn't. I only got a glimpse. I think whoever it was wore shorts and a T-shirt of indeterminate color. The person's face was obscured by the binoc-ulars. I looked away quickly because it startled me, and then Ann came back up."

"I'm worried about this thing with the map that may or may not have been photographed. If you'd told Deputy Biffle the story immediately, it would have more credence." Johnny tapped his pen on the yellow pad, where he'd jotted down a few notes. "Deputy Biffle will definitely be questioning that. He'll think you concocted the story after the fact." He gazed at me.

"He could think that we concocted the story

anyway. It might give them more reason to charge us," I said.

"I think we should pass this information on to Deputy Biffle this morning," Johnny said.

I shook my head. "I promised Ann I wouldn't."

"Okay. But my advice is to tell Deputy Biffle sooner rather than later." Johnny set his pen down. "I heard that they found some baggies of drugs at the condo where Enrique was staying."

I couldn't imagine how he'd gotten that information, but it must be why people said he was a shark. "What kind?" I did my best to keep my voice calm, but it shook just a little.

"That I don't know yet."

"Did they find anything else?"

"A couple of laptops and some electronic equipment. I'm sure they'll be trying to get access to all of it." Johnny stood, so I did, too. "It's likely that Deputy Biffle will call you back in for questioning. Don't talk to him without me present."

Oh, great. Just what I wanted to do was talk to Deputy Biffle again. I felt guilty enough withholding information from him as it was. I might not be able to do it twice. "Is there a cause of death yet?"

"The autopsy is set for tomorrow morning."

I nodded.

"And remember, *do not* under any circumstances talk to Deputy Biffle or anyone else from the sheriff's department without me present."

I wanted to say, "I got it the first time." Instead, I nodded again and left. My unease was growing by leaps. This morning, I'd been hoping I'd feel better after I met with Johnny. I'd been involved in varying degrees with three other murders during the past ten months. But I'd never been hauled to the sheriff's department or represented by a lawyer. I had to figure things out, and fast.

CHAPTER 15

The day passed swiftly, and the bad weather drove people inside, so the bar was hopping. Finally at three, the sun came out, and people poured outside, but that just meant the deck was busy. I didn't hear any new gossip, but didn't have much time to think about my predicament, either. Around 4:30, we had a lull. Joaquín called for me to come to the bar.

"What?" I asked, eyeing the tray he'd covered with a clean white bar towel. It had suspicious-looking lumps and bumps under it.

"We need to start your training for the barback competition." He waved a hand at the tray. "I've gathered a series of ingredients, and you need to make an original drink with them."

"I think Vivi just called for me." I gestured toward her closed office door.

"She's out," Joaquín said, narrowing his eyes at me. "Are you trying to get out of practice?"

"Yes. Yes, I am. I won't be any good. I'll let you and Vivi down. I'll bet no one else is practicing." Did I sound whiny or what?

"Everyone is practicing." Joaquín whipped the towel off the tray. "You have sixty seconds. Starting in three, two, one."

There were three bottles of various sizes. None of the bottles were labeled. There were also peach slices, limes, and lemons on the tray, as well as a rocks glass and a flute. I opened one with what looked like alcohol and sniffed. No smell. It must be vodka.

"Fifty seconds," Joaquín called.

Good grief. I grabbed the peach slices and dropped two in the rocks glass. I took a mortar and squished the heck out of them. Joaquín would call it *muddling*. I grabbed the medium-sized bottle, opened it, and sniffed. It smelled like simple syrup—a sweetener often used in drinks. I poured some over the peaches and squished it all together. Then I poured in a healthy amount of vodka, scooped ice into a shaker, dumped the contents of the rocks glass in, gave it a good shake, and strained the mixture into the flute. I dropped in another slice of peach and stepped back.

"Disqualified," Joaquín said.

"What? You haven't even tasted it."

"You were five seconds over."

I shook my head. "Why didn't you warn me?"

"No one's going to warn you in the actual competition." Joaquín picked up the flute, took a sniff like it was fine wine, and then tasted it. I swear he was letting it roll on his tongue like this was some highfalutin competition. His face was neutral.

He'd give Deputy Biffle a run for his money with that expression.

Joaquín handed me the glass. "Taste it."

I took a cautious sip. Hmmm, not bad.

"Anything you would have done differently?" Joaquín asked.

"I think a squeeze of lemon juice would have offset the sweetness with a bit of acidity." Personally, I loved a sweet drink, but I'd been reading up on making cocktails and balancing ingredients over the past few months.

Joaquín beamed at me. "Absolutely right."

"A little rosemary or basil would have been nice, too," I said. I wasn't big on herbs in my drinks, but it was a thing in the cocktail world right now.

Joaquín grabbed me, gave me a spin, and dipped me. "Look at little Chloe, learning the bartending trade."

I shook my head. "I'm part owner of the bar. What do you expect?"

Joaquín's face became serious. "For reals? I keep waiting for you to grow weary of small-town life and hightail it back to the city."

"Really?" I was surprised. "I moved all of my stuff down here last January. I'm in a relationship and own a house, boat, and part of a bar. And you think I'm not going to stay?" I paused. "Does Vivi think that, too? Is she just waiting me out so she can have the entire bar to herself?" Had they been talking about me when I wasn't around? I was hurt. Way more than I would have thought.

"No. No!" Joaquín pulled me to him for a moment.

That was a relief.

"Life can be slow here. There's no museums or theater."

"There's the Indian Temple Mound Museum in Fort Walton Beach and the Destin History and Fishing Museum. And Northwest Florida State College has plays and symphonies. There's culture here if you want it. You are not getting rid of me that easily."

"I'm sorry. I don't want to get rid of you. I just know that when I first moved back here, I missed some of the excitement of Los Angeles."

"I miss my family. Some days. But I love it here. It suits me, and I would have never known if it hadn't been for Boone."

"I'm glad, Chloe. Really. Let's try another challenge."

I whisked an order pad off the top of the bar. "Oh, look." I pointed out to the deck. "Someone out there is probably ready for another round." I smiled sweetly at Joaquín and took off.

I was home by six and went for a long run, heading east, away from the Sea Glass. After missing my runs the last two mornings, this felt good. As my feet pounded the firm sand, I took in the tangy smell of the salt-spiced air, the whoosh of the waves that curled onto the beach, and the calls of the seagulls as they circled a family who threw food up to them. That made me shudder; being circled by hungry birds wasn't my idea of fun. I'd watched the movie *The Birds* with my grandmother and had never looked at birds the same way again.

I'd been running about twenty-five minutes when I spotted Lisa Kelley running toward me. Her strides were long and looked effortless. I hoped she had just set out, or else it meant she was in way better shape that I was. That depressed me a little, and it wasn't just about the barback competition. Nope—I realized I was a little prouder about my running prowess than I'd ever realized.

Lisa didn't notice me at first. Probably because the sun was to my back and getting lower in the sky. When she got close enough to see me, she broke her stride for a minute. I stopped and ran in place until she came up beside me.

"Come on," she said. "I might as well check out the competition."

I turned and ran with her back toward my house. Lisa was a couple of inches taller than me, which meant I wasn't going to match her stride for stride. When she sped up, so did I. This is usually why I ran alone. I liked to set my own pace, based on my mood, not anyone else's. I lagged behind only by about a half step. After five minutes, we were both panting and sweating.

Lisa slowed, so I did, too—no need to show off, and maybe she'd think I wasn't much competition to worry about. A cool April breeze blew from the north, and even though I was hot from running, I almost shivered.

"So you're staying in the competition?" I asked Lisa.

She glanced over at me. "Of course. Why wouldn't I?"

"I just thought since you were close to Enrique, you might not want to go on with it."

"Whatever gave you that idea? That we were close?" She almost snorted.

"Pictures and stories online."

Lisa shook her head, dismissive-like, but not before an expression somewhere between anger and frustration passed over her face. "That was a long time ago."

"It looked pretty volatile."

"Enrique." She shook her head again. "He said the publicity would be good for us. He called a couple of tabloids so they knew where we'd be."

"So you threw a glass of wine in his face for publicity?"

This time, she did snort. "No, that was because he was a cheating bastard. Him. Cheating on *me*. I should have known better than to fall for his charm."

We were even with my house at this point. Normally, I'd peel off, but I really didn't want Lisa to know where I lived. It was one thing to run with her out on a beach dotted with other people waiting for the sun to set, but there was a possibility she had murdered Enrique. The less she knew about me, the better. Out of the corner of my eye, I saw Rip, sitting on my back steps. He stood when he saw me. I dropped behind Lisa for a moment and waved him off before catching back up.

"Men can be scum," I said. "Enrique seemed to have quite a fan base, though."

"I don't care. I got over him a long time ago."

She may say that, but her body language was tense and her voice close to sputtering with fury. I didn't think I should point that out to her. And I knew it didn't take her off my list of suspects.

"I'm the one who got him the gig with Two Bobs."

I almost stopped in my tracks at that. "Really?" Was that so she could kill him out here, where it was less likely people would find out they knew each other?

CHAPTER 16

"We stayed in touch over the years. I knew he was in between things, so I let him know."

None of this was adding up for me. "You're a better person than I am."

Lisa took a deep breath. One that seemed to calm her. "Holding grudges in Hollywood gets you nowhere. I try to apply that to my life."

She had a point about grudges. They weren't useful, but I'm not sure I believed her. "I'm surprised someone like you—with your stuntwoman skills—would enter a small-town barback competition."

We were passing the coastal dune lake where they'd found my ex-fiancé's body in January. I was finally to the point that I didn't burst out in tears every time I passed this spot. I heard someone running behind us and glanced back. It was Rip. He came up even with us and kept running, like he didn't know who we were. He must be worried about me. A small smile crossed my face.

"Now that's a fine example of a perfect male specimen," Lisa said. She turned up her speed a notch. She let out a long sharp whistle.

Rip glanced back and let a slow smile spread across his face. Damn, he was one fine-looking man. It's a good thing he kept running, or Lisa would know from me leaping on him that we were in a relationship. And like with my house, the less she knew about me, the better I'd feel.

I accidentally-on-purpose crossed in front of her, slowing Lisa down. "Oh, sorry. I was so busy staring, I wasn't watching where I was going."

Lisa slowed. "I'm almost to where I parked." She pointed to the beach access point on the west side of the lake. "How about you?"

"I'm parked by the Sea Glass." I was a good liar.

"See you later, then." Lisa walked up the beach and was soon out of sight.

I turned and headed back toward my house. My legs ached from the run, or the tension of talking to Lisa, as my feet pounded against the sand. My breath was coming out in pants, not only from exhaustion, but from a bit of panic over the situation I found myself in. How was I going to find out more about Lisa? It wasn't like I could call up Gal Gadot for information. I slowed my pace to a walk. It wasn't long before Rip showed up by my side. It eased some of the stress I was feeling.

"Thanks for running by," I said. "I felt safer." It

was unlikely that Lisa would try to harm me out here, but still. I smiled at him. "Lisa was impressed. She said you were a fine male specimen. Not a bad compliment from a woman who worked with stars in Hollywood."

"Were you impressed? Because that's all I care about."

Honestly, if it was possible for a human to actually melt, I would.

"Who was that?" he asked. "And why did you wave me off?"

"It's Lisa Kelley. She's in the barback competition, representing Gray's Tavern over in Grayton Beach. She was Gal Gadot's stuntwoman for the Wonder Woman movies."

"Oh, so she does know about impressive men. And she thinks I'm one of them." He laughed.

I rolled my eyes at him, but she wasn't wrong. Rip had deep green eyes, curling dark hair, and a sculpted body that came from hard work and the gym. I shook my head at him. "Lisa went that away." I pointed behind us and took off at a run toward my house.

I heard Rip running behind me and grinned. Moments later, his arm looped around my waist, and he planted a kiss on me that had me clinging to him. Someone on the beach whistled, and another person yelled, "Go for it."

We broke apart.

Rip stared down at me. "Seriously. You are the only one I want to impress."

"Lucky me."

Rip laughed.

"Did I actually say that out loud?" My face warmed. I was probably bright pink.

"I'm the lucky one."

My heart boomed around in my chest. Words were close to the surface and ready to spill out. My stomach rumbled, breaking the moment.

"Let's go get some dinner," Rip said.

Thirty-five minutes later, we sat outside on a picnic bench, freshly showered and waiting for our food. We'd come to the first place we'd ever eaten together. A food truck right next to the ocean in Emerald Cove. Maria and Arturo made the best Mexican food in the Panhandle. Arturo fished in the morning, and Maria used whatever he caught to whip up tasty delights. By this time of night, the fresh seafood was gone, but Maria could turn any meat into something delicious. We were having Mexican street tacos with steak, fresh pico de gallo, Maria's homemade special sauce, and a side of Mexican corn. It had been grilled before being sliced off the cob and dressed with queso fresco and some other tasty sauce.

A string of lights waved in the soft breeze. At any other time, I'd thoroughly enjoy all this, but tonight I was working on a sticky problem. Most of the time after a dinner like this, we'd go dancing somewhere or out to a movie, then always back to my place or Rip's boat. But Ann was picking me up at six, and even though she and Rip were close—so close that last June, I assumed they were a couple—Ann didn't want anyone else knowing what we were up to. However, this was Rip, and I wasn't about to ruin my relationship with him for Ann. I had to figure out a way to honor both of them.

"What?" Rip asked.

I looked up at him, surprised. "What do you mean?"

"You quit eating, but earlier you said you were starving. I know this corn is your favorite, so something must be bothering you."

"It's been a rough couple of days."

Rip hugged me to him and kissed the top of my head. Yes, we were the obnoxious couple who sat side by side instead of across from each other. Especially at places like this, where on one side of the table, you could see the ocean and watch the sunset, and on the other side, you couldn't.

"It has been," Rip answered. "How can I help?"

I told him about my conversation with Lisa and about her relationship with Enrique. "Lisa still sounded upset, even though she said she wasn't."

"Maybe she came here to rekindle things with him and found out he wasn't interested."

I munched on my taco while I thought about that. "Or that he wasn't only going to be interested in her," I said when I finished. "From what I saw and what I've heard, Enrique wasn't ready to settle down with one woman."

Rip looked at me. "Maybe he just hasn't found the right one."

Thank heavens I didn't have any food in my mouth, because I'm pretty sure it would have fallen out and ruined the moment. Car doors slammed behind us, which made me jump. Moment ruined anyway.

"I'm exhausted. I won't be good company later tonight," I said as we walked to Rip's car.

"I don't care."

Rip was so understanding. I bet if Greg, the unhappy motorcycle-riding doctor, had a wife this understanding, he wouldn't be so unhappy. I'm not sure how I got this lucky. "I have to get up early to help out a friend tomorrow morning."

Rip's expression was puzzled, until he smoothed out his face and nodded. He knew how to pull a neutral face because of his past as a lawyer. To hide his thoughts. He gave me a light kiss. "No worries."

He said it, but did he mean it? Was I being more loyal to Ann than Rip? But maybe I was just being me, without regard to loyalty to one person over the other. I said I'd help Ann. I said I'd keep it quiet, so that's what I was going to do.

Tuesday morning, we launched from the same place we had the day before. Only the boat we were on today was bigger with fancier equipment.

"The police still have the other boat as part of their investigation," Ann explained as we puttered off.

"You have more than one boat?" I asked. Or had she borrowed one from someone?

"Lots of people do down here."

There'd been more than one boat at the dock yesterday. I just didn't think they were all Ann's. The only other people I knew who had more than one were Joaquín and Michael. They lived on one, and Joaquín fished with the other.

"Is that your house?" I asked, pointing back at

the large house. The Gulf side had tall windows on both floors. The views must be incredible.

"One of them."

Yeesh. More than one boat, more than one house. Ann had a lifestyle I couldn't even imagine. "Right. Lots of people down here have more than one."

Ann laughed. "Not lots, but plenty. Some they use as rentals. Or they have a place at the beach and then a place somewhere quieter."

I got that. The beaches could be packed at various times of the year, but I also knew you had to have money to do that. A lot of money.

The sun was barely a glimmer on the horizon. But unlike the last time we were out here, there were no clouds in sight.

"Is that the house where the break-in occurred?" I asked.

"It is." The wind blew her hair back like she was a model facing a fan. "Dex is talking to the people who own the security company. However, so far they haven't been too forthcoming."

Talking to. Interesting word choice when she probably meant Dex was interrogating them. "You know Dex can be a little intimidating. Maybe that's why they aren't talking."

She narrowed her eyes for a second. "You could be right. Will you talk to them? You've got that wholesome Midwestern nice thing going on."

I'm not sure that's how I wanted anyone to describe me, but it was probably true. Even in Chicago, I'd be the one tourists would come up to and ask directions. I had some friends who tried to teach me to be less friendly, but it just never worked.

"I wouldn't even know what to ask. All I know about security systems is how to turn one on and off."

"I'll prep you."

"In that case, why not?" I really needed to work on saying no to things. But that Midwestern nice always got in the way.

We rode in silence for a few minutes. Probably both regretting that we'd come up with this cocka-mamie plan to have me go talk to the security people. The wind blew my hair around. It was too short for a ponytail, but long enough that it was in my face. And I certainly didn't look like a model.

"What about security cameras? Did you catch anyone on them?" I asked.

Ann shook her head. "I don't have any. They are too easy to hack, and I like my privacy."

I could understand that, but was still a little surprised. "It seems like we're going a different direction this morning," I said. We were heading due south today.

"I ran more calculations last night, adding in variables that I hadn't the first go-round."

"Did you include the storm from the other night?"

Ann nodded. "I did. The problem is the Gulf is so big and, when you take into account all the storms over the past three hundred years, trying to find a treasure is improbable."

"And yet, we're out here."

"I said improbable, not impossible." Ann grinned at me.

I couldn't help but smile back. Something about her spirit was captivating. The song from the Pirates of the Caribbean ride at Disney World started playing in my head. The pirates' life for me, indeed.

Ann stopped the boat.

"Is this where you're going to dive?" I asked.

She pulled two pairs of binoculars out of a console. She handed one of them to me.

"This is where we make sure no one is following us."

We did a silent survey. Water gently hit the boat, making us rock in the small swells. I didn't spot any boats nearby. There were some nearer the shore and some farther out, but no one close.

"I don't see anyone," I said, putting the binoculars down.

Ann did a quick scan of the sky. I shaded my eyes to see what she was searching for and then flashed a questioning look her way.

"Drones," she said. "But I don't see any."

Yikes. Drones. This day just kept getting weirder.

Ann stored the binoculars, then turned the boat east. She turned on a couple of fancy-looking screens. "Normally, people use these to find fish."

"That doesn't seem quite fair."

"It is if that's how you have to make your living. It's not only the commercial fishermen like Joaquín who use them, but the charter boats. Nothing worse than a charter boat full of unhappy customers."

"I get that, but it still seems like it gives the fishermen an unfair advantage."

"I can also watch for abnormalities that might indicate the wreck."

That piqued my interest, and I watched the screen with fascination. We saw a lot of fish over the next fifteen minutes, but not much else. Ann slowed the boat down. The sun was warm on my face, and I was regretting not having any sunscreen with me. I freckled and burned all too easily.

"We're close to the spot that I charted on my computer last night," Ann said. "Keep an eye out on the screen."

"There," I shouted. "What's that?" I was seeing a rectangular shape. It definitely wasn't fish or any other sea creature I could think of. It didn't appear to be moving.

Ann slowed and made a couple of passes over the object. "I'm going in to check it out." She didn't sound very excited. "It might be a waste of time, but this is why we're here."

Ann got in her gear and jumped off the back of the boat. The motion set us rocking. There was a quiet out here like nothing I'd ever heard or, in this case, didn't hear. On land, there's always the background noise of cars or boats or people or birds. Here, it was a bit of wind and a bit of wave. If I wasn't on edge, it would be delightful.

I grabbed a set of binoculars and did another scan around us. Nope. No boats. No drones as far as I could tell, either. Just me and the boat. It didn't take long for Ann to resurface, and she had something tucked under one arm. A small box of some sort. *What?* I put my hand down to her and noticed it was shaking. She grasped it, and I pulled her out of the water.

Ann set the box on the deck. It was a small treasure chest with a humped top. It was about twelve-by-eight, black as night. Ann quickly removed her scuba equipment. We knelt down beside the box. Ann flipped the top open, and we stared down in shock.

CHAPTER 17

The box was filled with rocks. There was a plastic envelope with a note inside it that read *Too late*. With a smiley face. Ann started pacing and waving her hands around.

"Someone hacked not only my security system, but my computer, too. It's the only way they would know to come to this spot."

I thought over what I knew about Enrique. About all the people who'd left messages when the news of his death had hit social media. Some of the condolences had been from people who were proud geeks and computer nerds. While Enrique was anything but a geek, maybe it hadn't always been that way. "Johnny told me that there were two laptops and other electronic equipment in Enrique's condo. Maybe he was the hacker."

"In high school, he was good with computers." Ann paced back over and stared down at the chest.

"Someone got here before us and stole the treasure."

"Wait a minute," I said. "Take a closer look at this chest." I picked it up and dumped the rocks overboard. "It's not really old. It's lousy construction with new nails that someone painted to look old. The hinges aren't old either, and the wood looks too new to have been underwater for hundreds of years."

Ann squatted beside me and studied the chest. "You're right. You're a genius, Chloe."

"Maybe not a genius, but observant." Calmer, too, for once. "Did you see any signs that there may have been treasure down there? Something that was actually worth finding and stealing?"

"No. I was so excited by the chest, I just brought it right up."

We both stood and looked down at the water.

"I'm going back down there. Maybe there will be some clue as to who is doing this."

"You don't have any ideas?"

Ann shook her head as she put her gear back on. "None. But they'll regret it when I track them down."

"They must be connected to Enrique in some way, right? It seems unlikely that two separate groups could access your computers and find the spots where the treasure might be." Unless Ann had lousy security on her computers, which seemed unlikely.

Ann frowned briefly. "I hope you're right."

Fifteen minutes later, Ann was back up. She shook her head as she climbed back onboard.

Water flowed off her dark hair, making it look like a black waterfall. "Either they cleaned up so well that there's no sign of anything, or there never was."

"Let's go with the assumption that there never was anything. It doesn't seem possible that some-one could find a shipwreck and make all evidence of it disappear so quickly."

Ann nodded. "I think you're right."

"Maybe they were hoping that you'd just give up, if you thought someone else had the treasure."

"I guess they don't know me at all."

"Exactly what I was thinking."

"Because then I would go after them."

Well, that was a little scary, but not entirely un-expected. "How about we turn the tables on who-ever did this to you?"

"How so?" Ann stripped out of her wet suit.

"Why don't you fake a chart on your computer, and then we can lie in wait for whoever shows up?"

Ann put a hand to her chest. "Well, I do declare, Chloe. Under that Midwest nice, you are just dia-bolical."

Two hours later, just after 8:30, I arrived at Aymar Security. I'd dressed in a black knee-length skirt (the black a nod to Ann always wearing black) and white silk blouse with flowy sleeves. I'd once worn this outfit to a meeting with the head li-brarian of the Chicago Public Library system. Why I'd moved this outfit down here was a mystery, but I was grateful that I had. I wore fake horn-rimmed black glasses and carried a briefcase. I introduced myself as Elizabeth Bond and said I worked for Ann. I was starting to feel like I actually did, considering all the time I spent with her the past few days.

The office was small, neat, with neutral walls, cheap furniture, and not a speck of dust to be seen. Robin Aymar herself was much the same, except for her bright turquoise hair. Ann had given me a list of questions. I asked all of them, more than once, in varying ways. According to Robin, the only possibility was that someone knew Ann's code.

Robin walked me through how the system was set up and controlled. Frankly, most of it went right over my head, but I nodded a lot. I think they were a little afraid of Ann, because Robin said she had her best person looking for signs of hacks, backdoor entries, or anything else that could have allowed someone access to Ann's house. They'd found nothing yet, so either the people involved were so good that they hadn't left a trace, or Robin's people were incompetent.

"You have to understand," Robin said, "that clients don't get notifications when someone enters their house and turns off the alarm system in the required amount of time. An amount of time the client specifies."

"They don't?"

"Think of all the times someone might go in and out of their house a day and multiply that by thousands of clients. Not to mention how annoying that would be. However, there are exceptions to that if the client has a video doorbell or has specifically had their system set to notify them. That would alert them anytime someone entered or left. But Ann's system isn't set up that way."

And Ann didn't have a video doorbell. I pulled up a picture of Enrique on my phone. "Have you ever seen this man in your offices?" It was a long shot, but maybe Enrique had charmed his way in here somehow and accessed Ann's system.

Robin studied the photo. "No. I haven't seen him."

"Would you please check with your staff?" I asked.

Robin took my phone, and I followed her around the office while she asked people. Everyone denied seeing him. While I was no expert on liars, it seemed like they were sincere.

Back in Robin's office, I looked at her over my glasses. "Ann will be sending someone of her own to help you."

"That wouldn't be allowed. Our systems are proprietary."

I stood, picked up my empty briefcase, and walked to the door. "I believe you are familiar with Dex. He'll be by at two to go over your system with you. Ann would appreciate your cooperation."

Robin took a look at me and paled slightly. "Okay. Whatever Ann needs."

I stood by my car with a half-smile on my face. Being a badass was kind of exhilarating. I hated the stereotypes set up around librarians—that they were geeky nerds who wore cardigans with a tissue tucked up in the sleeve. Librarians were misinformation slayers. Just because we used databases and words instead of swords and guns didn't mean we never fought a good fight. But, I had to admit to myself, being on Ann's team was next level in some way.

I got in the car, started it, and called Ann. "Dex has an appointment to go over the system with Aymar's today at two. I hope that's okay."

"How did you ever manage that?" Ann asked. "Those people are tighter than Scrooge."

Oh! I'd thought that was the expected result. "I just told them that's what was going to happen."

Ann laughed. "Chloe, you are something."

"I've heard that more than once and never know if it's a good thing."

"Trust me, it is." Ann paused. "Are you coming over?"

"On my way."

Thirty minutes later, I knocked on Ann's door. I went to the door on the side of the house that faced the Gulf, unsure if that was the normal entrance or the one on the side that faced the drive. I heard locks clicking and took a good look at the unusual lock. It was keyless. Ann opened the door. She wore a black tunic top with black leggings.

"Your locks are electronic," I said. "Do you use a key fob to get in or your phone?" My voice rose as I asked her.

"A key fob. They're very secure. Plus, I keep the key fob in a Faraday bag when I'm not using it."

A Faraday bag blocked radio signals that could be used to access your credit cards, key fobs, or phone. "They can be duplicated."

"Someone would have to be nearby to do that, and as you can see, there aren't any bushes or trees near the house where someone could hide. And trust me, that is by design."

"Or they could plant a device that would pick up the signal when you came or went. Then all someone would have to do was pick up the device and make a duplicate. It happened at one of the libraries in Chicago."

Ann paled. "I thought it was safe enough with the way my house is situated."

We went outside and did a quick search through the flowerbeds near the doors to see if we found anything. We didn't, but there was an area near the door where some flowers had been trampled and the dirt disturbed.

"I'll have Dex check into this and call a locksmith to get these changed just in case."

"Maybe you should call Robin and see if there is any way they can tell if a fob has been duplicated."

"Good idea."

We stepped into a foyer with a front hall that cut down the center of the house. The hall was wider than my bedroom. The floor was wide-planked heart of pine wood, glossy enough to almost see your reflection.

A broad staircase was to the right, with an old-looking banister that made me think more than one kid had slid down it over the years. There was one doorway to the right and many down the hall to the left.

"Wow," I said. "This is unexpected."

Ann smiled. "What were you expecting?"

"To tell you the truth, I always kind of pictured you living on a three-masted ship that sat in a secret lagoon somewhere so that you could take off at a moment's notice."

"Yes. Well I have one of those, too."

Just one? I wasn't sure if she was joking about the ship or not.

I noticed the security system panel to the right of the door. The light was green. The system wasn't on. "Do you use a key fob for that, too, or do you manually type in a code?"

"I can do either."

"Where do you keep the key fob?"

"On the same ring with my car keys. They are in the Faraday bag with the key fob for the house." She shook her head. "So it could have been compromised, too. What a mess."

Ann turned and led me to our left. We walked into a room with huge arched windows that faced the Gulf. The walls were lined with floor-to-ceiling shelves filled with books—old and new, hardback and paperback—*objets d'art*, and the occasional painting.

There was a couch with chairs flanking a wood-burning fireplace that was probably only needed once a year. Although people had thin blood down here, and if it got below fifty, everyone was pulling out heavy coats. The room ran the length of the house and had windows on either end. A thick Oriental rug in deep blues and reds covered the wood floor. In a corner sat a Queen Anne–style desk. Of course, I thought, glancing at Ann. There was even a library ladder to reach the books on the top shelves. It was pretty much a room that I always dreamed of owning. Now if only one of the shelves led to a hidden staircase, it would be perfect.

"Robin Aymar thinks someone got the code to your security system."

"That's impossible."

She'd hesitated just slightly before she said that. I decided not to push it, because I was convinced the key fob had been cloned. That was Ann's problem and not mine. "Have you started running programs to find a new spot to go to?"

"Not yet. When I do, they're going to know I didn't buy the message in the treasure chest."

"Wouldn't they have been more suspicious if you did buy it? They must know you're smarter than to be taken in by something like that."

"You're right. It's maddening to know that someone is in my system watching me."

"Any ideas of who?"

"No. But I'm very carefully tracking things, so maybe I can trace who is in here without alerting them to the fact that I know they are there. A cousin has been helping me. It's complicated."

"I can't begin to imagine." Now it was my turn to hesitate. "You're sure you can trust your cousin?"

"Absolutely. Although he's my cousin, he's more like a brother. We were raised together."

"Does he know about the shipwreck?"

"Not that I know of."

"You didn't tell him? You said he's like your brother." I paused. "Maybe he found out you kept this from him, and he's mad enough that he's screwing with you."

Ann hesitated. *Again.* I studied her face, but it gave nothing away. I knew a lot of thoughts were swirling around in her brain. Thoughts she didn't seem inclined to share with me.

"There's a lot of pressure on a person when they are a Lafitte. Our family fortunes are like the waves out on the Gulf." She flung her arm toward the view. "There's the occasional big roller, but more often, the tide is out, and we are just little ripples trying to make our way to the shore."

"You seem to be doing okay." This house was one thing, but she either owned or had access to boats and vehicles and land.

"I work hard."

"I never said you didn't. You've never heard any family talk about a shipwreck?"

"Of course. So many shipwrecks, especially between New Orleans and Pensacola. It's one of the reasons I'm keeping this one such a secret. There's been too many hopes raised and dashed over the generations. I don't want to do that." She shook her head. "There were scallywags who pinned all their dreams and brought their families to ruin seeking treasure."

Scallywags. Not a term you heard every day, especially when talking about one's family. "Maybe someone else also found the map but put it back."

Ann snorted out a short, bitter-sounding laugh.

"Too much of my family is all for one and that's it. If someone had found it in New Orleans, they most likely wouldn't have put it back."

"What if they wanted you to find the map because you have the resources to do the search? Maybe it's a little too convenient that you suddenly found those papers."

CHAPTER 18

Ann twirled a long piece of her hair. I'd never seen her do that before. Once she realized she was doing it, she hastily stopped. It might be a leftover childhood habit that indicated stress.

"It's a possibility, although they'd been cleverly hidden. I suppose someone could have gone through my room once I found them."

"Either way, perhaps someone hopes you'll lead them to the spot, and then they'll snap up the treasure."

Ann frowned. "Now that sounds all too possible. I have an endless supply of cousins and distant relatives that might be up to something like that. Too lazy to search for themselves."

"Maybe you should make a list of most to least likely and just do a little checking on them."

"That's not a bad idea, Chloe. First, I'll go through the clever lazy ones and then the lazy ones with shady pasts."

"You have a very interesting family."

"You have no idea."

I stood and cast another longing glance around the room.

"You're welcome any time and can borrow any book you want. Why don't you come back at nine tonight if you still want to be involved in this mess?"

"Of course I do."

Ann nodded. "I'll have the trap set by then, and we'll wait and see if they take the bait." She looked at my outfit. "Wear all black."

I thought about saluting and saying "yes ma'am" but managed a nod instead. Now I needed to focus on who killed Enrique and who drugged me. "Aren't you worried about the possible murder charge?"

"Worry is unproductive. I'm going to give our attorneys a couple of days to see what they can come up with."

She might trust them, but I couldn't let it rest.

After going home to change into leggings and a light top, I parked by the Sea Glass and headed down the walkway to Two Bobs. I turned and looked up one of the branches of the walkway to where Rip docked his boat. It was there. Maybe I'd stop and see if he was home once I was done at Two Bobs.

Two Bobs was quiet this time of day, just before lunch. Soft rock was playing through speakers. The deck out front was the most crowded. I ordered a beer in a bottle and watched them uncap it. Less chance of anyone slipping something in my drink that way.

"Is Cindy here?" I asked as I laid a twenty on the bar for the bartender. "Keep the change." Was I trying to buy information? You bet I was.

"She's gone."

"She quit?" I hoped he didn't mean she was dead, but he was pretty casual about it.

"I'm a little fuzzy on the details. She either quit or got fired."

"That's too bad. This is a tough business."

"Some people here think she brought it on herself."

"How so?" I'm so glad this guy was the male equivalent of a chatty Cathy. Maybe a chatty Carl?

"Did you hear about that dude Enrique who was killed?"

"I did."

"From the minute he showed up, it was trouble around here. One employee after another threw themselves at him. Personally, I don't get it. He seemed creepy to me. But the females around here dug what he was dishing out."

"What was he, um, dishing out?"

"Compliments and his body." The bartender looked around, grabbed a towel, and swiped at the bar. Maybe he wanted to look like he was working instead of just talking to me.

The bartender sounded a little bit jealous. He was good-looking enough. Curly black hair, slender, nicely defined biceps. Strong enough to kill Enrique? With the element of surprise and enough rage, probably. Problem was, he didn't seem rage-filled. More mildly irked. That didn't seem like a good enough reason to kill someone. But I'd be mentioning this guy to Deputy Biffle.

"I'm surprised there weren't any catfights breaking out. You throw in the customers that were into Enrique, and it was chaos. But I didn't wish him ill."

Maybe, maybe not.

"I'm glad he's gone, though." He leaned across the bar. "I told Cindy she might want to stay out of town for a few days. It's not going to look good for her that she fought with Enrique and then he was murdered."

"They fought?"

"Oh, yeah. She was almost steaming when she got back."

"Got back from where?" I asked.

"She disappeared in the middle of her shift, and we were so busy that night, too."

"Do you know what they fought about?"

"Probably the usual. Enrique's harem."

An older man walked up to the bartender. "The supplier just came. Can you go help unload?"

The bartender nodded and took off. It left me facing the older man, who looked none too happy.

"I don't mind customers flirting with our staff. It's why we hire attractive people. But you looked like you were interrogating him, not chatting him up. He's a nice kid, but not the sharpest cocktail pick in the drawer. And I don't like people taking advantage of my employees."

He'd been observing us from somewhere. I'm sure there were plenty of security cameras around. The Sea Glass had them, and it was much smaller than this operation.

"We were just talking. Are you a manager here?"

"I wish. I'm one of the co-owners." He was thin, balding, and deeply tanned. Probably in his fifties. He had a slow, soft Southern accent.

"Bob?"

"Bobby Boggs. And you are?"

"Chloe Jackson."

He nodded. "You work for the Sea Glass and are entered in the barback competition."

"Correct. And I think I was drugged here three nights ago."

Bobby paled and looked around to see if anyone had overheard me. "Let's go talk in the office."

I nodded and followed Bobby toward the harbor side of the bar. There was a door with a PRIVATE sign on it. Bobby took keys out of his pocket, unlocked the door, and held it open for me. A gentleman.

The space was cramped with two desks, but everything looked neat and new. Monitors ran along one wall with various views of the bar. Harbor deck, beach deck, several angles inside the first-floor main space, and two views of the top deck. Bobby pulled out a simple stainless chair with a red cushion for me at the back desk and then went around and sat across from me.

"That's a very serious charge," Bobby said. "And something we take seriously. But what's your angle? A payoff?"

"I don't have an angle except making sure people are safe."

"The women that come here know to ask for

our angel martini. There are signs in the women's bathroom."

An angel drink was something lots of bars had taken to using. It alerted a staff person that the woman ordering the drink was in some kind of trouble. The staff could then help that person out. We had a similar thing at the Sea Glass. The drink didn't appear on the menu.

"Could we watch your security footage from the night I was here?"

"We don't normally do that."

I stood. "No problem. I'll just alert the sheriff's department and my reporter friend."

I took two steps to the door.

"Wait. I'll do it."

I resettled in my chair. "Thank you." I told him the day and time I was here. Fortunately, he had a system where he could type in that information instead of us scrolling back through hours of video. We watched as I ordered my drinks and the bartender whipped them up. It didn't look like he did anything suspicious. I carried the drinks to the stairs and started up. The next piece of video was me at the top of the steps on the deck.

"What happened to the part when I was walking up the rest of the stairs?"

"We have a dead space right there. Someone took the camera out, and we haven't gotten a replacement. But it would make a good case that you could have doctored the drink off camera if you sue us."

"Again, I'm not going to sue you. But if you look at the time on the two pieces of video, I didn't have time to stop and do anything."

"You could have had it in your hand."

While I was getting annoyed, part of me understood that he didn't want any legal repercussions. "Yes, and Santa Claus could have come down my chimney, but neither of those things happened. Let's continue watching. A waitress named Cindy brought us two more drinks."

Bobby grimaced for a moment. I'd get back to that after we were done watching. Again, nothing seemed off when the bartender poured the two drinks. He put them on a tray, and Cindy picked it up. She said something that made the bartender laugh. She slinked off with a sway in her hips that the bartender focused on until she started up the stairs. Cindy stopped on the stairs, but by that point, we could only see her ankle. A few moments later, she popped up onto the top deck. We watched her bring us the drinks and put them down. It was hard to tell from the angles if she dropped something in them or if Enrique could have while I was looking up at her and then over at the ocean. It wasn't anything I was even aware I'd done at the time. We watched as Enrique and I chatted. At one point, we were both staring out at the ocean. His hand moved around my drink, but there wasn't anything definitive to go on.

"She could have done it." Bobby frowned at the monitor. "Or he could have."

"I heard she was fired. Why?"

"Ever since Enrique showed up, she'd been on some kind of emotional roller coaster. Fighting with other staff members. Alternately flirting with them." He paused and shook his head. "Cindy would disappear in the middle of her shift, and I suspect she was sneaking off with Enrique. She took off again the night Enrique was murdered. When she came back, I told her she was finished. She was a good employee until Enrique showed up."

"Will you give me her contact information?"

Bobby stood. "That's a no. I hope you are okay. There's no proof you were drugged here."

I stood, too. Unfortunately, he was right. But I couldn't let him get the last word in. "There's no proof I wasn't."

CHAPTER 19

Rip wasn't on his boat. I was starving and needed some companionship, so I decided to head to my favorite restaurant, The Diner. But first I sent a text to Deputy Biffle, telling him what I'd learned about Cindy at Two Bobs. I waited for a few minutes but didn't hear anything back. After starting my car, I drove to the heart of Emerald Cove. I loved the town center. There was a big circular common area with a tot lot, gazebo, and picnic tables. Palm trees, which weren't native to this area, along with magnolias, surrounded the space. Today, someone was flying a kite, and people were playing chess on one of the picnic tables. A group of people had set up a game of cornhole, and people cheered as a young girl scored.

Five streets spun off of the circle, and I'd heard that from above, Emerald Cove looked like a starfish. I found a parking spot half a block from

The Diner and walked back toward it. I hoped Delores or her husband Ralph would be there. We'd become good friends since I'd moved here.

Delores greeted me as soon as I walked in. "Ralph's near the back if you're looking for company. Otherwise, take a seat at the counter."

The place was buzzing. I recognized some of the locals, but there were also a lot of tourists in here today. Delores had bright red hair and lipstick to match. She wore a pink dress with a white, frilly apron. The perfect look for a diner.

"Thanks, Delores. I'll find Ralph."

"Here, take a menu with you, we're swamped."

I took the menu and headed to the back. Ralph was seated at a booth for four, all by himself. I was surprised he wasn't out driving the trolley, but his son and daughter worked with him, so one of them must be on duty.

Ralph beamed at me as I slid into the bench seat across from him. "How's it going, Chloe?" Ralph had been slimming down since Delores had put him on a strict diet last October.

Ralph and Delores had been high-school sweethearts until their families intervened in their relationship. Back in the sixties, in this area, interracial relationships were frowned on. They'd both married other people but got back together several years ago. It seemed to me that I would be hard-pressed to find a couple happier than them. Maybe my parents, but only by a hair.

"It's good to see you, Ralph. Have you ordered? What are you having?" I wasn't sure what I was in the mood for.

Ralph frowned. "I'd like that oyster po'boy, but not with Delores supervising my meals, so a chef's salad it will be."

Oysters were one of the only foods I flat-out refused to eat. If you ever wanted to get information out of me or to torture me, all you had to do was bring out a platter of oysters. I'd confess to anything to avoid their sliminess.

"I'll have that, too. I need to get into fighting shape for the barback competition."

Ralph laughed. "That sounds about right. You could have told Vivi and Joaquin no."

"I suppose so, but if you'd seen their faces, you wouldn't have been able to turn them down, either."

"I've known Vivi a long time and know how persuasive she can be."

Delores stopped by the table. "Ralph, you're having the chef's salad, house dressing on the side."

Ralph winked at me and mouthed *told you*.

"I'll have the same, please," I said.

"Don't you want a side of fries with that or onion rings?" Ralph asked.

"He just wants you to order them so you'll share," Delores said.

Yeesh, the pressure. Who to please? "Just the salad." Delores for the win. She was scarier than Ralph.

For once, Delores didn't argue with me or tell me what she thought I should have. That was new. Delores bustled off.

"How are you doing? A dead body and possibly being drugged within a couple of days sounds pretty rough to me."

Not to mention being a suspect in a murder. "I'm keeping busy to keep my mind off things."

"Busy investigating? I heard Deputy Biffle thought you and Ann might actually be involved."

"I know. It's unbelievable."

"What were you doing out on the Gulf that morning?"

I hated lying to friends. "Ann wanted to go diving, and I rode along to make sure she was safe."

Ralph made a *hmpf* sound. "Kind of a coincidence that you ended up at that exact spot."

"Major coincidence. But they do happen. All the time. Once I was out in Denver eating at a restaurant, and a college friend was at the very same spot. Another time, I was at a library conference, and my aunt was staying at the same hotel."

Ralph nodded. "They do happen. Just usually not to Ann."

"Have you heard anything about Enrique?" Ralph and Delores had access to a lot of resources, not only because of hearing things here, but through the fire department and emergency call center.

"Not much."

A waitress brought us both large glasses of iced tea and our salads. I took a sip of my tea. It was sweet tea. Just the thing I needed to keep me going. We dug into our salads. I was surprised Delores hadn't added a bowl of gumbo to my order. She usually did, but things were busy.

"Not much but something?" I asked in between bites of ham, cheese, lettuce, egg, kalamata olives, and radishes. All I needed was some little nugget of information to get me going again. Of course, I still had Cindy to track down.

Ralph finished chewing and then nodded his head.

"Are you going to tell me?" I asked.

"I heard the last person who was seen with Enrique was that Lisa Kelley woman."

Oh, wow. Bad for Lisa along with the other things I'd found out about her and Enrique, but good for Ann and me. It kind of made sense, since she was at the Sea Glass with Jean Claude and Enrique the night before Ann and I found him. I should track down Jean Claude and see if he knew anything.

"Do you ever go to Two Bobs?" I asked.

Ralph snorted. "That place is a meat market."

I laughed at Ralph using the term. "Or a m-e-e-t market."

"I'm too old for that stuff."

"And Delores would kill you."

"You can bet on that. Why do you ask?"

"I'm trying to track down one of the waitresses who worked there. Her name is Cindy Reynolds."

"I know Cindy's mom. She lives over in Dune Allen off Thompson Road."

That wasn't too far from here. Maybe I could run over there after lunch. Ralph looked over my shoulder and smiled.

"Can I join you?"

Rip. My heart did its happy dance thing. I scooted over. Rip sat down, and I could feel the warmth of his left leg next to mine. He snagged an olive from my salad. I'd been worried I'd messed things up last night sending him home on his own, but he seemed his normal self. *Whew.*

"What are you two talking about?" Rip asked. "You looked as serious as a cop during an interrogation."

"Enrique," I said. "Ralph heard Lisa was the last person seen with him."

"Doesn't mean that's the last person he was actually with," Rip said.

That was a former criminal defense lawyer in action. "True."

A waitress brought Rip a cheeseburger and a plate of fries.

"I called in an order, but saw you two and decided to eat here." He dipped a fry in catsup and ate it. Then he laughed. "You two should see your faces. You look like kids with no money staring into a candy shop. Help yourselves."

Ralph took a quick look around. Apparently, Delores was busy elsewhere, because he grabbed a couple of fries and ate them quickly. I was able to eat them at my leisure. Delores's salads were so good that I really didn't miss having fries—too much, anyway.

"Are you volunteering tonight?" I asked Rip in what I hoped was a casual voice. It would make my life easier, since I had plans with Ann. Plans no one was supposed to know about. Again.

"I am. What are you up to?" Rip asked.

I couldn't tell him I'd be with Ann, because she wasn't really the "come over and watch a movie with me" kind of friend, if we were even friends at all. "I'm helping out a friend."

"The same friend who needed your help this morning?" Rip asked.

I nodded.

"Still can't say who?" Rip had a small line forming between his eyebrows.

"Nope. Sorry."

Ralph and Rip exchanged a look like they knew whatever I was up to wasn't good.

"How's the training going for the competition?" Ralph asked.

It broke the tension I was feeling. "Okay." Really, whatever Ann and I did tonight might in some way be construed as competition prep.

"I heard Michael was afraid to try to train you," Rip said.

"Oh, please. I'm a little bitty kitty."

"One with sharp claws," Ralph said.

"Better you saying that than me," Rip said.

"Oh, stop. I'm just fine to train."

The waitress came back by with three pieces of Delores's famous mile-high pie.

"Strawberry is my favorite," I said. "And Ralph, you get one too."

"It's a miracle," he said.

The pie was thick as could be and topped with a huge layer of homemade whipped cream. It was sweet, but not sickeningly so.

"Delores makes the best pies in the world," I said with a happy sigh.

"You've got a bit of strawberry above your lip," Rip said.

His intense stare made me think that in another situation, he'd be licking it off me, and I felt my face grow hot.

"Come on, you two," Ralph said.

We laughed. Talk turned to the upcoming very busy tourist season until we finished our pie.

"I'm going to need an extra long run after that," I said as we got up to leave.

"I could help you with a workout," Rip whispered close to my ear.

"I wish," I murmured back. We paid our bill and at the door, I kissed Ralph on the cheek. "Tell Delores the food was delicious."

"Will do. You two stay out of trouble," Ralph said.

I was hoping to get *into* trouble with Rip, but unfortunately, he was going back to the fire station. Maybe that was for the best, because I had to track down Cindy's mom.

CHAPTER 20

When I got to my car, I looked up Mrs. Reynolds in Dune Allen and found her address. It was only about seven minutes away. Before I started my car, my phone rang. It was Vivi's doctor. My breathing accelerated.

"Chloe here."

"Chloe, I have some troubling news."

That wasn't a good way to start a conversation when it was a doctor calling. Was I dying? "Okay?"

"The lab for some reason hasn't received your test. I'm terribly sorry. If it doesn't turn up, we can take a snippet of your hair, but we have to wait for seven days after the event."

Event. That was one way to put it. It had happened four days ago, which meant waiting another three before they could take a sample of my hair. Not knowing for sure what had happened that day was harder than I imagined it would be. I'd always been very careful about what I drank when I was in public. But I wasn't as careful as I should have been that day. While I knew on some level it wasn't my fault, another part of me was yelling that it was.

"Thanks for calling."

"I'll let you know if the sample turns up and gets tested."

I didn't want to sit around and worry, so I decided to go talk to Mrs. Reynolds to take my mind off this last bit of news.

After the short drive down 30A, I stood in front of a neat-looking, two-story brick front townhouse. It had a small palm tree planted in the front yard. A cheery flag with a giant pink flamingo stamped on it waved in the breeze by the front door.

I rang the doorbell, and minutes later, a small woman who looked like an older version of Cindy opened the door. She wore green cat-eye glasses with rhinestones embedded in the frame and blush so bright it was almost fire-engine red. Tight capris and a low-cut top completed the look.

"Can I help you?" she asked.

"Hi, Mrs. Reynolds. I was hoping to catch Cindy. Is she here?"

Mrs. Reynolds narrowed her eyes at me. "What do you want with Cindy? You with the sheriff's department? You people got to quit pestering me."

That was interesting that she was feeling pestered. It was good to know that Deputy Biffle was looking at other people of interest. That term always drove me nuts. Suspects. I was a suspect.

"No, ma'am. I work at the Sea Glass Saloon. We are looking for a new employee." I'm not sure where that came from, but it worked.

"Why do you think Cindy needs a job?"

Oh, rats. Hostility bristled off Mrs. Reynolds. "A mutual friend who works at Two Bobs mentioned that Cindy was looking." I didn't like lying and always thought of Amy Dunne from the novel *Gone Girl* when I did. But at least I felt guilty about it because Amy sure didn't.

Mrs. Reynolds finally relaxed a little. "You always go around to visit people at their houses trying to find employees?"

Whoops. I guess she hadn't relaxed after all. "No ma'am. This is a first, but my friend assured me that Cindy would be worth the effort."

"Well, she's not here."

I couldn't help myself. I looked over her shoulder and into the house. Unfortunately, I couldn't see beyond the foyer because of a staircase. "When you talk to her, tell her give me a call, and I'll set up an interview." If I couldn't find Cindy out and about, maybe I could make her come to me.

The woman studied me for a moment, and I held my face in its neutral librarian look.

She finally nodded. "I'll tell her. I don't want her freeloading off me."

Back home, I did some much-needed house-keeping chores like scrubbing down countertops and floors. Once things were clean, I decided to go out for a run. I needed the extra training for the barback competition. And since apparently everyone, including Michael, thought I'd be difficult, today I'd do it by myself. It was lovely out, and after my normal run, I went up to the softer sand and practiced some high stepping that I hoped might imitate what it would be like to step through the tires.

My calves and quads ached as I got back to my house. I turned when I got to the screened porch and looked back over the view. It was stunning as usual. I loved it even on rainy days and was grateful to be here. I looked skyward and thought of Boone. "Thank you." My phone rang, interrupting my reverie. It was Johnny. I hoped he had good news.

"The autopsy report is in," he said.

"I'm surprised you have it already."

"Now, Chloe, what kind of lawyer would I be if I didn't find things out that could be pertinent to your case?" The lilt of his accent was such a contrast to the lawyer he was.

My heart was thrumming harder than it had been when I'd been working out in the soft sand. "I hope you have good news."

"Enrique was dead before he went in the water. His lungs were clear."

"So it was definitely a homicide?"

"That's what the sheriff is thinking."

I was disappointed. Part of me had been hoping, even with the diver's weights, that Enrique had died of natural causes and tumbled into the water. Although since he'd been out there and no boat was around, it had seemed unlikely all along.

"Do they have an official cause of death?"

"A head trauma."

"Do they know what caused it?"

"Not yet. They've brought up the diver's weights and are studying them."

"Do they know where the weights came from or who they belonged to?"

Johnny didn't answer for a few seconds, which was worrying.

"It's the kind Ann uses on her boats, but before you get all worried, they're a very common brand."

"What's all this mean for me? Is it good news or bad news?" I realized that I was almost holding my breath and tried to relax. Going out treasure hunting with Ann, working, being around Rip, and training for the barback competition eased my anxiety and kept my mind off the situation. But the anxiety was always there, trailing around like a wraith.

"Ah, now Chloe, for the time being, it isn't good or bad. It's just information that we know and will use to our best advantage. Don't you worry, or at least try not to."

"I haven't heard anything from Deputy Biffle. Do you think he still wants to talk to me?"

"I'm sure he will. He's going to try to rattle you. Don't let him."

We hung up. It was easy for Johnny to say not to be rattled, but it wasn't that easy not to be.

By 9:00, Ann and I were in an inlet to the east of her house. The entrance to it was narrow, but as far as I could tell, it widened and went north and to the east for quite a while. It was surrounded by trees and underbrush. We were in a black boat, wearing our black clothes, and waiting under a dark, moonless sky. The engine of this boat didn't purr like a kitten because it was electric. While the engine was quiet, it was impossible not to hear the water moving around it. Still, the potential for stealth was better with this boat. According to Ann, Dex was out on the Gulf somewhere in a similar boat as backup.

Birds rustled in trees, frogs did their ribbiting thing, and I'd heard the whine of bugs more than once. At least I hoped it was birds and not snakes in the trees. Ann had explained to me at her house that she'd deliberately mapped a spot close to shore so we'd have a place to hide while we waited. Ann had planted her own version of a fake treasure chest earlier in the evening and scattered coins around. If whoever hacked Ann's computer relied on radar to find things, they would spot something.

"Tomorrow, I'll have my new computer and security system up and running," Ann said in a low voice. "I'll have new maps if you are still game after tonight and all that has happened."

"I'm game." Although, I hoped tonight was quiet and calm. We settled in to wait. I hoped my plan worked and we could get this all over with. A couple of boats had gone by, but none stopped or seemed curious about the area where she'd buried the fake treasure. Although maybe they were doing recon and planned to come back by. My mind circled as we waited. What if some innocent happened into our trap and stopped? It would be thoroughly embarrassing to chase the wrong boat.

We both wore earpieces that connected us to

Dex. He let us know he was to the south, looking like he was night fishing.

"One of the boats that passed by five minutes ago is heading back this way," Dex said. "Speedboat. About fifteen feet long."

"Let us know if they slow down."

We waited in silence for a few moments.

"They're going on by," Dex said.

I let a breath out, softly, of course.

"Wait, they're circling again."

"Circling you?" Ann asked.

"No. They seem to be buying that I'm just out here fishing. They're headed your way."

Soon we heard the motor. It wasn't very loud, either, but not as quiet as ours.

"Are we going out there?" I asked Ann. Suddenly, this all felt a little more over my head than I'd expected.

"Not yet," Ann said. "You can stay on shore if you want."

It was as if she read my thoughts. Or maybe my voice had wobbled. I looked over the dark woods surrounding us. "No. I'm good." But I hadn't thought this through. Maybe I never thought my plan would actually work. It seemed like a great idea in the bright light of Ann's library. I was still a little stunned that Ann invited me on this type of reconnaissance mission. And more than a little stunned that I said yes. I'd been doing a lot of things in the last few days that I never thought I'd do.

"They stopped," Dex said. "I'll head that way."

"Come in slowly," Ann said. Her voice barely above a whisper. Water carried voices almost better than a telephone line. Secrets were hard to keep out here.

"I think there are two people on the boat," Dex told us.

Two of them and three of us. That sounded okay, but my heart was pounding harder than someone pounding a steel drum. Ann started the motor, and we motored out of the inlet like black smoke. The boat was about fifty yards southeast of us. I grabbed binoculars as Ann headed toward them. We weren't rushing.

"It looks like someone is getting ready to dive," I told Ann and Dexter. "I only see one other person, too."

"Go," Ann said to Dex.

She pulled the throttle back, and we bounced across the small waves toward the stopped boat. Dex's approach was noisier and covered ours. The two people on the boat turned toward him. One picked up a shotgun.

"Gun," I yelled. But by then, it was aimed and pointed. We heard a loud bang and heard an *oof* from Dex.

"Dex," Ann yelled, not trying to be quiet any longer.

The gunman whipped around, pointing the gun at us. I pushed Ann down, heard a bang, and something slammed into my chest. I tumbled overboard into the dark water.

CHAPTER 21

The cool water shocked me. I froze for a second, remembering being tossed from the boat on Lake Michigan when I was ten. Then, like now, I wanted to gasp in a breath. I kicked, hoping I was going upward. There was no moon to guide me in the right direction. For all I knew, I was going deeper, not up. My chest hurt. I wanted to breathe. I tried to push aside thoughts about blood and sharks and dying out here alone.

A light shone across the water in a bright sweeping move. I kicked hard and broke the surface, gasping for air. But what to do? I didn't know if the light was the bad guys hunting me down to finish off the job.

"Chloe," Ann shouted.

Thank heavens. "Here," I yelled over and over. It was like playing the most terrifying game of Marco Polo. The light beam hit me square in the eyes. Moments later, Ann was in the water next to me. She swam us to the boat, and hauled me onto it.

Two hours later, I sat next to Ann in her black truck as we left the hospital. Dex sprawled across the backseat. We'd both been hit, but it was with beanbag rounds instead of bullets. I remembered seeing such shotguns on TV shows. Cops used them as a nonlethal alternative to capture someone. While my chest hurt like heck, nothing was broken, and all the x-rays and scans showed that Dex and I were okay. On the way to the hospital, Ann had told us the people in the boat took off when she'd fired at them. Only she had real bullets.

Ann hadn't attempted to go after the other boat. After Ann had rescued me, she'd checked on Dex, got him in our boat, and tied his to ours to tow back to her dock. That's when she'd insisted we go to the hospital. After some initial protests, we agreed. I was more scared than I was willing to admit.

We had lied to the doctor by saying it was practice for the barback competition that had gone terribly wrong. That we'd lost control of the kegs we'd been trying to roll up the hill and they'd slammed into us. I'm not sure the young intern believed that tale, but he seemed too worn out and too busy to question us further.

"I can't believe you shoved me out of the way," Ann said as she drove toward my house.

"To tell you the truth, I can't believe I did it, either. It was like I was watching the whole thing from above and just reacted." I rubbed my chest. "Man, this hurts. I wish I *had* been watching from above."

I heard a little snicker from Dex in the back. I joined him, and pretty soon we were all laughing like idiots. Good grief, I'd never thought I'd be laughing at a situation like this. It must be a weird way to release stress.

"Did either of you find anything out about the boat or see the people on it?" I asked.

"Its name was the *Lazy Susan*," Dex said. "I'll track it down."

"Tomorrow," Ann said. "We've all been through enough tonight."

After Ann dropped me off, I took a shower, took a couple of ibuprofen, grabbed a beer, an ice pack, and headed out to the screened porch. The doctor had said a regimen of ibuprofen, ice, and time would be the best way to heal. I'm pretty sure he'd muttered something about idiots and competitions as we left.

I settled on the well-cushioned chaise lounge and pulled a light quilt over me. The sound of the waves on the shore was soothing. I wondered who had been out on the Gulf tonight, and could they have killed Enrique, and if did, why. I bolted up. I went over it all again in my head. Why had Enrique's body been left where Ann would likely find it? All this time, I'd been assuming the person who killed Enrique hated him for some reason. What if I was wrong, and it was that someone hated

Ann? Did the person who was also searching for the treasure hope to get Ann out of the way?

•

I woke up way too early. My chest still ached but not as bad as it did last night. I forced myself out of bed, put on my running clothes—a sports bra, T-shirt to hide the bruise, capri-length leggings, socks, and running shoes.

I headed down the beach until I found sand that was firm enough to run on. I went east this morning toward the rising sun. The sun was showing off with beams of light shooting out from behind pink and orange clouds. The air was warm, birds were waking, and sandpipers scuttled along the edge of the water, picking at something. I hated disturbing them. They'd run up the beach as I passed by.

Running wasn't as uncomfortable as I feared it would be. I took the pace nice and slow. This run was for pleasure instead of practice. And for all the treats I planned to indulge in today after surviving a scary night. I was already planning on a shake at The Diner, burritos at Maria's, and some of Wade's cheesy biscuits and gumbo. I laughed at myself for planning my meals while I was out here running.

I turned back toward home and took the run up a notch. If I ate all I planned to, I needed a fast run. Not to mention, the barback competition was looming ahead, and running fast would be one of my main skills. When I got close to my house, I slowed for my warm down. Before I turned to go up to my house, I paused and watched some dolphins arcing out of the water as they searched for food.

When I turned to head up to my house, I noticed Rip was sitting there. I smiled and waved, which made my chest ache. He was not going to like this at all. I couldn't blame him. If he told me that he'd been in a similar situation, I'd be furious. It was something we did in my family. If you were scared for someone, you got angry first, before you could express any sympathy. While we eventually got to the sympathy part, it wasn't pretty before that and included a lot of yelling and slamming doors. I might as well get this over with.

"Hey," I said when I got to Rip. "What are you doing here?" He wore shorts and a loose T-shirt that hid his beautiful abs. It's too bad it wasn't the eighties, when men wore those really short shorts, so I could admire all of his long, strong legs instead of just his calves.

Rip stood and crushed me to him. I held in the *oof* that wanted to come out from the bruise on my chest. Maybe I could get through the day without having to mention it, and it would fade enough so it didn't look so bad. Then Rip kissed me, and all thoughts of pain went away as warmth like a ray from the sun hit me. Hmmm, maybe I should just tell him, so we could take this inside.

We broke apart and headed over the walkway that protected the dune beneath it. We held hands and went onto my screened porch.

"I got off work and wanted to take you out to breakfast. I figured you'd be up."

I unlocked the door, and we walked into my living room. "Breakfast sounds good. I just need to take a quick shower."

"Want some company?" Rip asked.

Oh, boy. There was no way to hide the bruise from Rip any longer, because I did want company. I know Ann didn't want anyone to know what was going on, but I wasn't going to lie to Rip. I'd been evasive the past few days, but outright lying was where I drew a line.

"I have something to show you."

Rip raised his eyebrows at me and grinned.

"I'm okay."

Rip's grin disappeared when he realized I wasn't being playful.

"Nothing's broken or cracked. I went to the hospital last night to make sure." I took off my shirt, standing there in my sports bra and leggings. The black and blue bloomed on my chest like a Rorschach-test tattoo.

Rip actually paled a little. "What happened?"

"I got shot with a beanbag gun."

Rip sank onto my couch. "A gun. You were shot with a gun."

"Just with a beanbag. It hurt, but it's not lethal." I'm not sure trying to put a light spin on this was helping the situation. Guns terrified me.

"But it could have been a bullet, and it could have been lethal."

I had to admit to myself that I'd been avoiding thinking along those lines. I'd tucked all those kind of thoughts in the far recesses of my brain to think about another day. When I was ten, and had almost died from drowning and my best friend *did* drown, my parents had not only gotten me back in the water right away, they'd sent me to a therapist. She wouldn't approve of tucking away scary events to think about later.

After that, I'd thrown myself into water sports— always trying to reassure myself that I wasn't afraid of water. What would trying to conquer my fear of guns entail? Hours on a gun range, taking up skeet shooting, or training for a biathlon—the sport with shooting and skiing? At least I knew how to ski.

Rip frowned. "How come I didn't hear anything about this through dispatch or the news?"

"We wanted to keep it quiet and weren't truthful with the doctor." I sat down across from him.

"We?"

"I've been helping Ann with something."

"What?" His voice was deadly calm.

"I can't say."

"Weren't you the one who said trust is so important," Rip said.

I was. I'd told him that in October. "I did say that." I sighed. I was being yanked in two different directions. I didn't want to make a mess of things with Rip. I liked him too much. On the other hand, I'd lived by my father's philosophy that a promise made was a promise kept. It was the reason I'd moved down here in the first place. I'd promised Boone I'd help his grandmother if anything happened to him in Afghanistan.

"I don't trust Ann completely," Rip said.

That surprised me, because Ann had trusted him before.

"Ann doesn't have an off switch when she's after

something." Rip rubbed a hand across the back of his neck.

"I get that." I'd seen it in action the past few days. "It's just that I promised her that I wouldn't say anything about what she's doing."

"You and your promises," Rip said. "I admire your commitment and am scared by it at the same time."

Rip stood and pulled me to him. Pretty soon, I forgot that Ann even existed.

Rip and I parted ways after we feasted on breakfast burritos at Maria and Arturo's food truck. He'd held me a long time before he took off in his car. His tires had chirped as he sped off. I could tell he was worried, maybe more than worried. Scared. I was scared, too, but not because of Ann and our activities. It came down to being scared about all the feelings I had for Rip. Going along with Ann kept me from thinking about it and acknowledging that I was falling hard, even though I didn't feel particularly ready to.

Ann called minutes later as I walked back into my house.

"Are you up for trying something different?"

CHAPTER 22

O h, boy. Normally, I said yes to almost anyone. I was usually up for something new, but this was Ann speaking. What next? Skydiving? Free-climbing a skyscraper? Swimming with sharks in chummed water?

"What did you have in mind?" I knew my voice sounded tentative.

Ann laughed. "Nothing dangerous this time."

"Well, that would be refreshing."

"Would you mind getting hypnotized?"

That hadn't been on my speculation radar. "Hypnotized? Why?"

"My aunt is visiting from New Orleans."

Ann didn't pronounce *aunt* the way I did with my Midwestern *ant*. Her way sounded classier, but I felt funny using it myself.

"My aunt's a hypnotist. I was hoping if she hypnotized you and took you back to right before I found Enrique, maybe you could remember something more about the people on the other boat who were watching us."

"But it was just a glimpse."

"You'd be surprised the amount of detail you might have taken in with that glimpse."

I doubted that.

"Please," Ann said, "give it a try. It might help us find out who killed Enrique and who else is looking for the treasure."

I did want to find Enrique's killer. Walking around as a suspect wasn't much fun. "Okay. But I'd better not end up neighing like a horse or quacking like a duck anytime someone says 'tequila' in front of me."

"It's nothing like that. Trust me."

"When did you want to do this? I have to get to work."

"What time do you get off?"

"Seven."

"I'll pick you up at seven-thirty. My aunt's staying out at my camp."

Vivi was already ensconced in her office when I walked in at ten. That was surprising. She stood and stretched her arms up over her head when she spotted me. For once, instead of being dressed in a glamorous outfit, Vivi wore leggings and an oversize T-shirt. I'd never seen her dressed like that in here.

Vivi noticed me noticing. "I swung by here after

the gym. Yesterday, I posted a help-wanted ad on a job site so we can get someone trained before the summer rush."

"That's a good idea." We'd been so busy last summer that the three of us rarely took any time off. While people avoided Southern Florida in the summer, they flocked here. June, July, and August were when rents were the highest and businesses made the majority of their earnings for the entire year. Besides, that would mean I hadn't lied to Mrs. Reynolds about trying to hire someone.

"I almost worked us all to death last summer." Vivi shook her head. "I was so devastated over Boone's dying that throwing myself into work and keeping busy was the only thing that distracted me. It wasn't fair to you or Joaquín, though, with just the three of us working."

Vivi and I hadn't ever talked much about Boone dying or our shared grief. "Working that much helped me, too." I paused. "How are you doing?"

"I miss him every day."

"So do I."

"As much as I didn't want you here at first, it's a comfort to have you here now. At first you were a painful reminder of what I'd lost." Vivi smiled briefly. "But now, through you, I'm reminded of how much he was loved and valued."

I hugged Vivi. I had known she hadn't wanted me here—she'd made that abundantly clear when I first arrived, and I'd lied to her so I could stay. We'd both been shocked when the lawyer had explained Boone's will to us. It had been rough at first, but we'd finally come to an uneasy peace. Since then, though, we'd grown fond of each other.

"Well," Vivi said, "I'd like you to handle the initial interviews. Anyone you like, have them talk to Joaquín and then, eventually, me. How does that sound?"

I was surprised Vivi wanted me to take this on. "Sure."

"I've said experience preferred but not required. They have to fill out an online application and then stop by here. A couple of people already filled out the application. One is stopping by at ten-thirty and the other at eleven." Vivi picked up her purse—pale pink today. "I'm going to shower, and I'll be back around one."

"Okay. See you then."

"Take a look at the applications before they come if you get a chance." Vivi showed me how to access the website and then left.

I glanced at the applications and then hurried through the morning routine of pulling the chairs and stools off the tables and setting them down. I'd started to cut fruit for the drinks we'd make today when I heard a knock on the back door. At least it was locked. I took a quick look at the security footage on the computer. This must be our first applicant.

I hurried back and opened the door. "Kenn?"

"With two Ns," he said with a grin.

I'd seen that on the application, but whatever. "Come in, I'm Chloe," I said as I led him past our small kitchen, the bathrooms, and Vivi's office out into the bar. I sat at one of the high-tops, and he sat across from me.

Kenn was tall and muscled. Short blondish hair. He wore a loose sky-blue polo over white board shorts. A shark's-tooth necklace was dangling from his neck.

I opened my phone and brought up his application. "I see you're from Detroit originally. What brings you down here?"

"The weather. I'm so over the winters in Detroit."

"I get that. It doesn't look like you have any experience in a bar." In fact, it didn't look like he'd ever worked anywhere before. How was that possible? He was twenty-four.

"I've got plenty of experience in bars, if you know what I'm saying." He grinned at me again.

He must think his grin would charm me. It didn't. "I'm talking about work experience." I used my stern librarian voice that I'd used a few times over the years. "What makes you want to work here?"

"Free drinks and women," he said.

I started to chuckle but realized he wasn't joking. "We don't get a lot of free drinks. Plus, we discourage fraternizing with our customers."

He leaned in, and a waft of some kind of alcohol came off him. Oh, boy.

"How about the other employees? You're fire."

Lingo for he thought I was hot. "That's a no, too." I actually didn't know if any of this was against any policies we had.

"Working in a bar doesn't seem like as much fun as I thought it would be."

"It's a lot of hard work. You're standing most of the day and carrying heavy trays."

"Do you need a bouncer? I'm sure I'd be good at sitting and watching over people." He rolled up his shirtsleeve and curled his arm up so I had a better view of his bicep. "Sun's out, guns out." He kissed his bicep. Actually kissed it.

"We don't need a bouncer at this time. I'll keep your application on hand in case something opens up."

"Could I have a drink?" he asked. "A free one? I'd like to know the quality of the drinks at the place of my future employment."

"No. We don't serve until eleven, and I don't think we'll be needing a bouncer anytime soon." I stood and was relieved when he stood and followed me to the door. Since we closed at 9 p.m., we didn't usually have trouble with our customers. When we did, Joaquín and I had been able to handle it. "You might try Two Bobs down that way." I pointed to the left. "They have bouncers." Although, I suspected their bouncers actually worked.

"Excellent. Later."

"You might not want to tell them you're there for the free drinks and women," I called after him. He flashed me a peace sign, of all things. I guess that was better than a one-finger salute. I watched as he drifted off toward Two Bobs. Maybe hiring someone else wasn't such a good idea. Vivi, Joaquín, and I were a team. We worked well together without a lot of conflict. Would introducing some-one new upset that dynamic? The line, "He chose poorly . . . he chose wisely," said by the Grail Knight in *Indiana Jones and the Last Crusade,* came to mind. I hoped I was the latter.

CHAPTER 23

"Hello," a female voice said.

I turned to find a twenty-something woman standing beside me. I hadn't even heard her come up.

"Hi, I'm Chloe. Are you Heather?" Heather was the 11:00 am appointment.

She nodded. Her long brown hair fell almost to her waist. Her shift dress was a nondescript shade of beige but clean and neat.

"Come on in."

We settled at the same table where Kenn and I had sat. Heather looked down at her hands, which she clasped together on the table. They shook a little. I knew how nervous I used to get before an interview, so I would be gentle.

"Tell me why you'd like to work here," I said.

"Well, for one, I need a job."

"That's important." I hoped there was no trace

of snark in my voice because, come on. "Why this particular job?"

"I really like working with people, and I'm very good with them." Heather addressed this all to her hands, now folded in her lap. Her hair formed a curtain that almost hid her face from me.

Great. First Kenn, who was overexuberant, and now Heather, who fit the definition of painfully shy. How could she be good with people? I felt for her. "Do you have any experience in the hospitality industry?" If she did, she hadn't listed it on her resume.

"No. But I was a nanny to five kids, so I'm used to dealing with people."

I'd always figured kids and drunks weren't that different, but I'm not sure Heather could handle drunks. "Have you ever been in here before?" I asked.

Heather shook her head. "I don't frequent bars. Is that a problem?"

Yeesh, this just kept getting better. "Doris from the Presbyterian church was in here last week. She said they are looking for a part-time teacher for their summer camp. Maybe you should head over there."

Heather actually looked up at me and beamed. "Really? That's perfect for me." She slipped off her barstool. "No offense."

"None taken." I escorted Heather to the back door and watched her prance away. Really, she was almost skipping.

"Hey," Joaquín said.

I jumped and put my hand over my heart. "Don't scare me like that."

"Sorry, didn't mean to." He had on a pristine black Hawaiian shirt with tropical flowers in gray and white sprinkled across it.

I should be paying more attention to who was around me. Whoever killed Enrique was out there still.

"Who was that?" Joaquín said, pointing at the rapidly disappearing Heather.

"My second interviewee." We walked into the bar, and as I resumed chopping fruit, I told him about Vivi's plan to hire help.

"That would be great. How'd the interviews go?"

"Great. I suggested Kenn try Two Bobs. He was interested in meeting girls and free drinks. Kenn thought the perfect job for him was being a bouncer. And Heather claimed she loved working with people, but couldn't even look me in the eye."

"Then why'd she seem so happy leaving?"

"I told her about a job at the Presbyterian church."

Joaquín snort-laughed. "So you sent our two first interviews away for other jobs?"

"Yes, and you can thank me for that. I've saved us."

"You know you aren't required to find other employment for people. You can just tell them thanks for coming and you'll be hearing from us."

I shrugged. "It seemed easier."

"You're something, Chloe."

Hmmm, Ann had said that to me too. "If I had a hundred-dollar bill for every time you said that to me . . ."

"You'd have a hundred dollars?" Joaquín asked, laughing.

"No, you say it at least once a week. I've been here ten months, and that's about forty-three weeks, so I'd have forty three hundred dollars. I could go on a nice vacation with that."

"Do you want to go on a vacation?"

"A girl can dream, right?"

"In this dream, where do you go?"

"Croatia."

His eyebrows darted up. "Why there?"

"I've never been, and it looks beautiful."

"Who are you going with?"

Rip popped into mind, and I grew warm.

"Ooohh, Chloe, you want to take Rip."

"More than you would ever know."

At 2:00, I was wishing we had a bouncer. Regrets, I've had a lot. Joaquín was off on his break, probably sitting peacefully on his boat watching the water, maybe reading a book. Vivi was out picking up supplies. This wasn't our busiest time of day or usually when people became belligerent. I faced the bear of a man who wasn't happy with a litany of things. I made lousy drinks, there wasn't a table for him out on the deck, he wanted to sit at a high-top table. Did I know who he was?

"I don't know who you are, but it doesn't really matter, does it? Because we are a first-come, first-serve place." My voice stayed calm. My librarian people skills really were coming in handy lately. I hoped he wasn't the governor or one of Vivi's close friends in high places.

"I could buy this place three times over," he said.

"It's not for sale."

"Listen, sis." He poked a finger towards my nose.

I grabbed his big meaty hand, which felt like a boxing glove, and pushed back on the finger he'd so recently had in my face. "I'm not your sis, and if my brothers ever acted like you, I'd be appalled. And if you have a sister, I feel sorry for her."

"You tell him, Chloe," a customer yelled. Another customer clapped.

He deflated. "I'm so sorry. I've lost all my manners. The drink wasn't really that bad, and while I'm disappointed there's no seating outside or a high-top, that's no excuse for my behavior."

I let go of his hand and stepped back. If only finding Enrique's killer and Ann's treasure were as easy. I looked around him to survey the bar. "There's a high-top opening near the doors to the deck. You'll have a lovely view and the sea breeze."

"You're not going to kick me out."

"I believe in second chances."

Joaquín walked back in as the man turned to sit at the table. "Everything okay? You look a little red."

"Just peachy," I said. "I'm going to check the hiring site and see if we have any more job applicants after I check on tables."

I did a quick round, took orders up to Joaquín, and poured beers and wine while he made the mixed drinks. Soon, they were delivered, and I opened the hiring app. It showed that three new applications had come in.

There were two good possibilities. Both had worked at their places of employment for a couple of years. Both lived in the Panhandle. The last application was from Cindy Reynolds. She was the waitress from Two Bobs, the one who had possibly put drugs in my drink. The one who had possibly killed Enrique in a fit of jealousy. I couldn't believe my plan of luring her to me had worked.

I set up three appointments for tomorrow. I put the first two in at 10:15 and 10:45. Cindy, I scheduled for 4:00. There'd be plenty of people around then, including Vivi and Joaquín. Between now and then, I needed to decide if I should tell them who she was and what she might have been up to.

CHAPTER 24

At 7:25, I was waiting for Ann in what I decided was appropriate wear for being hypnotized—capri leggings and a flowy, white top. I'd taken a quick shower, and my damp hair was curling around my ears. I'd also applied a little bit of makeup for courage. Might as well look good when entering the unknown. I laughed at myself. Was I dramatic or what?

When Ann pulled up in her battered Jeep, I set the alarm system, went out, and got in.

"How's the bruise?" Ann asked.

"Not bad. How's Dex doing?"

"Whining like a two-year-old. He's staying out at the camp with my aunt."

"Why's she staying out there instead of your house on the Gulf?" If I knew someone with a house like Ann's, I wouldn't stay anywhere else.

I'd been to Ann's camp once last fall. It had been pitch dark, but I don't remember seeing any kind of structure. Maybe her aunt liked to camp. April was usually good for that from what I'd heard, not too hot and not too cold. Although Leah Hickle had told me about a camping experience she'd had where an unexpected cold front had dropped down from the north, and they'd almost froze.

"She thinks the house is too bright and that there's no privacy on the beach. I think she's half vampire." Ann chuckled like she was very fond of her aunt.

I just hoped the woman wouldn't bite me while I was hypnotized. We took a left out of the driveway, over to 30A, then a left on 98 heading toward Destin. We passed Silver Sands Outlet Mall. Their parking lot was full. A night of shopping sounded way more fun than being hypnotized. We turned right, heading past Destin Commons, which also teemed with shoppers. Beyond that, we started up the long Mid-Bay Bridge, which took us over Choctawhatchee Bay. Far below the water was black, almost forbidding, or maybe it was just my mood.

I still had no clue who'd killed Enrique or who was messing with Ann. Maybe I just wasn't the right person for finding out either of these things.

"I've been thinking about who killed Enrique and why," I said.

Ann paid the toll with cash, smiled at the toll collector, and said thanks. "Have you come up with anything new?" She took the first exit to the right.

"What if this wasn't about someone who was angry at Enrique, but it is about someone setting you up?"

"Angry at *me*?" Ann took a left onto a small, paved road. She sounded kind of incredulous.

"Yes, at you. Can you think of anyone who might be out to get you? Or wants to shut down your business or has an old grudge?" The paved road became a dirt road, which wound around until I wasn't sure which direction we were headed. Talk about a metaphor for my life. "I can think of a couple of people from last fall when we were investigating."

"I suppose there are people out there."

"Any recent threats?"

"Nothing out of the ordinary."

So Ann did get threatened. We drove through a stand of tall pines, occasionally passing a house. But soon there weren't any more houses.

"Nothing I took seriously."

"Are you going to tell me about them?" I asked.

Ann shook her head. "No reason to. But to make you feel better, I'll check them out."

At least she'd do that much. "Did Dex find anything about the boat named *Lazy Susan*?" I asked.

"Nothing. It's not registered to anyone around here."

People came from all over to fish here. The boat could be from anywhere. Another dead-freaking-end.

Ann turned into the woods on a trail that could barely be called that. We came to a gate locked with chain link and a padlock. A sign on the gate read, PRIVATE—NO TRESPASSING, with a skull and bones under it. The first time I'd come out here with Ann, I'd barely known her, and she intimidated me. She still kind of did, but not like back then.

Ann jogged to the gate and had it open in minutes. A few night insects made their low sounds. Something small skittered in the pine straw to my right. I couldn't see it when I looked.

Ann climbed back into the Jeep and drove through the gate.

"Want me to close it?" I asked.

"That would be great," Ann replied.

I slid off the seat landing in pine straw, hoping I didn't come across a snake. It was dark out here with only the moon and stars for light. I crunched over, closed the gate, and reattached the padlock. I guess we were staying awhile if she wanted the gate closed.

We drove another forty yards or so. In front of us was a small, flat area on a smaller bayou or creek. We'd launched a boat from there last fall. Ann took a left on a road I hadn't noticed the last time we were here. The only light came from the headlights. There was no sign of anyone else living out here. We wound around trees, bumping along the rutted road until it came to an opening.

A two-story house on tall pilings sat on a wide bayou. Calling this a camp house was like calling the mansions in Newport, Rhode Island, cottages. It had a wide, sweeping staircase, deep verandas on the two sides I could see, and it was ten times bigger than my place. I was expecting some little half-tent, half-house kind of structure.

"This is a camp house?" I asked as we parked.

Ann laughed. "It used to be a little more rugged.

Now it even has an elevator to take groceries up in."

When we got to the top of the stairs, I turned and looked out over the bayou. The moon reflected on the water. It was languid-looking but probably had a swifter current than one would expect. There was a deep, earthy scent of growing things and wet soil. A mosquito buzzed at my ear, and I swatted at it.

"Let's go inside before we get eaten," Ann said. "Mosquitoes are the downside of living on the bayou."

One of many downsides, as far as I was concerned. I needed more civilization around me. I was a city girl at heart, still adapting to small-town living, which turned out nothing like I imagined. For one thing, I hadn't expected murders, and another, I assumed people in small towns were open books. Some of the people here were not only closed but locked and loaded.

Like Ann's other house, the inside of this one wasn't what I expected, which would have been a small, rugged, rough-hewn place. There was a long hallway cutting the house in half. Marble tile floors, thick Oriental rugs, and another staircase that begged for someone to slide down its banister. We went into the first room on the right. The marble floors and thick rugs continued in here. There were lit silver candlesticks on the mantel and pink roses in a matching silver bowl.

A petite woman, who looked to be around Vivi's age, sat in a wingback chair by a fireplace with a small fire going. She had Ann's thick black hair with some silver streaks, but hers was piled in a loose bun on the top of her head. Dex sat across from her in a matching wingback chair. He was reading *A Tale of Two Cities* by Charles Dickens. Somehow its first line—"It was the best of times, it was the worst of times"—felt very appropriate for how conflicted I was feeling.

Ann's aunt rose. "I'm Angelique Lafitte. It's lovely to meet you." Her voice had a deep Southern accent with a melodic lilt.

We shook hands. Her grip was firm, her hands cool and dry.

"It's nice to meet you, too. Hey, Dex. How are you feeling?"

"I'll survive."

"Dex, why don't you let Chloe have your chair so we can chat," Angelique said.

Dex stood with a little grunt and swept his hand toward the chair. I perched on the edge of it. Every muscle in my body was clenched, even muscles I didn't know I had. Then my right leg started jiggling up and down at about the speed of a hummingbird wing.

Angelique smiled at me, and a dimple appeared on her right cheek. "Will you be comfortable there, or is there another place? Perhaps lying on a couch?"

"This is fine," I said. Hard to picture going into any kind of relaxed state.

"I'm a certified hypnotherapist," Angelique said.

I nodded. Stiffly. Getting anything to move in my clenched state seemed like a good sign to me.

"Have you ever meditated?" Angelique asked.

"Yes, but never on a regular basis. I usually use some kind of app."

"Being hypnotized is much the same. It's a state of heightened awareness and relaxation."

I unclenched just a bit. Okay, that didn't sound so bad. "Are you going to use a gold watch on a chain and tell me I'm getting sleepy? Because I don't feel the least bit sleepy."

Angelique laughed, as did Dex. I glanced over my shoulder at him.

"Perhaps you'd be more comfortable without an audience," Angelique said. She gestured toward Ann and Dex, who were hovering around me.

I nodded.

"Dex and Ann, if you could just excuse us for a bit." She said it very politely, but there was an undertone of a command in there.

Ann looked at me. "I could stay if that would make you feel better."

I knew she'd want to be part of the process, but this was awkward enough without an audience. I glanced over at Angelique. She made a shooing motion with her hands.

"Leave us," she said. They walked across the room, left, and closed the door.

I turned to Angelique. "I'm nervous."

She smiled. "Really? I would have never guessed."

That made me smile and unclench a bit more. I relaxed back into the chair. "Okay. Let's do this."

"I'll be very careful with guiding you back to the day of Rick's death. I don't want to put any suggestions in your head about who you saw."

I nodded.

"We'll start though with a simple relaxation technique."

Angelique talked me through relaxing my body first, starting with my toes, releasing the stress until we worked up to my head. By the time we were done, I was feeling much better than when we arrived. She continued to talk to me, her voice as languid and calm as the bayou outside. I floated along with it.

Pretty soon, she had me back on the boat. I picked up the binoculars and looked through them.

"What do you see?" Angelique asked.

"Binoculars. Someone is looking at me."

"Gender?"

"It's a man. Thick black hair. Black T-shirt. There's a logo. But I can't tell what it is." It was frustrating.

"It's okay." Angelique's voice calmed me. "What else do you see?"

"He's wearing black shorts. No socks; black running shoes. He has a tattoo on his inner ankle. It's about the same place as Ann's."

"Can you tell what the tattoo is?"

"No. It's too far away."

"Anything else?"

"No."

She counted backwards, and I was fully awake, blinking at Angelique. "He looked like a male version of Ann." I shook my head. "I must have just mixed up two memories—one of the person on the boat and one of Ann."

Angelique didn't look as serene as she had before. "Will you get Ann and Dex, please?"

I walked across the plush rug and opened the door. Ann and Dex almost fell into the room. I guess they were listening at the door, although I don't think they could hear anything through the solid wood. I sat on the couch facing the fireplace. Ann sat next to me and Dex in the wingback chair.

"Did you remember anything?" Ann asked.

The door must have been so thick, and our voices so quiet, that it had made eavesdropping impossible.

"I'm sorry. I mixed two images together."

"How so?" Ann asked.

"I described a man who looked like a male version of you, right down to the tattoo on your ankle."

Ann slammed her hand down on the arm of the couch, which made me jump.

CHAPTER 25

"Antoine." Ann practically spat out the name. Angelique nodded. "I thought so, too."

"Who is Antoine?" I asked.

"My no-good cousin. We used to be very close, thus the same tattoo." Ann shook her head. "It was one night in college. One drunken night." She glared down at the tattoo. "He could talk me into almost anything back then."

It was hard to picture Ann out of control, but who knew what seethed under that normally calm façade. "What happened to cause you not to be close?"

"He almost got me kicked out of Tulane for stealing my papers and submitting them. We were both getting degrees in international business. Fortunately, they believed me after questioning us both, and he was thrown out. Since then, Antoine never seemed interested in doing any hard work."

"Is he the cousin you said was helping you with your computer security?"

"No. I have a large extended family."

"How would he know about the map?"

Ann stood and started pacing back and forth waving her hands. I'd never seen her so agitated.

"Antoine wasn't above looking through our grand-parents' things and helping himself to anything that was valuable. He probably found it and put it where I would find it. Just like you'd suggested." She muttered something to herself. "He wouldn't want to do the hard work of interpreting the map to find out where the shipwreck was. Oh, no. He would just let me do the work, follow me, and scoop up the treasure."

I looked over at Angelique.

She was nodding her head. "It's true."

"Ann, does he know you well enough that he could guess your computer and security-system passwords?" I asked.

Ann shrugged. "It's unlikely but maybe not impossible."

"But we shouldn't jump to conclusions," I said. "I may be wrong, and like I said, confused the memories."

Ann paused in her pacing. "You're right. I'll find out where he's been." She shook her head. "He was friends with Enrique for a while in high school."

"Could they have been working together?"

"It makes me crazy to think that's the case, but it might have been." Ann flopped back down on the couch.

"Maybe Enrique got greedy and tried to cut Antoine out. Maybe Antoine killed Enrique and left his body for us to find." I'd be sorry for Ann's family if that were the case, but relieved to be off the suspect list. "Or maybe he was just following you to see if you found the treasure and didn't know that Enrique's body was there."

Ann jumped back up. "I have to find Antoine. This town isn't that big for someone to hide out."

"Emerald Cove isn't that big, but the area is. It seems to me it would be easy to avoid you. I mean, look at all this land you have, and there's more like it all over the Panhandle," I said. Forestry and paper mills had once been big business here. There were still lots of undeveloped tracts of land.

"Dex, do you mind driving Chloe home? I'm going to track down Antoine. But first I'm going to do a sweep of my property to make sure he hasn't been hiding under my nose."

"Has he been here before?" I asked.

"A couple of times, and there are so many places to hide."

On the way home, Dex was quiet as usual.

I interrupted his thoughts and told him about my theory that someone who didn't like Ann was setting her up by killing Enrique. "What do you think?"

"It's a possibility."

Headlights flashed across his face as we drove down Highway 98. He didn't look happy.

"Can you think of anyone in particular?" I asked.

He thought for a few moments before shaking his head. "I can't."

"Will you at least think about it?" I asked.

"Of course."

"And let me know if you think of someone?"

Dex nodded. "Sure. You know Ann doesn't get close to many people. I'm glad she's getting close to you. Thanks for trying to help her out."

"Back at you."

At home, I wasn't content to let Ann search for Antoine by herself. I looked him up on social media. He used the last name Lafitte, which was much easier to track than the last name Williams. I found his social media accounts. He had some great dance moves on TikTok. It didn't look like he was a bad cook, either. He had so many followers on Instagram, he was almost famous. His dark good looks made him popular with women. Everything he'd posted was in the New Orleans area. There were no pictures of him with Enrique. But I noticed he'd quit posting and turned off his location tracking about a week and a half ago. That was before Ann's house was burglarized. Did he not want her to know where he was?

I sent Ann a text telling her what I'd found. She might have already figured that out, but just in case, it was better to let her know. I took a screenshot of the best picture of Antoine.

I didn't want to just sit home and not do anything, so I sent a text to Rip, asking him if he wanted to go to Sandy's for a drink. My phone rang two seconds later.

"You want to go to Sandy's for a drink?" Rip asked. "I can think of a lot of much nicer places to take you than there."

"You don't have to come."

There was a pause. "You're trying to find someone."

"Yes. Jean Claude."

"And you're going with or without me."

"Yes."

"I'll pick you up in thirty minutes."

"Thank you." I was so lucky. I hoped tonight ended better than last night had. As long as no one shot at us anything would be an improvement.

CHAPTER 26

Thirty minutes gave me time to change into bar clothes and add a bit more makeup. Not that Sandy's required anything fancy, but I at least wanted to look nice for Rip. I put on an off-the-shoulder, one-piece romper that was high enough it covered my bruise. It was comfortable and sexy at the same time. It was a pain if I had to go to the bathroom, but I hoped we wouldn't be there all that long.

Rip looked around once we entered Sandy's. "Wow, this place hasn't changed a bit, and that's not a good thing."

"You used to come here?"

"Every high-school kid from Pensacola to Panama City came here at one time or another. They weren't particular about IDs back then. If the cops showed up, we'd all just run out the back. Bar or table?"

That must be why the back door had been locked when I'd been here with Dex—to keep people from running out. "Bar." I'd rather have my back to the wall at a table, but Jean Claude had already spotted me from behind the bar. I'm fairly certain if we sat at a table, he wouldn't swing by to say hi. The place was about three-quarters full. Someone was setting up a guitar and amplifier over in the right-hand corner. It smelled of old beer and sweat in here.

We worked our way up to the bar and settled on two barstools. Jean Claude loomed over us. His muscles bulged, his arms were scratched and cut, his eyes unfriendly, and if he were green, he'd have reminded me of the Incredible Hulk. The scratches looked like he'd been in some kind of a fight—here, or with Enrique?

"We don't serve your kind here," Jean Claude said.

My brows popped up in surprise. "What kind would that be?"

"Nosy liars."

"What are you, nuts?" the bartender next to Jean Claude said. "As long as they have money, we serve any kind." He looked over at Rip and me. "You do have money, don't you?"

"Yes," we said in unison.

Rip got out his wallet and put a twenty on the bar. It warmed my nosy, lying heart. He didn't want me to come here, but supported me nonetheless.

We ordered local beers. Jean Claude glared as

he poured them, and I noticed Rip's jaw was starting to set. I picked up his hand and gave it a squeeze. He looked over at me and relaxed a little bit.

"What are you doing here?" Jean Claude asked as he set the beers in front of us. "Trying to stir up more trouble?"

"No. I came to tell you I'm sorry you lost your friend Enrique." That sounded way better than saying *I was here to find out if you killed your friend Enrique.*

Jean Claude's massive shoulders relaxed a little. "We weren't friends. I barely knew him."

"But you, Lisa, and Enrique all came in together to confront me." I took a sip of my beer. It tasted very good, a little hoppy.

"Lisa asked me to."

Do you do everything Lisa asks you to? I held that one in too.

"She said it would be more intimidating if the three of us came in together."

"Lisa was right." I smiled to show there were no hard feelings. At least on my part. "Have you known Lisa a long time?"

"Long enough. Do you believe what that woman said about Enrique assaulting her?" Jean Claude asked.

That was another surprise. "Yes. She's not one to make things up."

"I've got three younger sisters. The thought of someone hurting them . . ." He shook his head. Jean Claude picked up a bar towel and twisted it to the breaking point. "That's not right. But I guess he won't be hurting anyone else."

What if this was an act? Jean Claude seemed sincere enough, but I didn't know him well. Maybe he'd been enraged when he heard Ann call out Enrique. Maybe he thought about those three sisters of his and killed Enrique so Enrique couldn't hurt anyone else. But how would Jean Claude know to dump Enrique in the very spot that Ann and I would find him? I'd have to think about all of this later. I pulled up the screenshot of the photo I'd taken of Antoine. "Did you ever see Enrique with this man?"

Jean Claude looked at my phone for a couple of seconds. He shook his head. "I don't think so. Like I said, Enrique and I weren't friends."

He was lying. His eyes had shifted back and forth before he answered, like he was nervous. He really had no reason to be forthcoming with me. But what was he lying about? His relationship with Enrique, or knowing Antoine? He moved away from us out into the bar. And as much as I wanted to follow him and insist he give me more information, I knew that wasn't going to work.

I looked over at Rip. "What do you make of all of that?"

"I think he has a thing for Lisa."

I told Rip what I'd found out about Lisa and Enrique's past together. "Maybe that gives Jean Claude a motive for killing Enrique."

"Love triangle." Rip nodded. "It's possible. Who's the man in the picture you showed him?"

"Ann's cousin Antoine. Have you seen him any place?" I handed Rip my phone.

"Wow. He and Ann look like twins." He looked at me. "I haven't ever seen him before. Does he have something to do with what Ann is up to?"

"It's possible."

"Want to finish these beers and get out of here?" Rip asked.

"I don't even want to finish mine. Come home with me?"

"Ann doesn't need you tonight?"

Darn. I guess I had hurt him. I took his hand. "Nope. Just little old me in my big old bed."

Rip grinned. He squeezed my hand. "Let's go."

At seven in the morning, my phone rang. I rolled over and snagged it. Joaquín. I hoped nothing was wrong.

"Why aren't you fishing?" I asked.

"Engine problems—so meet me outside the Sea Glass in fifteen minutes for some training."

"Fifteen minutes? No way."

"Tired from your run?"

I glanced over at Rip. He was asleep on his stomach, an arm flung out to the side. "Something like that."

"Okay. Then thirty."

I groaned. "I'll see you then." I could have said no. But darned if I didn't want to win this stupid competition. As I got out of the shower, I smelled coffee. Rip must have woken up. I dressed in a

T-shirt that covered my bruise, which didn't seem to be fading, but at least I wasn't as sore. Rip had done his best to kiss it all better last night. I smiled at the memory. I tucked a jumpsuit into a bag to change into for work when Joaquín finished my training. Fortunately it, too, would cover my bruise.

Rip was leaning against the kitchen counter with a cup of coffee in his hand when I left the bedroom. He was shirtless and barefoot, wearing his jeans. Now that was a sight I could get used to seeing. There was a to-go cup sitting by him. I crossed the room and reached for the cup. Rip looped his arm around my waist and pulled me to him.

"Do you have to go?" he asked.

Was training really that important? For some reason, the thought *yes* answered. Ugh. What was wrong with me? Warm, sexy man, or being shouted at by Joaquín?

"Joaquín has engine problems."

Rip was feathering kisses down my neck. "Ummm. That's terrible. What's it got to do with you?"

"Training for the barback competition." Which was seeming less important by the second. A quick glance at my phone told me I was going to be late. I pulled away and grabbed the cup of coffee with a sigh so loud and long, it made Rip laugh.

I hustled across to the door to put some distance between us. "Lock up and set the alarm for me if you leave, please," I said.

He cocked an eyebrow at me. "If I leave?"

Oh, boy. I wasn't ready for this conversation and was wondering why I'd put it that way in the first place. My subconscious must be on overdrive. "When." I whirled out the door and ran for my car. I swear I heard Rip's deep, sexy chuckle following me.

CHAPTER 27

After reading me the riot act for being late,
Joaquín led me to the beach side of the Sea
Glass. He had on khaki shorts and a teal Hawaiian
shirt with Corvettes on them. Each Corvette was a
different color and had a different person in the
driver's seat.

"What the heck are those?" I asked, pointing at
circles he'd drawn in the sand. There were ten of
them staggered left and right. At the back of each
was a ruler stuck into the sand.

"Since I don't have actual tires for you to practice with, this is the best I could come up with. An
average tire is twelve-and-a-half inches, so you have
to step over the ruler to pass the test."

Taller people would have an advantage with this
one. "Got it."

Joaquín went to the end of his course and
pulled a stopwatch out of his pocket. "When I yell

go, give it a try. We'll practice without the beer mugs first."

Ugh. I'd forgotten all about the beer mugs. I channeled my inner Jodie Foster from the opening of the movie *The Silence of the Lambs*, where she was training on the FBI practice course at Quantico.

I took a stance like one I used when I ran track in high school. Joaquín yelled "go," and I took off. I was done in under thirty seconds. All but one of the rulers was knocked over. Joaquín and I walked back and studied all the circles.

"You would have stepped on the third, fifth, and eighth tire." Joaquín pointed to where my foot had landed on the outer edge of the circle. "You probably would have fallen or been disqualified. You certainly would have sloshed a lot of beer out. It's not necessarily about being fast but also about being accurate."

I liked fast. It's why I didn't run long distance in high school. And I had been terrible at the hurdles. My short body wasn't made for sailing over hurdles. I tried again and again, and then Joaquín added in beer mugs. Three in each hand filled with water, because why waste beer?

It was almost 9:30 by the time Joaquín was satisfied with my performance. I was a sweaty mess, but had managed to quit knocking over the rulers and didn't spill as much water. I felt like I was getting the hang of it.

"One more time," he said.

My arms ached from carrying the beers. My legs ached from the high stepping. But I wasn't going to be a quitter. I ran the course again. When I finished, someone started clapping behind me. Joaquín frowned, and I whirled around. Lisa. She was leaning against the deck of the Sea Glass.

"Not bad," she said, strolling over. "Mind if I give it a try?"

Joaquín and I exchanged *whatcha gonna do?* glances.

"Sure," I said. Maybe she'd be terrible at this, too.

We refilled the water mugs and set up the one ruler I'd knocked over. Lisa picked the beer mugs up with ease and stood at the start line with a determined look on her face. Joaquín trotted back to the finish and, seconds later, yelled *go*. Lisa took off and finished quickly. That was no surprise. She was, after all, Wonder Woman. It did give me some satisfaction that one ruler tilted to one side a bit, and it looked like she'd stepped on the edge of one imaginary tire.

Lisa handed the mugs off to Joaquín. "Thanks."

Joaquín and I watched her trot off down the beach with a wave back to us.

"Don't say it," Joaquín said.

"What?"

"That you can't compete with Wonder Woman, because you can."

I didn't have his confidence, but it was time to go to work. "I can't work like this, and I have interviews set up for this morning." I gestured to my glowing-with-perspiration body.

"Yeah, you're a mess." Joaquín winked to show he was joking. He took keys out of his pocket and tossed them to me. "You can go shower at our place. Michael left for Pensacola at eight and won't be home until dinnertime."

"Thanks. I'll be back in a little while."

When I arrived back at the bar, Joaquín had most of the opening duties done. He looked over my jumpsuit and tilted his head.

"You've certainly been more covered up lately."

"What's that supposed to mean?" I knew very well what he meant, because I was trying to keep my bruise hidden.

"You've just been wearing higher necklines lately." He widened his eyes. "It's a hickey, right?"

"Ugh. No, I'm not fifteen. I like this jumpsuit." It was a stretchy navy blue capri-length romper with a mock turtleneck and short sleeves. "I wanted to look professional for the interviews."

"Whatever you say," Joaquín said, clearly not believing me.

"It's not like I wear low-cut tops to work." I knew some waitresses said that equated to more tips, but I was not one of them. I believed in using my winning personality. Ha. I mostly relied on Joaquín's charm and good looks. Not that I'd tell him that.

"I didn't say you did. I'm going to run home, and I'll be back at noon for my shift. Text me if you get busy and need help."

I kissed his cheek, because I felt bad for keeping things from him. "My head is saying thanks for training me, and my body is saying *ouch*."

Joaquín laughed as he left.

*   *   *

At 10:15, I sat across from a pink-haired twenty-three-year-old named Tonya. She wore a turquoise dress with a huge, full skirt with lots of slips underneath. Her midnight-blue glasses were studded with rhinestones. For that matter, her ears were studded with rhinestones, too. I'd never seen that many piercings in one ear. She had a bright smile and looked around the bar with interest. Finally, a possibility.

Tonya had been working in a bar in Navarre for the past six months but wanted to work closer to home in Destin.

"The commute's killing me, and I know it will be worse this summer."

I read over her application again. "You went to culinary school?" She must not have liked it if she was working in a bar. There were always restaurants in the Panhandle searching for chefs.

"Yes. It's my passion. I went back and forth between cooking and bartending at my last job. I was hoping to do the same here."

I held in a sigh. "We don't have a kitchen. All of our food comes from the Briny Pirate next door."

She looked sad for a moment. "Maybe I'd be okay just bartending."

"Wade, who owns the Briny Pirate, is looking for a sous chef. Go over and tell him I sent you."

"Really? Thanks so much." She bounded out the front and disappeared from sight. We may never get summer help, but I could open up my own employment agency.

*   *   *

While I waited for the next interviewee to show up, I did a search on my phone for links between Jean Claude and Enrique. Just because he said they weren't friends didn't mean he was telling the truth. But my search yielded nothing. That was frustrating. Then another idea popped into my head. I searched for Lisa and Jean Claude. And *bingo*, there were pictures of them together. The pictures were from not long after Enrique and Lisa had split up. A lot of pictures, from innocent shots of them jogging together to them making out at a club as they danced. Lisa had even taken him to a premiere with her a couple of years ago. Well. that was interesting. Did they have some kind of love triangle going like Rip and I had talked about last night? Did Lisa arrange for them all to be here in the hopes that Jean Claude would kill Enrique in a jealous fit? He'd been upset at the thought of Ann being hurt and mentioned his sisters. Would he protect Lisa, too, or some other woman?

CHAPTER 28

My next interviewee, Bev Meyers, showed up just then, and I didn't have any answers, anyway. Bev's face was rutted with lines of hard living. Her eyebrows were drawn on, she wore blue eyeshadow, and her hot-pink lipstick was bleeding into the wrinkles around her mouth. Bev had the tan of a long-time Floridian who eschewed sunscreen. Her bleach-blond hair was piled up in a messy bun. According to Bev's application, she was fifty-two but she looked older than Vivi. She had a killer smile and a firm handshake.

"It looks like your most recent job was in Cheyenne, Wyoming," I said. She worked at a bar there for two years and also listed jobs such as ranch hand and cook. What brought her down here? I guess I'd have to reassess my speculation about her tan.

"Lived there all my life, but my daughter married an Air Force officer and then landed here. She just had a baby, and I wanted to be closer."

Her voice sounded like she gargled daily with shards of glass, but I'm guessing she used to be a smoker. Bev certainly didn't reek of smoke now.

"That's lovely. So are you really looking for a job as a cook or wanting to work as a ranch hand?" Finding her a job as a cook wouldn't be hard, but the ranch hand would be more of a stretch. Although last winter, Vivi had tried to set me up with a man who owned a ranch. Maybe he needed help. I don't know why I felt the need to find everyone who came in the perfect job.

Bev gave me a funny look. "No, honey, I like working in bars. I like being around interesting people, and bars are full of them. My mom always said I was born with the gift of gab."

She looked me right in the eye as she said it.

"The view sure is pretty, and this place seems homey. It looks like a good place to work."

"I enjoy being here."

"Where are you from originally, because you talk faster than the natives I've met?"

Ten minutes later, she knew pretty much my entire life story. Bev was a good listener. I hadn't told her about the murder that occurred last summer or that I was part owner. That could come later if we called her back for another interview.

We stood. "Thanks for coming in," I said. "I'll be in touch when we've completed our interviews."

"Thanks, hon. It was nice talking to you," Bev said.

"You, too." I smiled as she left.

* * *

I opened the bar, and Tonya walked back in. I was surprised to see her. She plopped at the bar.

"A prosecco, please," she said. "I'm celebrating and came to toast you."

"I take it Wade hired you?" I opened a bottle of prosecco and poured the bubbly liquid into a coupe glass.

"Fancy glass," Tonya said as I placed it in front of her.

"You didn't have coupe glasses where you worked?" I asked.

"No, just flutes."

"Flutes definitely have their advantages. They are easier to hold and less likely to spill when you clink them together." I smiled at her. "It's rumored that the coupe glass was modeled after Marie Antoinette's breast."

Tonya laughed and held the glass up. "Hmmmm, I guess she wasn't exactly busty, judging by the size of this."

I laughed, too. "No matter where the design came from, the larger surface allows more air to interact with any sparkling wine, which in turn allows the flavors and aromas to develop. And then you get a more rounded tasting experience. Lots of people think the flute allows the wine to stay bubblier and that the bubbles go flat in a coupe, but that's a myth."

"Mine never lasts long enough to worry about the bubbles going flat," Tonya said.

I laughed again. "Mine either." More customers came in, so I moved away and got down to business.

* * *

Cindy came in at five to four. I'd asked Vivi if I could use her office for the interview since we were busy. I didn't tell her I wanted it for privacy or about Cindy's connection to Enrique. I might confess it all later, but for now, I wanted to see how things played out. Cindy's hair wasn't gelled up in spikes, and the red tips were gone. Her outfit was way more modest than it had been the day I'd seen her at Two Bobs. She had on a short-sleeved dress in a floral pattern that hit just above her knee.

I wasn't sure she'd recognize me from Two Bobs. It would be better if she didn't. So I let her approach Joaquín and pretended not to watch her say she was here for an interview. Joaquín waved me over.

"This is Cindy," Joaquín said. "She's your four o'clock interview."

"Great—thanks, Joaquín," I said. "Come with me." I led her into Vivi's office and closed the door most of the way. If things got ugly, I wanted to be able to make a fast exit.

"Are you interviewing a lot of people?" Cindy asked. "Thanks for seeking me out. That has to be a first."

We sat down. Me behind Vivi's desk and her across from me. She crossed and uncrossed her legs several times. Nervous. I was nervous, too, but I hoped it didn't show.

"Yes," I said. "We've had quite a bit of interest. Tell me why you are interested in this job." I wanted to get to more personal questions, but I also had to be careful about what I asked. The last thing I needed was to get sued for asking something I couldn't legally ask. I'd read up on interviews after the first two I'd done.

"I looked at your hours, and I think I'd like the schedule better than that of my current job."

Her resume hadn't been updated to say she'd left Two Bobs.

"Plus, I like the idea of a smaller bar. It allows you to really connect with the patrons in a way I can't at my current position."

That was a good answer. But it seemed like she connected with Enrique without any difficulty. Or maybe with a lot of difficulty, if she was jealous of his interactions with the other women there.

She tilted her head to one side. "You look kind of familiar."

Oh, no. I'd put on a headband to hold my hair back from my face in hopes of looking slightly different. I also had on a lot less makeup than the day she'd seen me. "People always say I look like Rachel Bilson."

"Interesting. I don't see it."

Whatever. "Tell me about a time you were in a difficult situation at work and how you handled it."

"I had a customer complain about a drink and then got them a new one."

Not exactly unheard of in the world of bars, and it didn't get me any closer to the subject of Enrique. "How about working with a difficult fellow employee?"

Her face reddened a little bit. "One of the bartenders kept asking me out and made some rude statements. But I told him it was never going to happen, and he left me alone."

Again, nothing useful. "Were you ever in a relationship with anyone at work?" I wasn't just skating on thin ice here. I'd gone through it and plunged into icy, dark water, but I was getting a little desperate for answers.

"Yes," she said, and then she started sobbing.

Oh, dear. I wasn't expecting that. "I'm sorry." I found a box of tissues in one of Vivi's desk drawers and handed it over to her.

She blew her nose and seemed to calm down. "I have a new no-man policy in place. I'm going to date myself for a while until I'm ready to venture out in the dating world. I have terrible taste in men."

"Been there, dated that," I said.

"Thank you. I'm sorry for my outburst. It's just this man led me on, and then he was murdered."

Now we were getting somewhere. "Are you talking about Enrique? I read about that online. I'm so sorry."

She nodded and teared up again. "He acted like I was the only one, and then I found out he was also sleeping with several of the other waitresses and who knows who else."

"When's the last time you saw him?" Way out of the realm of interview questions, but I think I could make the case that at this point, we were just having a chat.

"The night he was murdered. We met down at the state beach." She pointed to the right, toward where Vivi's family used to own land. "Another waitress showed up, and she caught us kissing."

"What was she doing there? How did she even know you'd be there?"

"Either she followed us there, or Enrique told

her where we'd be. That actually sounds like something he would do. He loved the competition for his attention."

"Was she angry at him?"

"No. That's what was really crazy. She was mad at me."

"I never get how women are mad at the other woman instead of the cheating sneaky man."

"Me either." She looked at me more closely.

Oh, oh.

"You were at Two Bobs with Enrique. I brought you up a Bushwacker."

She must be a good waitress if she remembered that. I squinted at her like I was trying to remember her.

"That was you?" I asked. "You look different."

"I needed a change after Enrique."

"I think he roofied me that day. Have you heard anything about him doing that to anyone else?"

Cindy got very pale. Was it guilt?

"Once I found out he'd been cheating, I started talking to the other waitresses, but I never heard anything like that. You'd have to be a monster to do that." She paused. "Were you seeing him, too?" Her voice wobbled a little.

I shook my head. "No. He was signed up for the barback competition, and I was just checking out who I was up against." That led me to another thought. "Do you know who Lisa Kelley is?"

"Wonder Woman? Of course."

"Did you see her in the bar the night Enrique died?"

Lisa thought for a moment. "She was in there

early in the evening with that guy with the French name. Maybe around eight."

"How about later?" Ralph had said he heard Lisa was one of the last people seen with Enrique.

"Not that I remember. The three of them left together around eight-fifty, and then Enrique came back alone around nine-twenty." She glanced down at the crumbled tissue in her hand. "I know it's pathetic that I'm so aware of his comings and goings."

"Have you talked to anyone from the sheriff's department about Enrique?" I hoped so, because Deputy Biffle must be looking at Cindy as a suspect, too.

"No. I left town after I walked out of Two Bobs that night. I needed to clear my head, so I went to visit a friend in Mobile. Then I heard about what happened to Enrique. I knew it wouldn't look good for me. They might think I killed him. One of my bartending friends at Two Bobs told me to lay low."

"You need to call Deputy Biffle. He's leading the investigation. Better to get it over with and get your name cleared." If her name could be cleared. While she looked all pathetic and sad, she might have left town to get her cover story perfected. I'd certainly be letting Deputy Biffle know that Cindy was back in town. And since I had her address on her application, I'd be happy to provide him with that, too.

"I'll do it." She paused. "I'm not even sure if I want to work in a bar anymore," Cindy said. "The whole thing with Enrique has traumatized me. I just don't have a lot of experience doing anything else."

"What do you like to do?" *Here I go again.*

"I like spending time with my grandmother and her friends. I take care of them when they need help."

I couldn't stop myself. I opened my phone and typed in a few key search words. "Some of the home healthcare places are hiring, and one of the assisted living places in Destin is, too. Maybe you should check them out before you make a decision." I hoped I wasn't sending them a killer.

"I'm going to do that. Thank you."

Cindy left. I sat in the office for a few minutes, thinking about my conversation with her. She didn't seem upset enough to have killed Enrique, but she might have been one of the last people to see him alive. And I didn't know her well enough to know if all those tears were for show or not. Maybe she recognized me right away and went with it.

I sent Deputy Biffle a quick text, telling him Cindy was back in town. I mentioned that Cindy and the other waitress might be two of the last people to see Enrique. I waited a couple of minutes for an answer, but there wasn't one, so I walked back out to the bar.

Joaquín looked at me. "She looked happy. Did you offer her the job?"

I didn't really want to answer that question. "No. Of course not. I wouldn't do that without having her talk with you and Vivi." I hoped that would throw him off the scent.

He shook his head. "You found her another job, didn't you?"

"More like I suggested another job," I admitted.

"And what about the applicants that came in this morning?" He raised one well-manicured eyebrow at me.

"One is starting as a sous chef at the Briny Pirate tomorrow."

"And the other?"

"I was thinking of calling her back to interview with you, but I wanted to talk it over with you and Vivi before I did."

"Get out. Chloe's employment agency might have found us an employee."

I shook my head at him, scooped up an order pad, and went back to work, but before I could, my phone rang. It was Johnny. Maybe this time it would be good news.

"Chloe, you have to quit contacting Deputy Biffle every time you think you know something."

He skipped the pleasantries and went right for my throat. "How do you even know I've been doing that?"

"Doesn't matter. If you have information to pass on, bring it to me, and I'll decide if we pass it on to Deputy Biffle or not."

"But I've always shared information with him in the past."

"I understand, but it's different this time."

"Because I'm a suspect?"

"Person of interest."

"Whatever. Deputy Biffle hasn't ever called me in for another interview. That must be good, right?"

Johnny sighed. "He will. Like I said before, don't go without me."

Every nerve in my body seemed to stab into a muscle, which then contracted. Fear. "I won't. Do you know why he wants to talk to me again?"

"Not for sure."

Johnny seemed to know everything else. Why not this? Something that was really important.

"My guess is that he's trying to shake you up. Don't let him. You're innocent."

With that, he hung up. I looked around the bar.

"Are you okay, Chloe?" Joaquín stared at me. "You're whiter than usual."

I managed a laugh at that. "I'm fine." There was nothing I could do right now, so I got back to work.

Vivi came in just before I left at seven. Things were quiet, and most of our customers were outside on the deck, enjoying the last rays of light. Joaquín and I were standing behind the bar, checking inventory.

"Really, Chloe, sometimes I just don't understand you," Vivi said.

CHAPTER 29

I stared at Vivi for a minute, thinking *Back at you*. "If it's about helping our interviewees find other jobs, I'm not going to apologize. None of them would have worked out here, anyway."

"I have no idea what you're talking about," Vivi said. "We'll get to that later."

"Then what are you talking about?"

"You were in the hospital and injured and didn't even tell us." She gestured to Joaquín.

My stomach cramped a little. How could she possibly know this? We hadn't called 911. We'd gone to the hospital in Santa Rosa, which was farther away. Even worse, if Vivi heard, would Deputy Biffle? What would he make of it? "Did Ann tell you?" I asked.

"Ann? Ann's involved in this?" Vivi asked. Her drawl got more pronounced as she spoke, which was never a good thing.

Why hadn't I kept my mouth shut until she explained what she thought was going on?

"What happened?" Joaquín asked.

"How did you find out?" I asked.

Vivi shook her head. "I just had dinner with a dear friend whose daughter is a nurse in the emergency room at Santa Rosa. I guess everyone there is abuzz with the two people who came in because they were injured in some kind of silly barback training accident."

"Training accident?" Joaquín's eyebrows raised in alarm.

"But somehow I don't buy that story, because why would you try to hide that from us? What really happened?"

I didn't want to lie about this. "Dex and I were shot. It was only beanbag rounds," I explained.

"Only?" Vivi said. "*Only*? It could have been much worse."

"Isn't that a violation of my HIPAA rights, to be telling people I was in the hospital?"

"That's not the problem here," Vivi said. "And she didn't have your name, just a general description of you and a man. Plus, you've been all covered up since that night. It doesn't take a prodigy to figure it all out."

"So I was right about you trying to hide something," Joaquín said. "You could have told me."

"It's just a bad bruise," I said. "It wasn't a big deal." It had been, but I needed these two to calm down. I didn't want them to know how scary it had been. How I'd felt the impact more than once in my dreams.

"I hire Ann now and then to take care of things

for me. I have no idea what you were doing with her, but please stop."

"I'm just helping her with something, and you can't ask me not to do that."

"I can, and I will. I care about you and can't bear the thought of anything happening to you."

Wow. I went over and hugged Vivi. "I care about you, too. I'll be careful. I promise."

"You'd better be," she said. Vivi glanced at her watch. "You need to clock out, but what's this about you finding our applicants other jobs?"

Ann was waiting for me when I got home from work around 7:45. This was becoming a habit, and I'm not sure it was a good one. All afternoon, I'd considered texting her and saying I was out, because too many people were worrying about me. Then I had to admit to myself that I liked the excitement, and then I worried about that part of me. But I hadn't called, and here she was. I couldn't deny I was eager to hear if she'd found Antoine, figured out who'd broken into her computer system, or located the treasure.

A few minutes later, I had the answers to all the above—a resounding *no*.

"I don't think Antoine is smart enough to disappear so entirely on his own. Which means he has partners, and probably ones he owes money to for one reason or another."

"That doesn't sound good."

"It isn't. Plus, with everything else going on, my resources are stretched. I don't trust that many people, and my core group is exhausted."

"What's next?"

"Everyone has the night off."

"But you."

Ann laughed. "You're getting to know me a little too well."

I agreed and again thought about if that was a good thing. "Are you going back out to look for the treasure?"

"I've been running more programs and learning more about shipwrecks. If the wreck was close to shore where we've been looking, it would attract a lot of fish, because it would become a reef system. That would attract people fishing, so it would probably have been discovered."

"And there's never been word of that happening?"

"Not unless it was so long ago, not long after the ship wrecked, and no one wanted to admit finding it."

I could think of lots of reasons someone would find a treasure and keep it to themselves. Personal wealth being first and foremost. I said as much to Ann, and she agreed.

"It could have been pushed over the continental shelf into DeSoto Canyon at some point, in which case we will probably never find it without attracting attention at least."

Joaquín had told me that the huge underwater DeSoto Canyon was one of the reasons the fishing was so good in this area. The canyon sent cold, nutrient-filled water up to the surface and supported tons of marine life. It was sixty miles offshore and three thousand feet deep.

"I'd need a bigger boat and better equipment.

And then would have to spend days running line grids."

"Line grids?"

"I'd superimpose a grid system over a map of the ocean floor and then have to slowly search each grid."

"People would notice," I said.

"They would."

"It seems like you have something else on your mind, too."

"One scenario that I ran pushed the wreck up onto shore."

"*Oh.* Do you think it's possible?"

"The programs I run are like the models for where hurricanes will go. There are always a few outliers in those spaghetti-strand models. That's what this one was."

"If it landed on shore, wouldn't people have seen it?"

"Unless it went into one of the inlets and was pushed deep into the woods where it's been rotting all this time."

Even with all the development in the Panhandle, there were miles of wooded areas around here. Also, the way vegetation grew here, if the ship and been pushed into a remote area, it could be covered in layers of underbrush and trees and sand. It was a possibility.

"The shoreline changes so much that it seems like that could have happened," I said.

"Exactly. Comparing the shoreline of the old map to the current day one, it's easy to see how much more land area there is right now."

"So what are you going to do?"

"I'm going to run more programs tonight, focusing more on how that scenario would have played out."

"Is it safe for you to do that?" I asked.

"Yes. I have a new computer and loaded new programs from different sources just in case whoever was in last time got in through one of the programs themselves. The encryption is NSA level."

That figured.

Ann grinned at me. "Up for another adventure?"

Deputy Biffle called at 8:20, not long after Ann left. Maybe she'd be getting a call, too.

"Chloe, could you stop by the station so we can have a chat?"

Chat. I didn't buy that for a minute. It would be an interrogation. "When?" I asked. I was surprised at how cold my voice sounded. I guess being terrified did that to me.

"As soon as possible."

"You mean this evening?"

"Yes."

I was tired and shaken. It didn't seem like a good combination for going up against Deputy Biffle. However, I might as well get it over with. "I'll be there in a little while." I ended the call and immediately called Johnny. I got his answering service and explained the situation to them. Then I went inside, took a shower, put on clean clothes—what does one wear to an interrogation? I decided to go with comfortable and put on leggings and a soft, blue sweater. For once, I took some time with my hair and makeup. Finally battle-ready, I headed out.

Johnny called while I was driving, told me he was on his way, and not to say a word until he arrived. I promised I wouldn't. Twenty-five minutes later, Deputy Biffle was already aggravated with me. We sat across from each other in one of the "interview" rooms, as he called it, for our "chat." Johnny hadn't arrived, and I refused to say anything in response to Deputy Biffle's questions. Unlike last time, the room was at a comfortable temperature, and Deputy Biffle had offered me coffee or soda or water when I'd first arrived. That had all seemed very suspicious to me.

"Look, Chloe, I think you just got caught up in something that was way out of the norm for your life." Deputy Biffle looked sincere and a bit exhausted. He needed to shave, and there were shadows under his eyes. He leaned forward, putting his arms on the table. "I don't believe you had anything to do with Enrique's murder."

CHAPTER 30

Relief flooded through me. My shoulders dropped, and I unclenched my hands. "I didn't."

"But Ann can be very persuasive. You seem like one of those people who is very loyal to their friends. Who cares deeply about them. I've seen that in you since we first met last June. It's why you're so well-liked here."

While part of me was warmed by his comments, another part of me was sending up flares of panic. Where was he going with all this?

"Just tell me what really happened out there. You won't be in any trouble."

Deputy Biffle was good. He was luring me in with his gentle voice and compliments. But that last line, "you won't be in any trouble," was a flat-out lie, proving he was a law enforcement officer first and last. I shouldn't have expected anything else.

"Look, Ann's an exciting woman. It's easy to get caught up in her world, but don't let that put you in jeopardy."

That was the most personal comment that Deputy Biffle had ever said to me. He was leaving everything on the table to try and get me to talk. There was a sharp knock on the door, and Johnny walked in, dressed in a tux. He gave a brief nod to Deputy Biffle before focusing on me.

"Are you okay, Chloe?" The lilt was strong.

"Fine. A little wiser than I was a few minutes ago."

Johnny and Deputy Biffle exchanged a quick look. Deputy Biffle's face all innocent, and Johnny's annoyed.

"I haven't said anything," I added. Although I'd been darn close to it. Too close.

"What questions do you have for Chloe?" Johnny asked.

"I just want to know what really happened out on the Gulf the morning that Chloe and Ann found Enrique."

"But I've already told you," I said.

"I'd like to go over it again," Deputy Biffle replied.

I looked at Johnny, who gave a quick nod. "Fine. But my story isn't going to be any different than it was the first time."

I spent the next fifteen minutes going over what happened. Deputy Biffle asked a few questions. I looked to Johnny before I answered any of them.

"The drugs in Enrique's condo were Rohypnol," Biffle said.

Roofies. I jolted back. More from the fact Deputy Biffle shared that than from shock of finding out Enrique had such drugs.

"You must have been angry when you found out that Enrique possibly drugged you."

"You don't need to answer him, Chloe," Johnny said.

Deputy Biffle had brought this up the first time he'd interviewed me, too. Did he think I'd forgotten? I hadn't answered him then. I hadn't liked not answering him. "I thought at the time I'd drank too much. I wasn't angry with Enrique."

"But you had a doctor test you."

"Routine," I replied.

"Enrique's attack on Ann must have made you angry, too."

"Don't answer," Johnny said.

I'd ignored his advice once, but I wasn't going to do it again. *Of course it made me angry,* I answered in my head. It would make anyone angry. I stared passively back at Deputy Biffle. It was hard not to answer, because in the past, I'd always shared information with him. I didn't like that things were different this time. It was uncomfortable at the very least and somehow felt wrong.

"We also found equipment in Enrique's apartment that enabled him to clone key fobs."

That wasn't too surprising, since Johnny had already told me that they'd found drugs and electronic equipment at Enrique's apartment.

"Ann likes her privacy. I'm sure the news that someone broke into her home upset her," Biffle added.

Deputy Biffle knew Ann better than I thought. I shrugged.

"We've kept this out of the public, and I'd appreciate you both keeping it quiet, but our divers found a knife on the ocean floor near where Enrique was found."

Johnny and I exchanged surprised looks that suddenly Deputy Biffle was sharing information. What was his angle?

"Do you know who it belonged to?" I could picture Ann with a knife strapped to her leg like a bounty hunter in the Stephanie Plum books by Janet Evanovich. Not that I'd ever seen her do that.

"It had Enrique's initials on it. Either someone tossed it down with him, or he had it in his hand when he entered the water."

"Did you find fingerprints on it?" I knew from my time as a librarian, when I'd helped an author do some research, that fingerprints could survive being submerged in water.

"Only Enrique's."

I sat up a little straighter as a memory entered my head. I glanced at Johnny. He tilted his head like *go on*. I figured he'd stop me if he thought I was saying something I shouldn't.

"Jean Claude had some cuts and scratch marks on his arm the last time I saw him."

"When was that?" Deputy Biffle asked.

"Yesterday." It seemed like days ago at this point. "I went to Sandy's with Rip Barnett for a drink."

"To Sandy's. You went for a drink at a place like Sandy's instead of one of the many other much nicer bars in the area."

Deputy Biffle sounded a lot like Rip for a moment. I didn't bother to add more.

"Anything else?" he asked.

"There are pictures of Jean Claude and Lisa on social media looking like a couple after she and Enrique had a thing." He probably knew this, but there was no harm in telling him. "Maybe Enrique was jealous or maybe Jean Claude was."

Johnny stood. "Let us know if you need anything else."

Deputy Biffle and I stood, too. Johnny opened the door, and we walked out together. Neither of us spoke until we got to my car.

"Why do you think he told us about the knife?" I asked.

"I'm mystified, unless he had some reason to think that would trigger something in you and you'd blurt something out."

"I come from a long line of people who don't blurt."

Johnny threw his head back and laughed. "I've worked with a lot of clients over the years, but you are one of a kind, Chloe."

People told me that a lot.

"And who knows," Johnny said, "there may not even be a knife, and he was hoping to trip you up."

I was getting a new view of law enforcement. I understood that Deputy Biffle had a crime to solve, but I didn't like being in the middle of it. "I'm sorry to have taken you away from whatever has you dressed in a tux this evening."

"Just dinner at home."

I looked at him with wide eyes.

"I'm kidding. You're saving me from a bunch of

boring lawyers drinking and bragging about their feats. All of which I've heard before." He held my car door open for me. "I guess that means I owe you one." He winked as I climbed in my car.

As I drove home, I realized that even if Deputy Biffle had shared something with us tonight, I still wasn't off the suspect list. I was relieved he either didn't know about Dex and me visiting the hospital, or he did know he had more important things to worry about. If only I could put all the ingredients of what I knew into a cocktail shaker, shake them up, and pour out the answers. If only.

Ann picked me up just after dawn Saturday morning. It was hard to believe an entire week had passed since I'd first heard about the barback competition and met Lisa, Jean Claude, and Enrique. It's a good thing I liked getting up early, but I was missing my morning runs. The morning was cool and cloudy. I dressed in old jeans and a thick, hooded sweatshirt over a long-sleeved T-shirt. If we were going to be walking through underbrush, I wanted to protect my skin as much as possible.

"Did your programs pan out?" I asked as we drove to her house. At least no one should be lying in wait for us out on the Gulf this time.

"It gave me some interesting information. Remember the inlet we were in the other night?"

How could I forget it? The bruise on my chest had yet to begin to fade.

"We're starting there and will head north."

I looked around the Jeep. "Did you bring a machete?"

"There's one on the airboat."

Airboat? I'd always wanted to ride on one. They skimmed across shallow water with their big motors on the back. I tried not to act like an excited little kid.

"I'm not sure how far we will be able to take it, but it beats hiking all the way."

We pulled up to Ann's house a few minutes later. I could see Dex waiting down at Ann's dock by the airboat.

"Let's go inside for a minute," Ann said. "I'll loan you a pair of boots."

We walked up to the back of the house, and Ann used a key fob to unlock the door. I was surprised, considering what had probably happened with the last one.

The door we went through into the house landed us in a mudroom. Ann handed me a pair of sturdy-looking lace-up boots. "Try these. They're snakebite-proof."

Snakes? Of course there could be snakes. I was right up there with Indiana Jones when it came to disliking snakes. "Are they alligator-proof, too?"

Ann shrugged. "They might slow one down."

Great. She was serious. I'd been hoping for some kind of reassurance that there would be no alligators around today. But that was life in Florida for you. I took off my sneakers, put on the boots, and laced them up. They covered my ankles but not my calves. They fit pretty well.

Thirty minutes later, at seven, we boarded the airboat. Dex was piloting and had a rifle slung across his back. I'm pretty sure it wasn't packing beanbags. Ann had a pistol with her, and I had my bare hands. They must be worried about trouble, even with Ann's precautions. And they were relying on me as their weapon of last resort. Lord help us all.

The airboat was noisy, but it felt like we were flying across the water for the first few minutes where the inlet was wide and deep with brackish water. We slowed as Dex navigated around old tree trunks. I spotted an osprey's nest high in a dead tree, but then realized I should be looking lower in the water and marsh for signs of the wreck. Or better yet, alligators or snakes.

Fifteen minutes later, Dex announced we couldn't take the airboat any farther north. The inlet stretched to the east and west on either side of us. That was disappointing, as the ground looked marshy here. It was ground that could hide lots of scary things. The woods were thick, as was the underbrush. Bugs whined, birds called, and the whole place smelled of damp and decay. Light was dim because of all of the trees.

Dex parked the boat in an area of thick trees and underbrush, which hid it fairly well. Ann grabbed a backpack and hoisted it over her shoulders. Dex got off the boat and extended a hand to help us off.

The ground was squishy under my feet, and I was grateful for the boots. My sneakers would have been soaked in minutes. Ann studied a map on her phone for a moment and then pointed the way she wanted to go. Dex went ahead of us, using the machete to whack at anything that got in the way. I brought up the rear. I kept glancing over my shoulder to make sure I was the end of the line.

We went slowly so we could look around, but it seemed like an impossible task. The forest and underbrush were just too thick. The ship could be feet away, and we'd never see it.

Ann set down a backpack she was carrying. "I'm going to send up the drone. You gave me the idea, Chloe. It's the only possible way. This will take hours. Days, even. Even with the drone, we won't be able to let it out of our sight for fear of it smacking into a tree."

Ann set up the drone, and Dex piloted it—if that's what you called flying a drone. Ann and I watched on her phone as the drone moved around trees, but we didn't see anything that looked like a shipwreck. Although a couple of times, Dex hovered over what turned out to be saplings that looked like a ship's mast.

An hour later, we trudged back to the airboat disheartened. The task was too enormous without a smaller area to search or more manpower. This time, Ann and I walked next to each other, and Dex lagged behind. We turned a bend. The airboat sat directly in front of us. A man lounged on it with a gun pointing right at us.

CHAPTER 31

Dark, wavy hair, black clothing, and I bet he had a pirate tattoo on his ankle. Antoine. I recognized him from his Instagram account.

"Put the gun away, Antoine," Ann said. "You're not going to use it."

"I might," he said. "No luck again today?"

"Oh, more luck than you might think," Ann said.

I glanced at her, surprised. Had she spotted something and not said anything?

"How's that?" Antoine asked. He stepped off the boat and walked toward us. The gun dangled in his hand at his side. "What did you find?"

"You," she said.

Dex burst out of some brush and tackled Antoine. They fell hard, both letting out *oof*s. Ann ran over, stomping on Antoine's wrist until he released the gun. She picked it up and pointed it at him.

"Get him up, Dex," Ann said.

Dex stood and grabbed Antoine by his shirt and hauled him up. He gave him a shake before he let him go.

"You might as well put the gun down. You're not going to shoot me," Antoine said, mimicking Ann's voice and words.

"Don't tempt me," Ann answered.

I had so many questions. Did Ann know Antoine would follow us? Was that what this was really about, and if so, why not tell me? However, with a gun out and emotions high, it didn't seem like the time to ask.

Antoine gave me a good looking-over. "Must be desperate times."

"How's that?" Ann asked.

He gestured toward me. "She doesn't look like she'd be much good in a fight."

Antoine was so right. However, I excelled at flight.

"You'd be surprised. She's quite resourceful."

That was lovely to hear, but I'd rather hear it at a time where no guns were being flashed around and some place safer than this swamp.

"How are you going to get me back?" Antoine said.

We all eyed the airboat. It would be a tight fit with the four of us. I noticed a small bass boat was parked behind it. That must have been Antoine's transportation.

"Who said I'm not going to leave you here?" Ann retorted. "We'll sink your boat, and you can figure your way out of this mess." She waved her hand, indicating the swamp around us.

Being left out here made me shivery. Would Ann actually do something like that?

"What would Angelique say if you left me?" Antoine said.

"Probably 'good riddance,'" Ann answered. "Chloe, would you mind getting the zip ties out of my backpack? They're in the front zippered pocket."

Zip ties? Who carried zip ties around with them? Was this a thing, and every woman had a stash in their purse "just in case?" Or was Ann's backpack the equivalent of Mary Poppins's magic carpet bag and had everything one needed in it?

"No problem," I said.

"Is she your latest recruit?" Antoine said.

I unzipped the front pocket and pulled out a few zip ties. I figured she'd need one for his hands, one for his legs, and maybe some to tie him to the boat. I held out three and stuffed the others in the front of my sweatshirt.

"She's a friend," Ann said. "Give the zip ties to Dex, please."

For the past few months, I'd been saying I wanted to have more girlfriends, but I'd pictured someone to go out for cocktails or brunch or a movie with, not zip-tying relatives and searching for lost treasure in the middle of a swamp. Moments later, Antoine was secured in the boat. I climbed up on the high seat with Dex. Ann sat next to Antoine, the gun still in her hand.

I heard the sound of another airboat off in the distance.

"Did I mention I brought along some friends?" Antoine said.

CHAPTER 32

Friends. Of course he brought freaking friends. Dex and Ann exchanged a glance. She patted Antoine down, found his phone, and lobbed it into the trees like she was a second baseman trying to get the ball home.

"Just in case someone is using your phone to track you," Ann said.

Antoine didn't seem too perturbed, but maybe he was a good actor. Ann gave a shrug. Dex nodded. His mouth was set in a grim line as he started the airboat. It wasn't exactly stealthy, and I had a death grip on the seat. Dex wheeled the airboat around and headed east, away from the sound of the other airboat and the entrance to the inlet.

We couldn't go all that fast because of all the trees and tree stumps sticking up out of the water and the low-hanging branches. I saw a huge black snake on one of them, its tongue flicking out. I managed not to scream. Not that anyone would hear me over the sound of the airboat. At least all these trees provided a lot of cover and would slow Antoine's friends down, too. Maybe they couldn't hear where we were over the roar of their own boat.

I kept watch behind us, looking for the other airboat, but so far, no sign of them. When we were on the far side of the inlet, Dex cut the engine. The motor ticked, birds called out, and the water moved sluggishly around us from our wake. We were on the edge of the swampiest part of inlet. If we headed for the mouth, we'd be out in the open, with only widely spaced dead trees for protection.

"What do you think?" Dex asked Ann.

"I don't like just sitting here," Ann replied.

"They won't have beanbags this time," Antoine said.

We all glared at him.

The biggest mosquito I'd ever seen was feasting on my hand, and I flicked at it. "I have an idea." I didn't really like my idea, but I didn't like any of this. We had three guns, but who knows how many they had or how many of them there were.

Minutes later, the airboat roared back to life and shot across the water. We heard an answering engine come to life, way closer than was comfortable. But we stood on the edge of the swamp, watching the boat zoom away from us. The throttle was tied open with one of the zip ties. As we started tramping through the woods, we heard shots ring out. I shuddered to think that they could've hit been us. It probably wouldn't take them long to figure out what we'd done, and then they'd be back searching for us.

Dex led the way. At first, we just pushed our way through the brush, swamp grass, and cattails, some of which were taller than my head, all while trying not to leave a trail that anyone could follow. But after the first ten minutes, Dex started using the machete as needed to chop a path. Antoine was behind him, followed by Ann, with me in the rear again. The sound of the other airboat would grow closer and then further away. I concentrated on the ground, not wanting to step on anything I shouldn't, like an alligator or snake. I didn't dare look up in the trees to see what was lurking there. Antoine was unusually silent, but the duct tape across his mouth helped. None of us wanted him calling out to his friends. Ann would have made the ultimate Girl Scout, because she was always prepared with everything we might need.

As I studied the ground, I noticed something that looked out of place. I bent to pick it up. It was a small shard of china. It had a light pink flower with a green leaf. No one seemed to notice I'd stopped. I stuck the bit in the front pocket of my sweatshirt. It could be nothing, but if it was some-how part of the lost shipwreck, I didn't want to mention it in front of Antoine. I needed to mark the spot in case Ann wanted to come back here later. I took out one of the zip ties and dropped it on the ground. Then I took a stick and drove it down in the center of the zip tie. That should stay put. We'd only been walking about fifteen minutes at this point. Hopefully, we'd be able to find this spot again.

Ann used her satellite phone to navigate us to a trail and then toward a road. She called someone and arranged for them to meet us out here somewhere. Thirty minutes later, we came to a dirt road. Five minutes later, a woman pulled up, in a minivan of all things. She wore a pink camouflage T-shirt and sweats. Hardly what I expected of a rescue crew for Ann.

"Sorry," she said. "I was dropping the kids off at school."

Dex prodded Antoine to the back and sat next to him, I climbed in the middle, and Ann took the front seat. A Barbie doll was on the floor along with a fast-food bag and a juice carton. Where did Ann find these people?

I settled in a corner of the van so I could study Antoine. His eyes were closed and his head tilted back, like he was sleeping. But I didn't buy that for a minute, because of the pulse jumping on his temple. Antoine was worried. Was he a killer? Had Enrique double-crossed Antoine, and he killed Enrique for it?

"Have you heard from Deputy Biffle, Ann?" I asked. "I got dragged in for another interview last night. Well, he called it a *chat.*" I watched Antoine while I said it. I thought there was a slight lift of one eyebrow. Normally, I wouldn't have this conversation in front of him, but I wanted to watch his reactions.

"I hope you had Johnny there with you."

"I did."

"What did Dan want to chat about?"

"He went with he knew I wasn't involved and

that I should tell the truth. Oh, this was the best one—that I wouldn't be in any trouble. And that was all before Johnny arrived." Antoine didn't open his eyes, but I swear his mouth turned up in a grin as much as one could grin while one's mouth was duct taped.

"I guess I'd better prepare myself for a call. Did he say anything else?"

I thought about the knife Deputy Biffle had mentioned. He'd asked me not to say anything. Johnny said it might not even be real. Ever since we'd found Enrique, it seemed like I was always being pulled in two different directions about who to tell what and where my loyalties lay. In this instance, in a rare move, I was going to protect myself.

"He had me go over the entire morning again. I'm sure he was disappointed that I didn't have anything to add or that he didn't trip me up."

Antoine opened his eyes to a narrow slit, head still tilted back. If he could flick out his tongue, he'd remind me of the snake I'd seen in the tree earlier. He didn't seem afraid. He seemed pleased, but why?

Ann nodded. Her lips were pursed, and her eyes focused above my head like she was seeing something that I couldn't.

Thirty minutes later, they dropped me at my house. Ann hopped out when I did and walked me to the door.

"I'm sorry about all of that. I really wasn't expecting it to go down that way," Ann said.

"You never do," I said. Part of me was mad. We'd

come too close to a really bad scenario this morning. There'd been moments of terror. "But it was kind of exhilarating." What was wrong with me thinking this was exhilarating? "Life is never dull around you." I leaned in for a moment. "I have something to tell you, but act casual. I don't want Antoine to have any hint about this."

Ann nodded but looked mystified.

"I found a small piece of china on the ground while we were tramping through the swamp. Maybe it's from the wreck. I have to get ready for work, but come by tonight around eight thirty, and I'll explain everything."

Ann laughed like I'd said something funny. What the heck? Oh, she was play-acting like I'd asked her to. I grinned back at her. "What are you going to do with Antoine?"

"I'll take him out to the camp and torture him until he tells me what he's done."

My eyebrows popped up.

"I'm kidding. I'll turn him over to Angelique. He'll tell her everything for some of her beignets and shrimp creole."

I laughed. "Tough guy, huh?"

"He likes to think he is." Ann walked back to the car and waved. "I'll be in touch."

I'm not sure I wanted her to be. Always with the push/pull lately.

I walked into work conscious of the scratches and bug bites on my face. I'd tried to cover them up with makeup as much as I could. But there was no denying I'd been up to something since yesterday. At least Vivi and Joaquín wouldn't be in until noon, so maybe everything would fade by then. I'd worn another high-necked shirt with shorts this time, because it was supposed to be hot today. At least my legs weren't all scratched up, too.

The worst part was none of this brought either Ann or me any closer to finding out who killed Enrique. Unless Antoine was involved. Hopefully, Angelique would get the information out of him. For the most part Ann seemed content to let our lawyers handle this. I was not. But I couldn't just take day after day off to search for Enrique's killer. I had to make a living and couldn't do that to Vivi or Joaquín, even if I wanted to. On top of that, I had set up more interviews for today and had Spines and Wines book club tonight. We'd set up our schedule months ago, but ironically, we were reading *Treasure Island* this month. It should have been a cautionary tale for me before I said yes to Ann. I yawned as I chopped fruit and set the stools on the floor.

Once I was done, I went out and sat on the deck to let the sun warm me. I sat in one chair and turned another so I could stretch my legs out on it. I closed my eyes and lifted my face to the sun. I analyzed everything I knew and suspected about Enrique. I knew he was a terrible person, that he had connections with Lisa and with Jean Claude through Lisa. Cindy seemed a bit unstable, and I couldn't discard her as a suspect in his murder, but it also seemed like there were plenty of other women from Two Bobs or around town who could be just like Cindy. Used and tossed aside by Enrique. I couldn't rule out Antoine either. He knew about the dive sites *and* he knew Enrique.

"Excuse me?"

I sat up with a start and blinked my eyes. I must have drifted off to sleep.

"I'm here for an interview?"

It was a man about my age who looked a little worse for wear. He had a sleeve of tattoos in amazing bright colors that swirled around his arm. If I wasn't afraid of needles, I'd love something like that myself. I'd almost passed out when I got my ears pierced.

"Have a seat," I said. During our short interview, I found out his passion was restoring cars. "I got my oil changed last week in Emerald Cove. They had a sign up that they were looking for help."

He was out of the bar seconds later.

After Joaquín and Vivi came in, I had another interview. I sent the woman to the Barnes & Noble in Destin, giving her the name of my friend, who was a manager there.

Joaquín was shaking his head at me when she left smiling and promising to come back for a drink soon. "Are you ever going to find someone to work here?"

Vivi looked at me. "Are you thinking of starting a side business as an employment agent? Should we be worried?"

"No. I just can't help myself. We don't want employees who don't want to be here."

They both looked at me, and it didn't take long to realize they'd noticed the condition of my face.

"I went on a hike this morning," I said.

"With Ann?" Vivi asked. Her voice was colder than our frozen drinks.

I'd gone through all this earlier in my head—lie, or tell the truth? I knew there would be questions. I'm an adult and can make my own decisions, even if Vivi didn't like them. And she certainly hadn't liked me dating Rip, but she was coming around. "Yes. Vivi, I have to make my own decisions about my life. I know who Ann is and what she does." Boy, did I know. I'd also decided not to mention guns or being chased by bad guys. Amazing that when I first met Ann last June and heard she was a fixer, I'd thought that meant she was a handyman—woman. "I'm helping her with something that's important to her. That's what friends do."

Vivi sighed. "You're right. I'll back off."

I went over and hugged her. I couldn't reassure her that I'd be safe, not after this morning or the other night. "Thank you."

At seven, I was off work and sitting at a table on the deck that I'd reserved for the book club. Joaquín had made a pitcher of rum-based, fruity deliciousness for us to drink while we talked. After our first meeting last fall, he'd taken to pairing drinks with our books. Pirates loved rum and needed fruit to keep away scurvy, so there you go.

The discussion was lively as the women all romanticized treasure hunting. In real life, it wasn't nearly as fun. However, it reminded me that I'd stuck that small shard of china in my sweatshirt this morning and then forgotten all about it in the whirlwind of getting ready for work. I hoped it hadn't dropped out somewhere and I'd have to search for it.

"You know there's always talk of unfound shipwrecks around here," one woman said.

"Maybe we should start looking," another suggested.

"I think you need a lot of fancy equipment," I said.

"I've got just the thing," the first woman said. "My husband bought a fancy fishing boat with all the bells and whistles. He took it out exactly once."

I smiled as they debated the merits of doing this and when they would start. "I'm sorry I can't join you because of work." I gestured to the bar.

"We'll give you a gold coin once we've found one, since your book group inspired us."

"Thank you." I stood. "I'm sorry, but I'm exhausted. It's been a long day. Stay as long as you like." If I didn't leave, I was going to be snoring on the table, and no one wanted to hear that.

The group said their goodbyes and then huddled back together, planning their adventure.

It was 8:30 when I pulled up to my drive. Not only was Ann sitting on the porch, but so was Rip. Their heads were bent together and snapped apart when my headlights hit them. Little prickles of jealousy rushed through me. I'd suspected they had a relationship in the past, but Ann had denied that they'd had any kind of romantic relationship. I sat for a minute and gathered myself. I was so tired that I really didn't want to deal with anyone. Rip was holding something. Eventually, I gathered my purse, got out, locked the doors, and approached them. They both stood.

CHAPTER 33

"I brought pizza," Rip said, holding up two boxes. The smell of cheese, grease, and garlic wafted out of the boxes. "The new place in town?" I asked. A small pizza place had opened in Emerald Cove recently. The family had tired of living in the city, moved here, and started the place. While it wasn't deep dish pizza, I'd heard it was good.

Rip nodded.

"Oh, thank you. I'm starving." I'd hardly eaten all day. I guess hiking, having a gun pointed at me, and being chased by bad guys in a swamp, had deterred my appetite.

"I brought beignets my Aunt Angelique made," Ann said.

Ah, then she'd probably also brought information with her, too. Torture by beignet must have yielded something from Antoine. And I could fill her in about the china shard.

I unlocked the door, shut off the security system, and turned to Ann and Rip. "Let's eat, but give me just a minute to change."

By the time I came back out, the table was set, and the pizza was still steaming hot. One pear, gorgonzola, walnut, and prosciutto pizza and one pepperoni. I opened a bottle of wine and set a pitcher of water on the table. I wasn't sure which I needed worse, but took a big gulp of wine. We didn't talk a lot while we ate. Other than muttering things like "this is so good" and "pass me another piece, please."

When we finished, Rip looked from me to Ann and back. "Should I go? Do you two have plans?"

"No," I said, somewhat more firmly than I meant to. But I didn't care what Ann wanted. I wasn't going anywhere tonight. "But Ann and I need to talk for a few minutes. We can go out on the porch."

"I'll watch soccer then." Rip settled on the couch with the TV remote in hand. He looked so good there, my heart felt as gooey as the cheese on the pizza.

"I'm going to grab my sweatshirt," I said to Ann. "I'll be there in a minute." I went to my room, grabbed my sweatshirt, checked for the bit of china. Whew, it was still there.

Ann was stretched out on the chaise lounge. I turned on a couple of side lamps. She looked almost as tired as I felt, which was unusual for her. I pulled the china shard out of the pocket of my sweatshirt and handed it to her. Ann swung her legs off the chaise lounge and onto the floor. She held the shard to the light and bent over it, her hair falling in waves around her face. She looked back up at me.

"I found it when we were hiking to the road. I picked it up because it seemed like an odd spot to find this."

Ann's face glowed with excitement. "It might be important. Can you find the spot again?"

"I hope so. We'd only been walking about fifteen minutes. I marked the spot with one of the zip ties and a stick."

Ann leaped up. "You're brilliant." She pulled me up and kissed both of my cheeks. "Do you want to go with me when I search, or are you over it? I'll understand if you say no."

Earlier today, the answer would have been no. But Ann's excitement was contagious. "I've gone this far, why not?"

"Tomorrow morning then?"

"Sure."

"I'll pick you up just before sunrise."

Of course she would. "How'd it go with Antoine?" I asked as I sat on the love seat.

"I wish you could have seen Angelique." Ann grinned at me. "It was a master class in interview techniques. Although it helped that Antoine has always been a tiny bit afraid of her from a dressing-down over not sharing when he was five. And that he was hungry."

"Did you find anything out?"

"You were right. Antoine found the map and hid it so I'd find it. He's too lazy to search for the shipwreck himself, and he didn't have the resources."

"It's too bad he didn't just come to you with the map."

"It is. So much trauma could have been avoided."

I thought for a moment. "Why was he out there that morning? It seems like he was either waiting for us to find Enrique's body, which meant he either killed him or somehow knew he was killed, or that he was watching to see if we found the treasure."

Ann frowned.

"And how did he know we would be out there?" I asked. Ann might believe in Angelique's ability to get Antoine to talk, but I wasn't so sure he'd be honest with them.

"Enrique—it's still so hard for me to call him that—hacked my computer."

"So they were working together."

A flash of sadness crossed Ann's face. "I told you that Enrique and I went to high school together, which meant Enrique and Antoine knew each other, too." This time, it was anger in her face and in her voice. "Back then, Antoine hated Enrique as much as I did. But at some point, they hooked back up again. Antoine needed help and told Enrique about the map and his plan."

"I'm so sorry." To be betrayed by a family member like that would be terrible.

"Enrique was always good with computers and apparently honed that skill over time. He must have cloned the key fobs so he could get in and out of my house. That's how they both knew about the spots where I thought the shipwreck might be. And Antoine knows me well enough to know I'm a 'first thing in the morning' person."

It hadn't taken long for me to learn that, but as far as I could tell, with Ann regularly showing up at my house in the evening, too, she was a "go hard at it all day long" person. "Let's think about who knew about the map. Antoine and Enrique. The two of us. And whoever was working with Antoine. You said yourself that he wasn't smart enough to pull this off alone. We didn't kill Enrique, and he didn't kill himself. That leaves them or someone who happened to follow Enrique that night." Unfortunately, that wasn't out of the realm of possibility. I could picture Cindy or someone like her following Enrique.

"Or someone Enrique took with him," Ann said.

"You're right. That's another possibility. But what if Antoine figured out that Enrique was trying to double-cross him? That seems like a reason to kill someone." My mind was whirling with thoughts. "Plus, Antoine had people shoot at us."

"With beanbags."

"Yes. But since the incident, I've read up on beanbags, and while they are meant to be nonlethal, people have been killed with them." I was afraid that Ann's feelings for Antoine—however complicated they were—could be coloring her reactions to him. She seemed to blindly accept whatever he was telling her. I could understand that on some level, because I couldn't imagine thinking my brothers would murder someone.

"What about the people who helped Antoine?" I asked.

"I'm trying to track them down. They might have run back to New Orleans by now. Since they haven't heard from Antoine, they must know something went terribly wrong." Ann shook her head.

New Orleans was about a four-and-a-half-hour

drive from here. They could easily be home right now. "They knew about the map. Do they know about the treasure?"

"They do know about the treasure. Antoine promised them a share."

"Maybe they are still out there searching for it. We might have been close to it today." Or the china shard could be from someone who'd lived on that land at some point, and it had nothing to do with the shipwreck.

"You're right. I'll send someone out to look around." She pulled out her phone and shot off a text, presumably to the someone who would go search for the thugs.

"How did Antoine feel about Enrique trying to cut him out of the deal?" If that was what happened. Someone was in Ann's house, or maybe it was two people—Antoine and Enrique. As I'd thought before, the old map was valuable in its own right. But why leave it? So Ann wouldn't suspect anything? They could have argued about it, and Antoine killed Enrique and then dumped him where he knew Ann would find him so she would look guilty. Or they could have taken pictures of the map to try to create interest and sell it. Maybe after they took the pictures, they decided to get a head start on the search for the treasure. While they were out there, they had an argument, and Enrique ended up dead. But I could speculate and guess all night long and not hit on the truth.

"He complained about no honor among thieves anymore."

"What about honor among your family?"

"He swore that he was going to work with me

once I found the treasure. That he would never steal from me."

"Did you buy that?"

Ann sighed. "I want to."

Ann had never seemed naïve before now. But I understood. Antoine was family, and even when someone screws up, you still love them and want to trust them. "Wanting to and believing are two different things."

Ann nodded.

"Did Antoine say why he was watching us the morning we found Enrique?"

"To see if we found the treasure."

It made as much sense as any of this did.

"Did you call Deputy Biffle and tell him about Antoine and his friends? They assaulted us. Things could have turned out much worse."

Ann gave me a long look. "It would complicate things. Dan would have had a lot of questions. Ones that I'm not ready to answer." She paused. "I thought about it. But it might look even worse for us as far as Enrique's death."

She had a point, but I had a feeling she'd thrown that last bit in so I would comply. "How so?"

"Because then we'll have to tell Dan about the map. He might not even believe us, since we didn't tell him at first."

"But you can show him the map and your computer projects. How would he not believe that?"

"He could think we threw this all together after the fact."

"And he could believe we're telling the truth and had a specific reason for being where we were."

"And more motivation to get rid of Enrique so he didn't find the treasure."

It was true. I was exhausted with all the speculation and what-ifs. I'd go along again. What choice did I have? I didn't know the name of Antoine's friends or what they looked like. Even if I went on my own to Deputy Biffle, what would I tell him? Still, part of me felt uneasy about this. I thought again about Antoine's grin in the van. How self-satisfied he seemed.

He had all those things that the police always talked about—motive, means, and opportunity. From what Ann had told me and what I'd observed, Antoine only seemed to care about himself. He'd almost gotten Ann kicked out of college. Maybe that smile had been about knowing he'd killed Enrique and it looked like he was going to get away with it. Antoine didn't seem like the kind of person who would let someone double-cross him and just walk away. He must have been furious with Enrique. Who wouldn't have been?

I threw my hands up. "I can't do this anymore. I want to go to Deputy Biffle and tell him the truth. I'm tired of being a suspect."

Ann nodded. "I get that. But at this point, a week later, it's not going to look good."

"I don't care anymore. All these secrets are wrong."

"Give me twenty-four hours. Please. If I haven't figured it all out by then, I'll go with you."

I sighed. "Twenty-four hours."

"Now go spend some time with Rip. He's a good man."

At least we both agreed on something. We

walked back into the living room. Ann headed toward the door.

"Enjoy the beignets," she said. "I'll see you in the morning."

I sent a quick text to Joaquín, asking if he could trade shifts with me so I wouldn't have to come in until twelve. He texted back that would be great. I stretched out on the sectional next to Rip. He pulled me closer and kissed my cheek. I waited for recriminations, but there weren't any.

"Who won?" I asked.

"Arsenal," he said. "They aren't my favorite, but they played a heck of a game."

"Thanks for bringing the pizza." To me it was more than just a pizza. It was an *I care about you* gesture. "It meant a lot to me."

"It was just a pizza."

"It was two pizzas, and it shows you care about me."

"That's what shows I care about you? I must be doing something wrong."

"Oh, no. You are doing everything just right."

I woke up at midnight. Rip's arm was around my waist, and we were as close as paper on a wall. It made me feel loved. *Loved.* I let that roll around in my head for a while. Had I ever felt like this before? No. For once, I didn't feel scared or obligated like I had when I'd been engaged. Then I'd been on pins and needles all the time, always afraid I was going to do the wrong thing. Now I was cherished, and I wanted to cherish in return. *You have it bad, Chloe.* The good thing was I was ninety-nine percent sure that Rip felt the same way. I smiled.

Another thought about love entered my head. Maybe I was looking at Enrique's murder all wrong. First, I'd been thinking about who hated Enrique and exploring that. Then I'd thought about who hated Ann enough to set her up. I'd gotten nowhere with that theory. But maybe this was about who loved Ann enough to kill someone who'd hurt her. And Enrique had certainly hurt her.

CHAPTER 34

I remembered that Ann had said there was a red rose on her porch the night of the break-in. Red roses were a symbol of love. The problem was, I didn't know that much about Ann. She could be in a relationship for all I knew. But wouldn't that person be out searching with her instead of me? I stretched my arm and grabbed my phone, trying not to disturb Rip. I'd never looked Ann up on social media. I spent a few minutes searching. Nothing. Zippo. At least on my Ann Williams. There were thousands of Ann Williamses out there. Is that why she went by Williams instead of Lafitte? I tried a quick search on Ann Lafitte. Nothing there, either. Ann might have one of those services that scrubbed all traces of you off the internet.

"What are you doing?" Rip asked. He kissed the back of my neck. "What's keeping you awake?"

I rolled over so I was facing him. We'd talked about trust earlier. Now was the time to trust him.

I had to talk this out with someone. I explained my thought process to him.

"Does that make sense?" I asked him. I felt bad for waking him, but his past as a criminal defense lawyer could be helpful here.

"It makes sense as much as anything does."

I was hoping for more enthusiasm. "Do you know if Ann's in a relationship with anyone?"

"She keeps to herself."

"Any rumors?" I asked.

"None that I've heard. Do you have any thoughts?"

Who could it be? Who did I know that loved Ann? "What about Deputy Biffle?"

"Dan?"

Rip sounded so shocked that I almost laughed. "Have you ever seen them together? There's something going on, but I'm not sure what. Maybe he isn't the straight arrow he appears to be." How well did I really know him?

"I'm fairly certain he's exactly who you think he is." He paused. "Wow. Dan and Ann? That's just wild."

"Ann talks about her large extended family in New Orleans. Some of them must love her."

"I'm sure they do," Rip said.

"Have you ever met her Aunt Angelique?"

"No."

"Angelique loves her and is in town. Why show up right now when all of this was happening?"

"Do you know if Angelique spends a lot of time here?" Rip asked.

"I don't. I was hoping you would."

Maybe Angelique had planted things in my head while I was hypnotized so I wouldn't figure this all out and I'd look in the wrong direction. However, even though I'd been hypnotized, at the time, it seemed like I knew, on some level, what was going on.

"I'm going to look her up." Rip and I lay shoulder to shoulder while I used my phone to look up Angelique Lafitte in New Orleans. Her website popped up right away.

"Her website looks legit," Rip said once we'd scrolled through a few pages of it.

"She has certifications with various professional organizations," I said.

"And there are lots of articles about her doing charity work in New Orleans."

"It looks like she's generous with her time and money." I kept scrolling. "Oh, look at this." I pointed to an interesting article that said she'd worked with the police on several cases by helping victims remember details that led to arrests. I frowned at my phone. "There's nothing here that makes her look sketchy." I would have to look elsewhere.

"That doesn't mean she isn't."

Rip would know better than I about that. I set my phone back on the nightstand. Rip cuddled up against me and was soon asleep. My eyes drifted closed for a moment as I scrolled through people who knew Ann. The heritage business owners. Rip. I listened to his even breathing. He sighed a small sigh. But then my eyes went wide again. What about Dex? Little pings started zinging around in my head. Pings that I couldn't ignore, but I didn't want to wake Rip back up to tell him.

I thought back over the conversation I'd had

with Dex the night he'd driven me home after Angelique hypnotized me. I'd told him my theory that maybe someone who was angry with Ann could have killed Enrique. He'd said that it was possible and that he'd think about who could have been mad at Ann. Had he been playing me? He hadn't ever followed up with names.

I didn't see any evidence of a romantic relationship between Ann and Dex, but they were definitely more than just employer and employee. Who knew what went on between them when I wasn't around? Now how to go about proving it, and did I even want to? Normally with this kind of strong feeling, I'd call Deputy Biffle and tell him what I suspected. But I couldn't do that to Dex or Ann. Not without some evidence to back up my concerns. How in the world was I going to get that? Wait. Maybe I did have a piece of evidence.

The security firm said there was no sign of a hack, but Dex probably had all the codes to Ann's house. He might have signed in and known how to erase the sign-in from the system. But there must be a trace of it somewhere. I'd been to Aymar Security once before. There would be no reason for them not to talk to me about the situation again. Dex might even have his own key fob for Ann's house.

Dex spent a lot of time at Two Bobs. It was more or less Ann's unofficial office. In the past, when I'd had to seek her out, I always went there first. Dex often sat and held a table for Ann, so he would have been able to hear and observe a lot of things. Maybe bad things about Enrique. Maybe even before he knew about Enrique's past with Ann. Dex was loyal to Ann. There was no doubt about that. How would I feel if I found out someone I cared deeply about had been hurt by someone I knew?

I would want to kill that person, preferably with my bare hands. I'd been shocked and angry the night Ann had called Enrique out. The night we'd found out he'd assaulted her, and not only her, but other women. I can only imagine how Dex must have felt. He might have snapped. I couldn't picture Dex killing someone in cold blood, could I? I could picture him confronting Enrique and them fighting.

That Enrique's body had ended up exactly where Ann had dived was another worry in all of this. Had Ann known Dex killed Enrique all along? Had she taken me with her on the boat that morning to throw everyone off about the real killer? I shook my head. Maybe I was crazy. Maybe this was half-asleep wild speculation. Plenty of people had a reason to kill Enrique. But oof, Dex felt right.

I finally managed to get back to sleep around two. My dreams were filled with people chasing me. Everyone from Enrique to Dex to Ann to Deputy Biffle. But by six, I'd had an early breakfast and a lot of coffee. I went back in the bedroom and kissed Rip's cheek.

"Please set the alarm and lock up when you leave." Then I did something I'd been debating ever since I woke up. I pulled a key out of the pocket of my jeans—black, of course—and placed it on the nightstand. "There's a key for you, if you want it." I turned and almost ran out of the room.

"Of course, I want it, Chloe Jackson," Rip yelled

to me. "And you've got to quit doing this when you're running out the door."

I was smiling when I climbed into Ann's truck.

The smiling didn't last long, because Dex wasn't with her. The one time I really wanted to watch them interact, and I wasn't going to have the chance.

"Where's Dex this morning?" I asked, hoping my voice sounded casual but not so casual as to pique Ann's interest.

"This seemed like a pretty low-risk task, since we know who's been chasing us."

I couldn't argue with that.

Forty minutes and one airboat ride later, Ann and I found the spot where we'd started our hike yesterday. The grass was trampled, and there were multiple footprints on the water's edge. Hopefully all ours. We headed in, following the trampled grass, footprints, and the occasional spot that looked like it had been recently hacked with a machete. Ann had brought another one with her. I hoped it was for underbrush and not because we needed a weapon. The trees formed a towering canopy over us, and the light was dim as the sun was rising. Sunbeams shot through small spaces between the trees. We walked about eight minutes, then stopped.

"This might be the area. If only I'd snapped branches along while we were here."

"Or left a trail of bread crumbs," Ann said with some mirth in her voice. "Don't worry. We've only been out here a little while."

We walked slowly. So slowly, we were almost not moving forward. We both had flashlights and scanned the ground thoroughly.

"It's here," I shouted. "Look." I held my flashlight to further illuminate the stick with the zip tie around it. I was jubilant, but then I deflated a little. "Now what?" The woods seemed huge around us. I couldn't hear any cars or even boat motors.

"We'll assume that the wreck isn't behind us," Ann said. "I did another chart last night based on your description of the spot and based on storm patterns and the shoreline shifting."

"That was smart."

"If the ship came into this inlet for shelter, the wind could have driven it farther north. So we'll look that way first."

We headed off the path from yesterday and into the brush. Ann hacked through some of it; we dodged around other bushes, and forced our way through yet others. It was dirty, unpleasant work at times. What the heck I was doing out here when I could have been home in bed with Rip? However, Ann didn't seem inclined to give up, so I trudged on, too.

We stopped for a water break.

"Did you bring the drone?" I asked.

"No. It wasn't useful yesterday. It's just too dense."

I spotted a tree with some low branches and pointed it out. "I'm going to climb up and see if I can spot anything."

"Knock yourself out," Ann said. "I meant that as a figure of speech."

I'd always loved climbing trees as a kid. I took a running jump to get to the first branch and snagged it on the first try. It was easy to climb, and soon I was about fifteen feet off the ground. I took a long look around.

"Ann, get up here. You're not going to believe this."

CHAPTER 35

Ann scrambled up the tree asking, "What? What do you see?" But I wanted her to see it for herself. Describing the sight wouldn't do it justice. When she was on the branch beside me, I pointed. There, sticking out of the murky ground, was the vine-covered bow of a blackened ship. Ann gasped, and we both just stood there, taking it in. Undergrowth draped off it like lacy living crochet. It would almost be impossible to see except from this angle.

"I can't believe it," Ann said. "I didn't think we'd ever really find it. I assumed it had been swept away or crumbled apart."

"Back then, lots of ships were lined with copper, which probably helped preserve it." Yes, I'd been reading up on shipwrecks ever since this adventure started. I was grinning, first at her and then the ship. "I can't believe it, either. Let's go take a closer look."

We scrambled down the tree, jumping the last bit and landing with soft thumps. We pushed and hacked and dodged until we stood in the small clearing. The ship looked way bigger from down here.

"Do you think the ship broke apart, or is more buried underneath?" I asked while we stood reverently taking in the boat. The timbers were blackened. A mast leaned precariously, no sails to be seen. Vines wrapped around it, and small plants had taken root in the rotting wood along with fungi. I half-expected a pirate with a peg leg and a parrot on his shoulder to come out and take us captive.

"I don't know." Ann's eyes were glowing, and she had the biggest smile I'd ever seen as she took it all in.

We walked around it as best we could, mesmerized. Ann put her hand against the old wood and just held it there like she could feel something through it.

"What are you going to do now? What are next steps?" I asked.

"I'll track down whoever owns the land and try to buy it."

"Are you going to tell them what's on it?" I asked.

Ann shook her head. "If they haven't figured it out, I'm not going to tell them."

"What about the treasure?"

Ann looked around again. "Chances are the boat's been stripped of anything of value by now. People surely looked for the treasure after the initial wreck. And others must have stumbled across it over the years."

"Then why doesn't anyone know it's out here?"

"Probably because whoever took things away wasn't supposed to be here in the first place. They might have been afraid of Jean Lafitte's wrath."

"Does that make you feel bad?"

"No. I don't really care about the treasure, but this"—she swept her hand at the ship—"this is family history."

As we drove back to town, I wondered if I should bring up Dex and my concerns. But I decided not to until I had more information. When Ann dropped me off, Rip's car was gone. I noticed there was a message on my phone. It was from Rip, saying his mother had fallen and he was driving down to Tampa and would be gone for a couple of days. He didn't mention the key or wanting to talk. I sent him a quick text, telling him I hoped she was okay and to let me know.

I hustled inside and approached my nightstand with trepidation. Rip had yelled that he wanted the key, but what if he changed his mind? I couldn't decide which would be worse—that the key I'd left him was still there or if it was gone. It seemed like if it was gone, our relationship had taken another step forward. It was scary and exhilarating at the same time. I shook my head. All this speculation was ridiculous. I marched into my room and looked at the nightstand. The key wasn't there. I sank on the bed. "What have you done, Chloe?"

The good thing was I didn't have time to sit around and ponder that.

*   *   *

An hour later, I was back at Aymar Security, dressed in a black sheath dress. Once again wearing the fake horn-rimmed glasses and carrying an empty briefcase. Back to my Elizabeth Bond persona. I had to admit, I kind of liked her. I sat across from Robin in her office.

"Thank you for seeing me on such short notice," I said, smiling brightly at Robin. I'd called her after Ann had dropped me back at my house.

"We're always happy to help Ann," Robin said. "She's one of our best customers and sends a lot of business our way."

Ah, so she feared losing a great customer. I would in her place.

"As we explained to Dex the day you set up his appointment, we don't know who turned the alarm off."

"That's right. Ann's system isn't set up that way."

"Ann explained her concerns about her key fobs being cloned. We have no way to know if that happened or not. Obviously, if it was cloned, whoever had them could get into Ann's house *and* shut off the alarm."

Robin looked over my shoulder, so I did, too. The door was still closed.

"I hate to speak ill of any of Ann's employees," she said.

"No worries." I waved my hand around. "Getting to the truth is Ann's top priority." At least I hoped it was. "Have you found any answers?" If she hadn't, I didn't know what kind of questions to ask next.

"As you know, Dex was in here after you came in. He went through our systems."

I nodded.

"Once he left, we started running programs. One of my employees realized she should match them against what had been stored in the cloud." Robin hesitated. "She found a discrepancy and just reported it to me this morning."

"What kind?"

"On the cloud, it showed that at two-ten, the alarms at Ann's house were manually turned back on."

I frowned. "Is there any way to tell who did that?"

Robin nodded. "Yes. Ann's system is set up so that anyone who has access to it has an independent sign-in assigned to them."

"So who reset the system?"

"Dex. And he also changed our system to cover it up."

CHAPTER 36

Oh, Dex. This was looking worse and worse for him. I realized how much I'd been hoping I was wrong about Dex. If only it were some relative of Ann's that I didn't know or care about. Anyone but Dex. Robin pulled out a report with a lot of graphs and went over them with me, showing me the comparison of the old and new data.

"Can you tell when the system was shut off?"

"Normally, we wouldn't pay any attention to that, but I pulled Ann's records and looked through all the data, so the answer is yes. That occurred at about one-forty-five."

"And was Dex the one who shut if off?" Was I all wrong again? Did Dex set up Ann and me on purpose?

"As I said, it looks like a key fob was used to turn if off, so it could have been anyone. Let me restate that. I'm assuming a key fob was used based on the information we have. There is a slim possibility the system was hacked, but we've found no evidence that occurred. I know it didn't happen through here. Someone very familiar with computers could have hacked the system at Ann's house. However, my gut tells me it was someone using a key fob."

"Does Ann know?" I asked. If she did, had she come to the same conclusion I had?

"Not yet. Since you were coming in, I decided I'd give you the update."

I translated that to mean that they should have noticed the alarm reset earlier, had somehow missed it, and were afraid to tell Ann.

"I appreciate that. She's in a very delicate negotiation this morning and doesn't want to be interrupted." If she was trying to buy the land the ship was on, that could be true. I thought the situation over again. Something was hinky about the whole thing. "Did you leave Dex alone to go through your systems?"

"*No.* Of course not," Robin sputtered.

"And yet he somehow managed to hack your system and then, very conveniently, someone came forward with new information this morning?"

Robin paled.

"It sounds to me like someone helped Dex change things, then had a guilty conscience, and came forward."

Now Robin flushed. "I'll be looking into that. I assure you." Robin stuffed the report in an envelope, handed it to me, and I left moments later.

Even if someone had helped Dex, it didn't let him off the hook.

* * *

My stomach was twisted in knots by the time I got to work. On the drive over, I'd debated whether I should tell Ann what Robin had told me or not. I decided I'd wait until I saw her in person. She'd shown up at my house almost every night for the past week, so she probably would tonight, too. And the new information didn't prove that Dex killed Enrique, but it seemed like another nail in the proverbial coffin. I had a million things I'd rather do than work, but I couldn't leave Joaquín and Vivi in a lurch. It made me realize all the more that we needed extra help.

I changed out of my dress into shorts and a T-shirt. Then I took a quick look at the latest round of applicants. I selected the two who looked like the best fit and scheduled interviews for this afternoon. After that, I got busy serving, cleaning, making a few drinks, and chatting with Joaquín when he came in.

The first interview was a bust. The girl was only sixteen, had lied on her application, and thought she could pull it off because her friends told her she looked older. They all had agreed that access to alcohol was the perfect answer to their social problems. If only it were that easy. She said that by working here, she and her friends could meet older men (college men) because they were so over high-school boys. I didn't want to dishearten her by telling her that college boys weren't much more mature than high-school ones. I explained to her the hazards of lying about her age and how much trouble we would have been in if we'd hired her. Even after I went through all of that, I don't think she understood that our employing her could shut down our business.

My second interview was with a man named Ted Wilson. He was in his mid thirties and had a long, stable work history in the hospitality business. He had brown floppy hair, light brown skin. Ted wore cargo shorts and a Hawaiian shirt. I took that as a sign—a good sign. He hailed from Birmingham, had a deep Southern accent, and wanted to live near the beach. When I got done talking to him, I went over to Joaquín.

"Do you have time to talk to Ted?" I pointed him out. "I think he's a good candidate for working here."

"What? Are you sure? All those interviews, and you've finally found someone for us to hire?"

I narrowed my eyes at him.

Joaquín laughed. "Let me just finish up making up these Bloody Marys."

"I'll serve them for you."

After I served the drinks, I called Bev and asked her if she could come in for an interview with Joaquín tomorrow afternoon. She said yes. Things were finally looking up in the employee department. A few minutes later, Cindy called.

"I took the job at the assisted living place. I wanted to thank you for telling me about it and to withdraw my application."

"I hope you love the new job," I said, but I wanted to talk to her about Dex. "Do you mind if I ask you a question that is completely unrelated to working here?"

"Oooookay," she answered.

"I'm going to text you a picture, and I want to know if you've ever seen this man." I shot her a picture of Antoine. As much as it looked like Dex had killed Enrique, I wanted to rule Antoine out completely.

"I've seen him."

Little chills ran up my arms. Maybe I was wrong about Dex. I hoped I was wrong about Dex. "Where?"

"I follow him on social media. He's hot."

"Have you ever seen him in Two Bobs or anywhere else around here?"

"I wish."

That was disappointing. "Do you know Ann Williams?" I described what she looked like.

"Yes. Of course. She's at Two Bobs a lot."

"There's a man she works with who is often there, too. Pretty brown eyes. Quiet."

"You mean Dex?" she asked. "He's quiet but a good tipper."

"Did you ever see him argue with Enrique?"

Nothing. Did Cindy hang up? "Cindy?"

"Not argue so much as watch him."

Interesting. "Do you remember when he did it or if it happened a lot?"

"Just once. Enrique was at Two Bobs the night he was murdered. We went back after our rendezvous on the beach. Dex was there, too. Enrique and I argued. Enrique laughed at me. He told me I was too clingy." Cindy paused. "Enrique walked off and Dex told me that Enrique wasn't good enough for me or anyone else." Her voice was shaky. "When Enrique left the bar, Dex followed him. Well, at the very least, he just happened to leave around the same time."

"What time was that?" I asked.

"Twelve-thirty or one? I got in trouble for leaving in the middle of my shift. I wish I would have followed Enrique out. Maybe if I had, he'd still be alive."

"Don't do that to yourself, Cindy. Maybe you would have walked into trouble, too." Or maybe Dex wouldn't have killed Enrique like I suspected he did. "Have you told Deputy Biffle all of this?"

"Should I?"

I guess that was a no. Part of me wanted to tell her that it wasn't worth mentioning, but that wasn't right. "Yes." It came out almost like a sigh.

"He's going to think I'm lying because I didn't tell him the last time we talked."

That could very well be. "Deputy Biffle needs the information. You want to know who killed Enrique, don't you?"

"Yes. It's just that I didn't even think about it in the moment. Lots of people came and went around the same time as when Enrique left. You're the one that got me thinking about Dex."

Great. Deputy Biffle would probably be upset with me about this for interfering. In my opinion, he should be thanking me. "Tell him about anyone else that you saw coming or going, too." It didn't have to be Dex. I hoped it wasn't.

My phone rang right after Cindy left. Vivi's doctor. I wanted to ignore it but decided I shouldn't. I'm not even sure the results mattered at this point.

"I got your test results back."

"And?"

"There were traces of Rohypnol in your system. As these things go, it really wasn't very much, but I know these things can be very traumatic. I can give you some information on counselors who could be helpful."

"I'm not even sure how I feel right now."

"That's understandable. Why don't I email you the information so you have it on hand?"

"Thank you. I'd appreciate it."

"And feel free to call me if you have any questions."

"I will." I disconnected, and that's how I felt, too.

"Excuse me," a man shouted. "We're ready for another round."

Sometimes work was the best therapy.

I waited until after work, after Vivi left; then, I pulled up the Sea Glass's security footage from the night Enrique had died. Two Bobs didn't have its own parking lot, so patrons had to use the public lot and walk past the Sea Glass to get there. I typed in 12:30—I had to start somewhere—and started watching. A few people went back and forth. A couple of men with fishing poles in their hands, who were probably heading to a boat. A group of rowdy-looking college-aged kids who were heading toward Two Bobs. They were laughing and pushing each other as they walked by.

At a few minutes after one, Enrique strolled by. He didn't seem agitated or worried about if someone was following him or not. He pulled out his phone, smiled down at it, and then started talking. Deputy Biffle must have his phone records and would know whom Enrique had talked to. Then Enrique walked out of sight of our camera.

Five minutes later, Dex hurried by. He was craning his neck, searching for someone. All I knew was that around a couple of hours later, he was at Ann's house, resetting her alarm system. I gasped when I realized he was carrying a rose in his hand. Was it the rose Ann found at her house? I'd been to bars where later at night, people came around selling roses. A guy had handed me one once.

He'd said, "I could buy you a dozen, but they still wouldn't be as beautiful as you."

"Does that line ever work for you?" I'd asked.

He grinned. "More often than you might think."

I'd just shook my head and walked off—with the rose.

Even with all of this, I still had no proof that Dex had killed Enrique, but I was determined to either find some or clear his name.

CHAPTER 37

As I was walking up to my house, a black truck pulled up the driveway. Ann. I trotted over to meet her, but Dex got out of the truck and slammed the door. I froze. It was a quiet night. I had no neighbors close enough to hear me scream. And Rip was out of town. I took a step back and another. There was no way I could reach my door before he got to me. Maybe Dex didn't know what I was thinking. I mean, how could he? I tried to relax my posture. To command my authoritarian librarian side. To remember what the heck they taught us in the self-defense class, but my brain was scrambling from one thought to another too fast to make sense of anything.

"Hey, Dex." I stuck my hand in my purse, digging around for my phone.

"I heard you were at Aymar's today," Dex said.

How could he possibly know that? My fingers brushed my phone, and I clamped my hand around it. If only there was some way to call for help without being able to see what I was doing. There wasn't.

"Yes. I was picking up something for Ann."

"I know that's not true."

"It is. I have the report in my car. Go take a look."

That would put more space between us. I could make a run for it.

"Chloe—" Dex's voice was patient, controlled, and it was scaring me.

I pulled the phone out of my purse. Dex put his hands up.

"I'm not going to hurt you. I'd never hurt you or any other woman. I despise men who do."

Of course that's what he'd say.

"When I was ten, a man kidnapped my six-year-old sister."

I gasped. "I'm sorry."

"We got her back. She hadn't been hurt physically, but she suffered a lot. Nightmares when she was young, drugs when she was a teen. Finally, therapy. She's doing good now. Has a kid and a boyfriend."

Was he making this up to lull me into a sense of security?

"I'm not going to lie to you. I just want to tell you my side of things."

"Okay. But don't come any closer."

"I won't. We're good."

I wasn't as confident of that as he was. I knew from the incident at Sandy's how fast he could move.

"Why don't you record this?" Dex suggested.

That made me uneasy. What was he planning to do that would necessitate the need for a record of what he said? "Why?"

"Because things don't always go as planned, and it would be better to have a record of our conversation."

"What makes you think I won't just dial nine-one-one?" I asked.

"Because I think you want to hear what I have to say."

Darn it all, he was so right. Since my phone was already in my hand, it was easy to start the record function. "Okay. Go ahead."

"When we were in the Sea Glass, and Ann said what she did about Enrique, I wanted to kill him. For hurting her. For hurting others. For possibly hurting you on my watch."

"So you did?" I asked.

"Yes, but it wasn't murder, it was self-defense."

That's what Ann had said about the man *she* killed. "Then why didn't you say so? Why let Deputy Biffle blame Ann and me?"

"I would have never let you be arrested or go to trial. I knew there wasn't any real evidence that you or Ann had killed him. Selfishly, I was hoping that it would all blow over, and no one would ever figure things out."

"But I did."

"How?" he asked.

"I thought about who loved Ann enough to kill for her."

"And I came to mind?"

I nodded.

"You aren't wrong."

"You love her?"

"Yes, but not romantically. Like she's family. We've been through a lot together. She's the one who finally got my sister into therapy, and she paid for it. But I didn't know about what had happened to Ann in high school."

That made sense from what I'd seen of them. "So what happened that night? I know you followed Enrique when he left Two Bobs."

"I tried to, but I lost him. Cindy told me he'd said that he was going to surprise an old high-school friend. How many old high-school friends did he have here? Likely only Ann. I didn't know that Antoine was in town then."

Cindy had left that part out when I talked to her. If she hadn't, I would have called Deputy Biffle and Dex, and I wouldn't be standing here.

"I went to the camp first, because that's where Ann was staying that night. There wasn't any sign of him, so I hauled it over to her beach house." He shook his head. "The front door was open. I still don't know how Enrique got past the alarm system."

"I think he cloned the key fobs."

Dex looked surprised.

"So, you found him in the house, you killed him, and planted the body." But why plant the body where Ann and I would find it? Even though I was scared right now, there was still a part of me that trusted Dex. I hoped that instinct was right, or I was in a lot of trouble.

Dex was shaking his head. "I did a quick search but didn't find anyone in the house."

"Why didn't you just tell Ann you found the door open?"

"My immediate thought was there was no need to worry her. I reset the security system. Then I heard a boat start up, so I ran down to the dock and saw someone leaving in a boat. I took one of Ann's, followed the boat to see what it was up to, and found Enrique anchored." Dex shook his head. "I wasn't surprised it was him. We argued. I lost it. I was so angry. He hurt women." He paused and took a breath. "I knew I had to get out of there or I'd beat him. When I turned to go, Enrique pulled a knife on me."

I was horrified but kept silent.

"I wrenched the knife out of his hand, and it tumbled into the water. We fought." He shook his head again, like he wished he could get rid of the memory. "Enrique was choking me, and I shoved him off me. He stumbled and slammed his head on diver's weights. It was like I watched it happen in slow motion." Dex paused and took a deep breath. "I yelled at him to get up and realized that he was too still. I checked for a pulse, but he was gone. I was in shock. And I . . . something kicked in, and I tossed him over with the diver's weights from his boat. At the time, I had no idea why he was in that particular spot or that he'd seen Ann's map. Hell, I didn't even know about Ann's map then." He shook his head again. "I didn't think he'd ever be found."

The pain in his voice cut through me. "Why didn't you just tell Deputy Biffle all of that?"

"It doesn't look good."

"It doesn't, but if it's the truth . . ."

"The Bible might say that the truth will set you free, but it doesn't always work that way in the justice system, Chloe."

"What happened to the boat Enrique was on?"

"I towed it far away and sunk it."

"Does Ann know all of this?"

"No. I haven't told her a thing."

I shook my head. "I don't understand why."

"I didn't tell her any of it right away. Ann trusts me to be upfront with her, and I broke that trust. It could have ruined everything. And it may have looked like Ann was involved, even if she wasn't."

"You were trying to protect her?" My voice was highly skeptical.

"It seemed like it in the moment." Dex rubbed his forehead like he wished he could rub away everything that had happened.

"I think Ann is more understanding than you are giving her credit for."

"And I know her a lot better than you do."

Touché. Ann wasn't stupid. She might have figured part of this out. We stared at each other for a few minutes.

I stopped the recording. "I'm going to call Deputy Biffle," I said. Why did part of me feel like I didn't want to do that?

"You do what you have to. You're a good person."

"Call Johnny McCellan, and then turn yourself in to Deputy Biffle. It will be okay."

Dex didn't answer. Instead, he turned, got in the truck, and drove off.

I stood there for a few minutes, hoping he would take my advice. A breeze hit me, and I realized how cold I was—partly from the wind, but more from all I'd just heard. My hand was shaking so badly, I couldn't even open my phone, and it was too dark out here for the facial recognition to work.

I went inside. Splashed some rum into a glass and shot it back. It burned down my esophagus and into my stomach. I almost choked. I rarely drank hard liquor straight and wasn't sure why I thought now was a good time to start. The warmth slowly spread, which made me think this was why it was a good time to start. My nerves were so frayed that I was surprised I wasn't shaking apart.

I took a deep breath. Several deep breaths. If only Rip were in town and I could talk this all over with him, but I didn't want to call him. He'd hop in his car and drive through the night to be here. His mother needed him more than I did. Instead, I sent him a text, telling him I hoped that his mom was feeling better. Seconds later, I got an "I miss you" with a heart emoji next to it. I missed him, too.

I shouldn't have had that rum. What if Deputy Biffle thought I'd been drinking and had made the whole thing up? Thank heavens I had the recording of my conversation with Dex. But would Deputy Biffle believe it? Maybe he'd think we made it all up. I brushed my teeth, rinsed with some mouthwash. I picked my phone up and stared at it for a long time—calculating and recalculating what to do. I thought over all Dex had said. Should I make the call? I had to. Dex had killed Enrique, even if it was in self-defense. Surely, a jury would understand that. I had to believe the judicial system would work.

I dialed Deputy Biffle's number. It rang several times. I started with each ring. Part of me hoped he wouldn't answer. That I could just hang up and sleep on all of this. But just as my finger hovered over *end*, he answered.

"What?" he asked.

"I know who killed Enrique. Can you come over?"

CHAPTER 38

I'd called Ann after I'd hung up with Deputy Biffle and told her the high-level version of my conversation with Dex. I also told her about my call to Deputy Biffle. She hadn't said much, other than she'd be over. Thirty minutes later, Deputy Biffle was sitting across from me in my living room, wearing jeans and a soft, old, white T-shirt. He wore worn cowboy boots instead of his highly polished work boots. His biceps bulged, and his brown eyes were sharp. I almost wished he'd put his mirrored aviator sunglasses on. That's how I was used to seeing him. He had eyes that drilled right into the gray matter in my brain. I wanted to put up a deflector shield like they did in Star Wars or Star Trek to keep him from sucking my thoughts out.

We stared at each other for a few moments before Deputy Biffle spoke. "Tell me what you know."

I felt like there was an unsaid *tell me what you think you know* in there.

"Who do you think killed Enrique?" he asked when I didn't tell him what I knew right away.

"Dex." I tried to be as succinct as possible, including how I'd come to suspect Dex and what I'd done since coming up with that theory.

"What evidence do you have?"

"Dex confessed."

"To you, so you say. An alleged confession would get you and Ann off the suspect list."

"You think I'm making this up?" I shook my head. "Dex had me record our conversation." I took my phone out and hit play so Deputy Biffle could listen. It was painful to hear all the things Dex revealed again. I watched Biffle, but his face didn't change at all while he listened.

When the tape ended, Deputy Biffle leaned back and studied me for a couple of moments. "He could have said these things to protect the two of you. He's very loyal to Ann."

I wanted to smack my head or him. "I take it Dex hasn't turned himself in." That's what I was hoping. That Dex would leave here, call Johnny, and turn himself in. At least that's what I'd told myself when I had procrastinated calling Deputy Biffle. More likely, I was thinking, "Run, Dex, run."

"Not that I know of, and since I'm in charge of the case, someone would contact me." Deputy Biffle laid another long look on me.

I did my best not to squirm. I didn't say anything.

"Why did you wait so long to call and report his alleged confession?"

I shrugged. "To give him time to get an attorney."

"Or to run?"

Wow, he really could read my mind. We heard a truck come up the drive, and we were both outside before anyone got out. I'm not sure which of us wanted it to be Dex more, but Ann climbed out. Her hair fell in luxurious waves around her. She had on a short black leather skirt and a low-cut silk tank top with a leather jacket over it. Ann wore peep-toed shoes with three-inch heels. I'd never seen her dressed like that.

I glanced at Deputy Biffle. Desire flashed across his face for a brief second or two. What was the story with them? Ann walked effortlessly toward Deputy Biffle. She stopped when they were inches apart and looked up at him. Either she was a great actress, or she wanted him as bad as he wanted her. It was awkward standing here, and I was afraid the sparks sizzling off the two of them might start a fire. I'd never seen so much being said without a word being spoken.

"Have you found him, Dan?" Ann asked. Her voice small instead of the usual low, sultry way she talked.

I couldn't tell if she was hoping he had.

"I haven't even had a chance to look. Any ideas where I should start?"

"No." Ann wobbled on her heels and put a hand on Deputy Biffle's chest to steady herself. He picked up her hand and pressed a kiss into her palm.

I took a step back. I didn't need to see this.

"He's not at the camp. I searched before I came over," Ann said.

"So you could turn him over to me?"

Ann didn't answer.

Deputy Biffle dropped her hand and took his own step back. "This is why we'll never work."

Ann's eyebrows shot up. "Why?"

"Because you are all shades of gray, and I deal in blacks and whites."

"Nothing is ever just black and white," Ann responded.

Deputy Biffle shook his head. "I've got to go put an APB out for Dex." He looked over at me. "Is there anything else you want to tell me, Chloe? I feel like there is."

I still hadn't said anything about the treasure, but with Dex's confession, I'm not sure it was even important anymore. Plus, I wondered if Ann and I could be in trouble for not mentioning it in the first place. I shook my head, because I didn't trust myself to speak. Without changing his expression much, I could tell that Deputy Biffle was disappointed in me. *Very disappointed,* and it didn't feel good. I thought about him telling me, that morning out on the Gulf when we'd found Enrique, that Johnny McCellan was underhanded. That's how I felt, too.

Ann and I watched as he climbed into his SUV and backed down the drive. Her shoulders were slumped, so I slung an arm around her.

"Want to come in?" I asked.

"Why don't we drive out to my beach house? On the way, you can tell me about your entire conversation with Dex. I want to know everything he told you." She glanced at Deputy Biffle's SUV, which hit the road and roared off. "And I want to find Dex, before Dan does."

* * *

Twenty minutes later, we were at Ann's house. Dex's truck wasn't parked outside. I walked with Ann through her entire house. It was enormous, with five bedrooms, all with en-suite bathrooms, two half-bathrooms, and an office. Everything was top of the line and beautifully decorated with a combination of modern and antique pieces. When we were in the kitchen, Ann grabbed two water bottles and tossed one to me. We leaned against the pristine marble counters and drank. The search had been very slow and deliberate. Every closet checked. Each bed looked under. I was beginning to get suspicious. "Do you really think Dex is going to be hiding under a bed, or are you just stalling?" I got the stalling. I'd done it myself earlier.

"Just trying to be thorough."

Thirty minutes after we arrived, we were in the library. Ann pushed on one side of a shelf, and it swung open. There was a skinny-looking safe built between the shelf and the wall. Ann typed in a combination of numbers, and it swung open. There was a business-sized envelope sitting in it.

"He's been here," Ann said. "His stash of cash and alternate identity passport and license were all in here." She stared into the safe for a moment before turning to me. "He's gone, and he's not coming back."

Ann sounded so sad, it almost broke my weary heart, but I wasn't sure I liked it or not that I knew all these things. I could already feel a moral dilemma coming on.

"How do you feel about Dex letting us look like

suspects?" I wanted to ask if she felt betrayed. They'd known each other for a long time.

"I suppose I should be angry. But I understand why he did it, and I know that he wouldn't have let us take the fall for him."

I was a bit surprised that Ann even answered. Even though we'd been spending a lot of time together, we usually weren't talking about things on any deep level. Oddly, that was my take on the situation, too. I would miss Dex and had only really gotten to know him over the past few days. I couldn't imagine the mix of emotions that Ann would feel.

She turned back to the safe, took out the other envelope, closed the safe, and pushed the shelf back into place. Ann handed me the envelope. "This is for you."

I opened the envelope with some combination of dread and curiosity. I took out the two items—a Florida license good for the next six years and a passport. My picture was on both with the name Elizabeth Bond. It was weird looking at them.

I looked up at Ann. "What's this for?"

"You just never know when something like that will come in handy."

I didn't know what to say.

"Just keep them somewhere safe and pray you never need them."

I stuffed them in my purse for the moment and would figure out what to do with them later.

"Let's walk down to the dock," Ann said.

"Okay." I hoped Dex wasn't waiting there for a ride someplace. I wasn't sure I could be part of that. Maybe he'd ditched the truck nearby and walked the rest of the way here.

We walked across the broad lawn. Ann didn't seem to be in any kind of hurry. The stars were bright in the sky. A light breeze gave the air a slight chill. The dock was empty except for some boats. I didn't know how many Ann had or how often she switched them out.

"One of my boats is missing."

Ann didn't sound upset at all.

"Are you going to tell Deputy Biffle any of this?" I asked. Was I?

"I'll call Dan when we're back at the house and tell him the boat is missing." She thought for a minute. "And about the missing money."

"What about the new ID?"

Ann turned to face me. "It would look bad for me if I knew that Dex had a fake ID. It's something I should have confiscated and probably told Dan about. Do you understand?"

"I'm not sure."

"Dex was in and out of jail and prison from the time he was sixteen. That's when he found his sister's kidnapper and nearly killed him."

Dex had left that part out when we'd talked.

"When he got out, he started hunting down other victims' predators. When he could, he turned them over the police."

"And when he couldn't?"

"He didn't ever kill anyone. Dex didn't want to be as bad as the criminal. But justice can be served in many different ways."

The gray areas Deputy Biffle had mentioned. We headed back to the house.

"When he got out of prison the last time, he was twenty-five. I hired him, and he's stayed out of legal trouble since."

"Work smarter, not harder?"

Ann laughed. "Something like that. If Dex went to trial and the old stories came out, it wouldn't look good for him."

"Did you know he killed Enrique? Have you been lying to me all this time?"

"No. Maybe I should have known. Maybe I didn't want to believe it." She stopped and looked back over the water. "I'm going to miss him."

Funny, but I was going to miss him, too.

When we were back in the library, Ann called Deputy Biffle and told him about the missing money and boat.

She held her phone out to me. "Dan wants to talk to you."

I wanted to run out the door and go hide in my bed. "Hello?"

"Did Ann leave anything out of her story?"

"No," I said. I didn't hesitate. It surprised even me. I handed Ann the phone back, and she hung up moments later.

"Why didn't Enrique take the map?" That had been bothering me ever since I talked to Dex.

"I think Dex's arrival scared him off, but we probably won't ever know for sure."

"What about Antoine and his thug friends? What is going to happen to them?"

"I was surprised you didn't tell Dan about them tonight."

"I think he'd have a lot of questions about why we didn't say anything earlier." Basically, we were screwed.

"I promise you, Chloe, that I'll hunt them down and keep an eye on them. Antoine, too. The whole family will. They won't bother anyone ever again."

I nodded. I'd leave it to Ann.

An hour later, I sat on my screened porch with a glass of red wine in my hand. The fake driver's license and passport were tucked in a drawer beneath my underwear. I'd sent another text to Rip. This time asking how his mom was. He'd replied that she was going to need help for a few days and that he missed me. I missed him, too. Especially tonight. I took a drink of wine and studied the Gulf. The waves rolled forward, over and over in a timeless move that would go on long after I was gone.

It wasn't always easy to tell who was the wolf and who was the lamb. There were all kinds of justice in the world, and not all of them ended with neat bows tied around a gift-wrapped box with the bad guy in jail and the good guy vindicated. I'm not sure Enrique deserved to die, but he was a terrible human, and Dex was a good one.

I chose to believe what Dex had told me. Even though part of me believed his fate should have been decided by a jury, I also knew he should have been found not guilty. Yet that might not have happened. Sometimes good guys go to jail. I didn't want to be part of that. Deputy Biffle said he lives in a world of black and white. Like Ann, I saw the grays.

My moral compass felt off north tonight, and I'd have to see how that felt going forward. Lying to Deputy Biffle meant protecting Ann and Dex. I hoped I could live with that.

CHAPTER 39

Two days later, I was focused on winning the barback competition. Seven of the obstacles were down. There were three to go. The air was warm but not hot. The Gulf dazzled, and the white sand sparkled. Finishing first didn't necessarily mean you won the competition. You got points for neatly chopping the fruit, points for how good your mixed drink tasted, and points for not spilling beer when you ran through the tires. You did get points for how quickly you finished, too.

The three judges had been brought in from Pensacola and vetted to make sure they had no ties to any of the bars that had people entered in the competition. The crowd was bigger than I expected. The chance to see Wonder Woman had created a lot of publicity. And Lisa didn't disappoint. She was dressed in a Wonder Woman costume, sans the boots. I felt frumpy in my shorts and SEA GLASS SALOON T-shirt.

Lisa wore one-of-a-kind Wonder Woman sneakers signed by Gal Gadot. After the race, Lisa was auctioning them off and donating the money to a charity that supported hospitality workers. It was a lovely thing to do. The crowd was definitely on her side. Although I heard a few *go, Chloe*s as I ran the course.

I stopped in front of the drinks station. The first one here, but I was sure Lisa was right behind me. We had traded back and forth as to who finished what obstacle first. Jean Claude was not far behind us. The stations were set up with partitions between them so no one could see what the other person was doing. Joaquín had told me if the drinks were bad, the judges would spit them out. I'd be humiliated if that happened.

I took the bar towel off the tray of ingredients. There were three vials with clear liquid and a fourth with a pale green liquid that was probably lime juice. There were also lemons, limes, and cherries. A knife and three styles of glasses—coupe, flute, and rocks. We got points not only for taste but presentation. I sniffed the vials. Gin, simple sugar, and another clear liquid with bubbles that had no smell. Probably club soda. There was also a bucket of ice. All of these ingredients would make a lime rickey, but I knew they wanted something original.

While the coupe glass was my favorite, I went with the rocks glass, a classic for a lime rickey. I put in some ice, added the gin, but instead of lime juice, I squeezed in lemon, simple syrup, and a splash of the club soda. I gave it a stir. Then I cut a twist out of the lemon peel and added a maraschino cherry.

I repeated the process three times. When I finished, a judge nodded at me. I took off for the next obstacle, not waiting to see if the judges spat the drink out. I glanced at Lisa as I ran by. She'd used the coupes, and there was way too much lime in her drinks. I could tell by the color.

The next challenge was carrying the six steins through the tires. I'd practiced with Joaquín the past few days, but hadn't improved much. We'd decided a slower time with less sloshed beer would be better. I ran twenty yards and picked up three steins in each hand, which was a stretch for me with my small hands. Jean Claude would have no problem with this one.

I was three-quarters of the way through when Lisa caught up with me. I could tell she'd spilled more beer than I had. Lisa set her beer steins down on the table, just as I made it through the last of the tires. I set my beer steins down and took off after her. The last obstacle was the keg roll up a hill. Someone had gotten up early and scraped sand from the beach to make a hill that had a twenty-degree incline.

Lisa was surprised when I ran past her on the way to grab a keg, and I was kind of surprised myself. But I'd made it this far, and I didn't want to choke on the last leg of the competition. I picked up a keg, hefted it to the bottom of the hill, and started pushing. The crowd was screaming. Mostly "Go, Wonder Woman," but I didn't care. I was doing this for me. Out of the corner of my eye, I spotted Joaquín, Vivi, and Michael jumping up and down and yelling, "Go, Chloe."

Darn it. I wanted to win. I started pushing the

keg up the hill. It wasn't easy. The sand was soft, which slowed the keg, and my feet sank into it. I was like the wolf in "The Three Little Pigs," huffing and puffing. I glanced back as I pushed, and Lisa was right behind me. Jean Claude was at the bottom, grabbing his keg. He made it look like it weighed nothing, but he weighed more than I did, which meant he'd sink into the soft sand more than me. I dug deep, got a rhythm, and rolled. Two minutes later, I crested the top with Lisa right next to me. We rolled our kegs down the other side, slipping and sliding after them. We crossed the finish line almost together. Although I think Lisa might have been a step ahead.

We both bent over, panting.

I looked over at Lisa. "We did it."

She laughed. "You're more competition than I thought you'd be."

It was nice to hear that from Wonder Woman. "Why'd you even do this?"

Lisa shrugged. "It was basically a paid beach vacation. I got to sit around and read for a month. I needed a break from Los Angeles."

I nodded. Someone handed me a bottle of water, and I chugged it as I walked over to Joaquín, Michael, and Vivi. They were still screaming, jumping, and hugging each other.

Joaquín threw his arms around my sweat-soaked body. "Great job, Chloe."

Michael hugged me, too.

Vivi sensibly patted my shoulder. "Well done."

Now it was over except waiting for the other eight contestants to finish and the judges to tally the scores.

Fifteen minutes later, the judges stood on a small platform, ready to announce the winners.

"Third place goes to David Grace."

Joaquín, Vivi, and I exchanged glances. He'd crossed the finish line in fourth place after Jean Claude.

"Second place goes to Lisa Kelley, aka Wonder Woman." The crowd went wild.

I was squeezing Joaquín's hand. What if I didn't even place?

"First place goes to . . ." The judge stopped and looked over the crowd.

I held my breath. I knew it was probably Jean Claude. He was an Olympic athlete, after all.

"Chloe Jackson."

Joaquín grabbed me and twirled me around. Then he and Michael hefted me on their shoulders and carried me to the platform. People chanted "Chloe, Chloe," and I felt like I was Rudy from the movie with the same name.

An hour later, the Sea Glass was packed, but for once, I wasn't running my rear end off. I was still serving, but we'd hired Bev and Ted. Bev only wanted to work part-time so she could help with her grandchild. Both of them were here today, and so far—fingers crossed—we were all working well together. Bev and Ted had completely different personalities, but both were charming in their own way.

The trophy gleamed on the bar, and everyone congratulated me or wanted to snap a selfie with me. It was kind of fun and flattering. On the other

hand, I couldn't help thinking about Dex and Enrique. Dex's picture was plastered all over the news
as a person of interest in the death of Enrique Laurier. Part of me hoped he was on an island somewhere, sipping a Bushwacker and staring out at
the sea with a smile on his face. It was unlikely that
he'd ever be found.

Ann slipped in around seven. She ordered Blan-
ton's on the rocks. We had these giant ice cubes we
used for this kind of order, because they melted
more slowly than smaller ice cubes and wouldn't
dilute the drink as quickly. I put the drink in front
of her and sat down across from her. Ann had an
ever-present book with her. This time, *Like A Sister*
by Kellye Garrett.

"I've heard that's good," I said, pointing to the
book.

"Hard to put down." Ann took a slug of her
drink. "I bought the land."

"Already?"

Ann nodded. "Turns out I'd done a couple of
favors for the woman who owned it. She also wanted
the cash I offered her more than the land."

Who knew what kind of "favors" she'd per-
formed, but I knew better than to ask. "Have you
been back out?" I asked. That I felt a little disappointed I hadn't been invited along surprised me.

"Not yet. We just signed the deal a couple of
hours ago." She took another drink. "Do you want
to go out with me when I go?"

"You bet I do."

"Congratulations on your win," she said, tipping
her head toward the trophy.

"Thanks. I realized I wanted to win it more than I thought."

"There's nothing wrong with wanting to be a winner. It's part of what makes you so great."

I think I turned a bit red. Fortunately, a group came up just then and wanted a picture with me. I waved a quick goodbye before rejoining the revelry.

I got home at 9:45 and was so tired my bones ached. Rip sat on the steps. Happiness surged through me—I didn't know he was coming home today. I took a deep breath so I didn't run over and plaster myself on him. Part of me felt awkward and shy. Rip looked up at me as I got out of my car and walked over to him. He was rolling the key I'd given him around in his hand. Then it hit me that he hadn't used it to let himself in. That couldn't be good.

"Why'd you give me this?" he asked. "And please don't run off again."

While ninety percent of me wanted to run, the other ten percent kept me rooted in place. It was now or never. "Because I'm in love with you."

"You're in love with me?"

Oh, no. Answering with a question wasn't good either. It sounded like the lawyer side of him was coming out. I'd been hoping for a return declaration or at least a "that's great." But it was too late to take it back now. I wasn't going to laugh it off and say "just kidding," although that ninety percent was suggesting just that. I nodded. "Yes. I'm in love with you."

Rip stood and crossed over to me. He cupped my chin and tilted it up. He hadn't burst out laughing, nor had he shoved the key at me and taken off. Rip looked into my eyes. A small grin tugged up the outer edges of his lips. Here came the laughter.

"Well, that's a very good thing," he said.

"Why's that?"

"Because I'm in love with you, too, Chloe Jackson."

Acknowledgments

Thanks so much to my editor, Gary Goldstein, for your faith in me. Not every author has an editor in their corner. And thanks to the team at Kensington, who take a Word document and turn it into a real book.

Along with Gary, my agent, John Talbot, has made my writing career possible.

As I say in every acknowledgment, I don't know what I'd do without the Wickeds—Jessie Crockett, Julie Hennrikus, Edith Maxwell, Liz Mugavero, and Barbara Ross. You lift me when I'm down, celebrate the wins, and mourn the losses.

Barb Goffman, independent editor, always reads an early draft of my books. Your advice, encouragement, and support mean the world to me. If there are mistakes, they're on me, not Barb.

Jason Allen-Forrest, thank you for your wisdom and for being my sensitivity reader. Your insights are invaluable.

Christy Nichols, thanks for reading for me and finding errors. You and your family bring so much joy into our lives.

Mary Titone, thank you for always dropping everything and reading for me. This book is so much better because of your contributions. I'm so lucky to have you as a friend.

Also, thanks to Jen—you are so much more than a virtual assistant.

And last but far from least to my family, who take care of me, put up with me, and make me laugh. Life would be dull without you.

Keep reading for a special excerpt!

THREE SHOTS TO THE WIND

A Chloe Jackson Sea Glass Saloon Mystery

By Sherry Harris

The third installment in Sherry Harris's Agatha Award-nominated series finds former Chicago librarian Chloe Jackson loving her new life as a bartender in Florida . . . until a surprise visit from her Windy City ex-fiancé ends with him blown away in the Panhandle!

Saloon owner Chloe Jackson appears to have a secret admirer. She's pouring drinks at the Sea Glass Saloon in Emerald Cove when an airplane flies by above the beach with a banner reading I LOVE YOU CHLOE JACKSON. She immediately rules out Rip Barnett. They are in the early stages of dating, and no one has said the L word. Then a bouquet of lilacs—her favorite flower—is delivered to the bar, followed by an expensive bottle of her favorite sparkling wine. It couldn't be . . .

Sure enough, her ex-fiancé from Chicago has flown down to Florida for an accountants' convention. But is he trying to mix business with pleasure and win her back? Unfortunately, he's not in a hotel conference room, he's floating face down in the lake next to her house, clutching a photo of Chloe. Who murders an accountant on a business trip?—it just doesn't add up. When Rip becomes the prime suspect, Chloe is determined to find the secret murderer. But if she isn't careful, it may be closing time and lights out for her . . .

Look for **THREE SHOTS TO THE WIND** *on sale now!*

CHAPTER 1

The whine of a plane's engine had become part of the music of my life working at the Sea Glass Saloon. They flew over day after day, pulling banners advertising happy hours, restaurant specials, and amusements such as water parks and minigolf.

"Chloe, you've got to get out here," Joaquín Diaz yelled. He stood out on the deck of the Sea Glass, gesturing wildly for me.

It was ten thirty and we'd just opened. I grabbed the three beers I'd poured, dropped them to patrons sitting on tall stools at a high-top table, and ran to Joaquín's side.

"What?" I asked, looking across the expanse of white sand to the Gulf of Mexico. Snowbirds, the flock of people who abandoned their cold, wintery states and provinces for the warmer climes of the Florida Panhandle, walked and sunbathed on the beach. No local would sunbathe in January. I scanned for something more interesting. Something that would make Joaquín sound so urgent. Last October a sailboat had run aground not far from here, but I saw no such boat now.

Joaquín pointed up. I shaded my eyes with my hand and squinted into the bright January sun. A small plane was flying over the beach with a banner. It read: "I love you Chloe Jackson." What the haymaker? My eyes went wide as I tried to sort through why such a sign would be flying over the beaches of Emerald Cove, Florida.

"Oh, Chloe," Joaquín said, "somebody loves you, girl." His eyes were the same aquamarine color as the Gulf on its showiest days. Dark hair tumbled over his forehead. "Do you think it's Rip?"

He gave me a hip nudge and did a little dance with his hands clasped over his heart. Joaquín was a former professional backup dancer for the likes of Beyoncé, Ricky Martin, and Jennifer Lopez. Now he was a fisherman in the early morning and a bartender the rest of the day, but, boy, he still had moves.

I'd been dating Rip Barnett on and off for the past few months. His real name was Rhett, but he'd gotten a nickname in the fall and it stuck. We were solidly in the like zone, with a touch of lust thrown in. But we definitely weren't in the love zone, and Rip didn't seem like the kind of man who went for wild public gestures like this. No man I could think of would do this. Although the proof otherwise was flying right over my head.

"It's not from Rip," I said, my voice sounding crosser than Joaquín deserved.

Joaquín whipped out his phone and started snapping pictures.

"Stop that, Joaquín," I said, making a grab for his phone.

He held it out of my reach, which wasn't hard because he was a lot taller than I was at my five four.

"You're going to want to remember this, Chloe."

I had a terrible feeling he was wrong, and that I wouldn't forget this no matter how much I wanted to.

"What's going on?" Vivi Slidell asked. She came out and stood beside us. "We have a business to run and thirsty customers."

Vivi Slidell was my boss, even though I owned a quarter of the Sea Glass. She was tall, slender, worked out regularly, and had a sleek silver bob. As far as I was concerned, she was the poster child or woman, as the case may be, for how to live your best seventy-year-old life.

Joaquín pointed up. Vivi went through the same routine I had of squinting, looking up, and eyes widening.

"Is this from Rip?" Vivi asked. Exasperation poured through her voice like beer through a broken tap.

Vivi and Rip's grandmother had a long-running feud that had started with a boy when they were in high school and had continued on from there. It had made dating Rip awkward and sometimes secretive. I often wondered if the rebellious part of me enjoyed the sneaking-around aspect of our relationship. Although you'd think at twenty-eight I would have matured beyond such actions. And I guess the sneaking was unnecessary if Vivi was asking if the banner was from Rip. Our jig was up.

"No. It couldn't be." I almost shuddered at the thought. "He knows I'd hate something like that. Something that would make everyone gawk at me. Maybe it's my brothers." They loved to tease me, and this stunt seemed right up their alley except for the fact they wouldn't want to spend the money to prank me. Plus, it would take a lot of work to do this and they had busy lives, wives, kids, and plumbing jobs back in Chicago, where I'd grown up. They'd taken over my father's plumbing business when my parents packed up, bought an RV, and hit the road.

My phone buzzed in the back pocket of my leggings. Normally, I didn't pull it out at work, but right now I needed answers. I had five texts. The first four were from heritage business owners—local people whose families, like Vivi's, had opened their businesses when Emerald Cove was barely on the map, hence the heritage designation. The heritage businesses had been in Emerald Cove since the nineteen fifties or longer. The Sea Glass was one of the heritage businesses, and often a gathering place for the other owners, which included the Hickle Glass Bottom Boat, the Redneck Rollercoaster, which was a trolley, Russo's Grocery Store, the Briny Pirate restaurant, and the Emerald Cove Fishing Charters. They all wanted to know who loved me. The fifth one was from Rip. Great.

Is there something you need to tell me?

I clapped my hand to my forehead and then shoved my phone back into my pocket. As Vivi said, there were thirsty customers inside. I would deal with the rest of this later.

* * *

An hour later, during a lull, Joaquín, Vivi, and I stood behind the bar speculating who could be behind the "I love you Chloe Jackson" banner. The Sea Glass was more tiki hut than saloon, with its wooden walls decorated with lots of historic pictures and its concrete floors, which made it easy to clean up the sand our customers dragged in.

"What about that guy, Smoke?" Joaquín asked. "He's been in here a lot lately."

Smoke was one of the few full-time employees of the Emerald Cove Fire Department. He was a good-looking man and a transplant like me. He'd moved down here from Minneapolis a couple of years ago.

"Ewww, no. We're just friends." We'd gone water-skiing a couple of times before the weather got too cold, and he'd been over to my house to watch football with some of the other volunteer firefighters. But that was it. There'd been the occasional friendly hug. It didn't mean we weren't just friends.

"I don't know," Vivi said, "you know what they say. Where there's smoke, there's fire." Her eyes sparkled as she said it. She'd be happy if I had a boyfriend as long as it wasn't Rip.

A woman came staggering in from the deck, which wasn't entirely unusual. Only this woman wasn't drunk, she was carrying an enormous bouquet of flowers in a ceramic pot almost as big as she was. Purple lilacs. My favorite flower. I had the same sinking feeling I had when I saw the banner.

"Is there a Chloe Jackson here?" she asked.

I wanted to run out the back door. "That's me." The lilacs' perfumey scent was already competing with the smell of salt air, beer, and the lemon cleaner we used. I hustled over to help her. Together we managed to get the arrangement on the bar top.

"Ooohhh, Chloe, your favorite flowers," Joaquín said.

"They are beautiful," the florist said. "And hard to come by this time of year."

"Thank you," I said. I gave her a tip.

She started to turn, but then snapped back around. "Are you the Chloe Jackson that the 'I love you' banner was referencing?"

Hey! Maybe there was another Chloe Jackson in town. "I'm sure it must be some other Chloe Jackson."

The woman started shaking her head. "I've lived here all my life and our family floral business opened in the seventies. I don't recall anyone else named Chloe Jackson."

"Have you ever had amnesia or a concussion?" I asked hopefully. Not that I wished her harm, just a temporary memory lapse so maybe she'd forgotten all the other Chloe Jacksons who lived in Emerald Cove.

"Sorry, honey. I'm known for my recall."

She left. I stared at the lilacs for a moment, but I couldn't resist their charm, so I put my face near one, breathing in their delicious scent. I fingered one of the soft flowers, while I stared at the card, trying to work up the courage to open it.

"Want me to look?" Joaquín asked.

"No. I'll do it."

Joaquín plucked the card from its clear, plastic holder that looked like a cheap, mini version of Triton's trident. "Here you go."

I opened the envelope, pulled it out, and stared down. *I love you, Chloe Jackson*. No signature. I handed it over to Joaquín, who handed it to Vivi. They both laughed. I'm glad someone found this situation was funny.

"Wait," I said. "The florist must know who bought these."

"Go," Vivi said.

I raced out the back door, ran along the harbor to the parking lot, and caught the woman as she started her van.

"Who bought these?" I asked. "The card wasn't signed."

She frowned. "He paid cash."

Of course he did. "What did he look like?"

"He asked me not to say. Said he wanted to surprise you."

"Trust me, I'm surprised. Please, tell me?" There was a little whine to my voice that I didn't usually have.

"Honey, the florist-client relationship is sacred. If I started giving away all the secrets I know, it would ruin my business."

Oh, good grief. It wasn't like she was a psychiatrist or a lawyer. There were no oaths. "Please?"

She shook her head and drove off.

Thank heavens we were having a busy day, so 90 percent of the time I could keep my mind off the banner and the flowers. Although the flowers were hard to avoid. Even though we moved them to the other end of the bar, they scented the air. Also, my phone kept buzzing away and I kept ignoring it.

At one forty-five there was a knock on the back door. I went to answer it, but no one was there. I started to step out, looked down, and froze.

Visit our website at
KensingtonBooks.com
to sign up for our newsletters, read
more from your favorite authors, see
books by series, view reading group
guides, and more!

Become a Part of Our
Between the Chapters Book Club
Community and Join the Conversation

Submit your book review for a chance to win exclusive
Between the Chapters swag you can't get anywhere else!
https://www.kensingtonbooks.com/pages/review/